WHEN THEY COME

COME

FOR

YOU

Short Story Collections

Paper Products
Over Exposure

Nonfiction

Hit Lit
Hot Damn!

JAMES W. HALL

WHEN THEY COME FOR YOU

THOMAS & MERCER

Text copyright © 2017 by James W. Hall
All rights reserved.

Published by Thomas & Mercer, Seattle

www.apub.com

Amazon, the Amazon logo, and Thomas & Mercer are trademarks of Amazon.com, Inc., or its affiliates.

ISBN-13: 9781477848678
ISBN-10: 1477848673

Cover design by Shasti O'Leary Soudant

Printed in the United States of America

For Evelyn

PART ONE

ONE

February, Coconut Grove, Florida

Spider Combs was parked five blocks east of the white wood cottage on Margaret Street in Coconut Grove where his target lived.

Behind the tinted windows of the stolen pickup, he spied on the residents of the cottage via the iPad in his lap. Last week, after a midday recon of the neighborhood, he'd slipped behind the house, jimmied a door, spent a half hour inspecting the layout, noting the proximity of neighbors, angles of sight, then searched for security alarms, hidden firearms, or other weapons.

It checked out fine. Neighbors shielded by thick walls of foliage. No guns in bedside tables, no baseball bats tucked behind doors, no security system. Sweet young pacifists. Easy pickings.

In the pantry, he spotted an oversize can of charcoal lighter. Which saved Spider the trouble of lugging his own.

When he finished his inspection, Spider installed four microcams, piggybacking on the young couple's wireless network, then planted a range extender behind the curtains near a front window. The extender projected the cameras' signals for several blocks, so Spider could park a safe distance away and access the live feed on his tablet.

For the past few days, he'd monitored their helter-skelter schedules, looking for patterns, getting to know them. Husband Ross, a newspaper guy, left and returned at odd intervals through the day, heading out before dawn some mornings, other days staying indoors in his sweatpants and T-shirt, typing on his laptop, making phone calls, then putting on jeans, polo shirt, baseball cap, and departing.

Wife Harper spent her days with the infant. When she wasn't breast-feeding the kid or singing to it or reading to it, the kid was sleeping in a crib and she was shut inside the spare bathroom that was rigged as a darkroom. Harper was a photographer. Black-and-white shots of famous people. Some so famous even Spider knew their names. Most nights she stayed at home, made dinner for hubby, read a book or watched TV, breast-fed the kid. Tonight was different. She was headed out, going somewhere fancy.

Spider would have to hurry to make it before she left.

She wasn't exactly his type. He preferred them short and plumpish, a little flab for handholds. But, hell, he'd make an exception for Harper McDaniel. Truth was, he had a goddamn crush.

Spider watched her dry off after her shower, then slip into her black bra and panties. Hubby appeared in sweatpants and a ratty T-shirt, and they had a quick back-and-forth that ended with Harper giving hubby's crotch a feel through the sweats. Watching that, Spider felt his hormones fire.

Hubby scooped the baby out of his crib and tucked the little guy into a body sling, then went back into the bathroom. Harper, still in her underwear, picked out a black cocktail dress from her closet, held it up against herself, looking in the full-length mirror. Something about her putting on her clothes layer by layer, leg by leg slipping into her panties, snapping that bra, shifting her breasts so they were comfortable, then sliding into the black dress—it was sexier than when she stripped them off.

Something else for his shrink to play with.

That black outfit was one of the few dressy items in her closet. Harper was a blue-jeans girl. Tomboy. Tee tops, shorts, workout clothes, sandals. She was tallish with shoulder-length raven-black hair, very thick with a good shine. She was long limbed and lean like some kind of athlete, marathon runner, high jumper. He couldn't say. The husband, Ross, was a couple of inches taller, curly black hair, hawk nose. The wife was clearly a nine, tilting toward a ten, while the guy was barely a six. A weird combo. From what Spider had seen, the guy survived on black coffee, Cheerios, milk, the occasional apple. No physical threat to Spider.

They weren't rich but doing okay, these two white-bread yuppies. Husband pulled down high five figures at the *Miami News*, and Harper brought in slightly more than half that as a photographer.

Thirteen thousand in a savings account, a piddling 401(k). A quarter of their monthly paychecks went to mortgage, taxes, and insurance. Didn't eat out much, a movie now and then. Ordinary financial situation, nothing that concerned Spider. He wasn't after their money. It was just part of his research, the usual protocol. He liked to know as much as possible about his targets to protect himself against hidden trip wires. Rich fucks could pose problems. The less income, the less likely anyone would come looking for their killer.

Though he knew he shouldn't do it, he saved the day's video feed to a file, then attached that to an e-mail and sent it to himself. Later he'd load that file onto his storage site out in the cloud, wherever the hell that was.

He never took that kind of risk. He always let everything he recorded go flying off into the wireless void. But he wanted to watch this one some more. Later on, when this job was finished, bring her back, feast on her face, her long, lean body, that hair. That goddamn hair.

This had never happened before, falling for a target. Spider was a pro. Clinical, detached. But this girl was graceful. He liked how she moved, how she held the baby, the kind of wife she was. The way Ross brushed her hair some nights, slow strokes through that long black mane. Brush, brush, and brush. Hypnotic to watch. Fuck if he could explain it. But there it was. He was going to miss watching the live feed, Harper McDaniel doing her daily rituals, the way she leaned close to the mirror and dabbed at the skin around her eyes like she was searching for wrinkles, the sexy way she fit the kid's lips to her nipples. The way she and hubby spooned after sex, holding each other like that until they fell asleep. Another thing to dump on his shrink. Someday, when he actually got around to seeing a shrink.

He sat back, tapping his foot, in a hurry now, eager to arrive before Harper left, have a few words with her, see her up close, a last look. He felt like he knew her, like they were old friends.

But he couldn't move until dark. He watched the last of the twilight drain from the sky. Watched people walking their dogs. Big dogs squatting to leave turd piles on lawns. People picking up the piles in plastic bags. Everyone all goody-goody.

He rolled down his window for some fresh air. Coconut Grove had good air, flavored with jasmine or something. Spider didn't know from plants. There were a lot of things he didn't know the names of: stars, insects, trees, shit like that. Not one of his skills. But he had other talents. The things he did to make his money. Cagey, industrious. How he survived. Where he got his name. Stringing his intricate web, snagging his prey.

When it was full-on dark, he rearranged the fit of his shoulder holster beneath the baggy Cuban shirt. He left the keys in the ignition so the truck could find its way back to its rightful owner. Spider was a hired gun, yeah, but he was no low-life car thief.

He got out of the truck and walked west on Margaret Street. He hadn't gone a block when his phone buzzed in his pocket. He stopped, took it out, read the text: **Okay, go.** He didn't bother answering. The fucker didn't need an answer. He shoved the phone back in his pocket and went on.

Two blocks from the McDaniel house, he checked to be sure nobody was around, then he smashed the iPad against a fire hydrant. Beat it until the screen shattered and the guts came loose. He dropped the remains down a sewer drain. With the pay from tonight's job, hell, he could buy a hundred iPads.

He walked on, staying on the shadowy side of the street, fitting on his leather gloves, a sticky silk thread spinning out behind him.

TWO

February, Coconut Grove, Florida

They said their good-byes, and Harper did a final check of her lipstick in the dresser mirror and was headed to the door when she caught a glimpse of Ross and Leo in the bathroom. An irresistible photo op.

She went back to her closet, took down her Leica from a high shelf, and returned to the half-open bathroom door. This was going to make her late, but screw it, the shot was too good to pass up.

Standing at the bathroom mirror, Ross angled the blade against his throat. Only a straight razor would do for Ross McDaniel. He'd inherited the blade, along with the leather strop and the badger bristle brush, from his father and generations of McDaniel men before him.

He worked the blade around his Adam's apple, then moved down row by row, scraping away his coarse beard. With the towel tight around his narrow waist, the sinews and muscles of his upper body swelled and flowed with each adjustment of the blade.

Leo was cradled in a sling on Ross's naked chest. Facing forward, Leo stared into the mirror as if trying to puzzle out the meaning of this odd ritual. There was a dab of shaving cream on Leo's cheek. A father's mischief.

Just beyond Ross's peripheral vision, Harper steadied her aim.

A side view of Ross's craggy profile, bent nose, the hard cheekbones, long lashes. A challenging angle. Beyond the window the moon was rising, its frail light filtering through palm fronds.

An edgy contrast between the moonlight and the ominous blade sliding across the throat only inches from the delicate skin of the child. The father's eyes, loving yet coolly workmanlike. The clash of serenity and risk, the mundane and peculiar. A photo Deena might have taken.

Harper slanted to the left, caught the perfect zing of light on that flat silver instrument, the upward tilt of the sharp steel. And depressed the shutter. Her mother's spy camera, the Leica's mechanism silenced for such stealthy shots as this.

She snapped a second.

Ross didn't notice.

Three tries were all her mother had allowed herself—her only aesthetic rule. If three attempts couldn't nail it, it probably wasn't there.

Harper focused on the blade scraping his throat, Ross working deliberately as if each stroke were a discrete lesson for their son. Leo's first drill in the art of patience and restraint.

On Harper's third snap, Ross sensed her presence, and his eyes ticked to the mirror and met hers, and his razor flinched. A dot of blood, then a dark trickle cut through the foam.

Baby Leo saw it in the mirror and reached out, swiping a hand toward his father's reflected face, fascinated by the red stream tracking down Ross's throat.

"Oh, shit, I'm sorry." Harper pushed open the door, came into the bathroom, and set the Leica on the edge of the tub. "I ambushed you."

"A nick," he said. "It's nothing."

"It was such an image," she said. "Leo learning the manly arts."

Harper tore off a piece of toilet paper and handed it to him. He applied it to the cut and smiled at her in the mirror.

"I thought you were gone."

"I'm just stalling," she said.

He nodded. Understandable. "Why don't you call them, tell them you're sick."

"I'm not sick, damn it. I'm fine."

Ross toweled off the last of the shaving cream, then Leo's puff of foam. The boy was grinning at Harper, delighted by the fuss, the three of them gathered in the small room. Something new.

"Don't rush it. It's still fresh. If you don't want to go, you're entitled to stay home. Relax."

Goddamn it, Harper felt her eyes muddying again. Another surge of grief for a mother who didn't deserve it. A woman who'd never shown her daughter even mild affection. Since Harper was old enough to speak, Deena had treated her with the cool practicality of a business partner, not the nurturing presence any daughter yearned for.

"Or, if you want, Leo and I can come along. We'll hang out in a back room, entertain ourselves until you're done. Send supportive vibes."

"I thought you had work to do."

"There's always work. The news cycle never sleeps."

"I'm okay," she said. "I need to suck it up and stop whining. You and Leo have your boys' night. You'd just make me self-conscious."

Harper picked up the Leica, enjoying the heft of the old R8, its reliable sturdiness. That camera was the one tangible item her mother specified in her will; the Leica should go to Harper. There was money too, a mountain of it, but the camera was Deena's prize possession and became for Harper a shred of evidence, however wishful, of her mother's affection.

Deena was a suicide. Caught in the steep downdraft of her latest depression, she'd managed to acquire a pistol in Paris and shot herself through the heart. Then lay dying in her hotel room with a **Ne Pas Déranger** sign on the door. The maids stayed away. No one heard the gunshot. How was that possible? The Parisian *médecin légiste* believed she hadn't died quickly. Might have been saved. Maybe lasted hours, bleeding out. Harper picturing it again and again. The ornate Hôtel de Crillon, her mother's favorite, on the Place de la Concorde next to the American embassy. High ceilings, thick walls, a former palace. Where she and Deena had stayed dozens of times, mother and daughter in Paris, working side by side on Deena's latest project.

Hours bleeding out. If Harper had gone along as usual, she would've heard the gunshot through their connecting door, gotten help in time, saved her.

But she hadn't made the trip. With Leo only seven months old, the fresh challenges of motherhood consuming her, she had a good excuse. But more than that, she'd needed time away from Deena's gravitational pull, time to consider her own direction. Did she truly want to follow in Deena's deep footsteps? Spend her life peering through the lens at the faces of the rich and infamous?

"You sure you can manage without me?" Harper said.

"Leo's easy, we'll be fine. We'll probably be in bed by nine." He patted his face dry with the towel.

"You have another early day tomorrow?"

He nodded.

"Who's the target this time?"

He gave her his customary chiding smile and waved off her question. Ross was deeply superstitious about his process, keeping his stories to himself till the research was complete and a solid draft was turned in to his editor at the *Miami News*. Only then might he confide a bit to Harper.

But this time there was something odd in his face. After the smile faded, she saw a crease in his brow, a shadow behind his eyes, a skittish look she'd never seen.

"What's wrong? You're worried, what is it?"

"Chocolate," he said.

"Chocolate?"

"Food of the gods," he said. "*Theobroma.* That's the Greek."

"You're writing about chocolate?"

"I know it sounds weird. But I've been wanting to tackle something new. This popped up. It's big. Different than anything I've done before. You ever realize chocolate is a hundred-billion-dollar industry?"

"That much."

"People have been consuming it since 600 BC. The Toltecs considered cacao beans so valuable they used them as money. Did you know that?"

"Cacao beans."

"Fascinating stuff, huh?"

"That's it? Tease me with that?"

"More than I usually say. I think I'm being very forthcoming."

She shook her head and smiled.

He opened his arms, and again she stepped into the embrace. Sandwiched between them, Leo gurgled, loving this new experience as he seemed to welcome everyone. So like his father. Two optimists, smiling their way forward into the fog of the unknown.

THREE

February, Key Biscayne, Florida

Two dozen men and women drifted across the spacious lawn with the 180 view of Biscayne Bay and the bejeweled skyline of downtown Miami. As Harper expected, the group was made up mostly of friends or fans of her mother.

Out of loyalty to Deena, they'd come to watch Harper perform, and after several flutes of champagne and sampling the platters of mushroom polenta diamonds, Spanish ham with olives and oranges, tuna niçoise crostini, and other exotic hors d'oeuvres, they would get out their checkbooks and donate to tonight's charity and receive a signed copy of Deena's final book as a gift.

Good people, community leaders, donors for a host of worthy causes. There was no reason for Harper to resent their condolences for her loss. No reason to squirm as some of them moved close to inspect her features, as if searching for signs of her own suicidal tendencies.

Dutifully, she mingled, nodded, smiled, attempted small talk. Sipped an exquisite chardonnay. Pretended to listen, thanked them for coming, for saying such kind things about her mother, for asking about her dad, replying as best she could to the well-intentioned banalities.

But Harper knew most of them would have preferred to be in the presence of the flamboyant Deena. Barely five feet tall, her mother had been a mouthy, street-talking, no-bullshit raconteur who could entertain any gathering with endless tales about the quirks and follies of the stratospherically famous folks she photographed. She'd also been an effortless entertainer. That is, when she found it necessary or amusing to conceal her aversion to the public and to socializing in general.

She could stand in any spotlight and perform her ass off, drop famous names with unaffected ease. Make the audience laugh, make them lean forward and listen, make them applaud. Like seals, she used to tell Harper, like trained barking seals.

It was when Harper was still in grade school that she'd realized her mother was a celebrity. Deena's photos of Hollywood actors, rock stars, avant-garde painters, glamour chefs, sports heroes, ballet legends, and the odd Vegas performer had won her national fame. That was her gig. Catching their essence. Stark black-and-white portraits, jolting in their intimacy. A fresh look at familiar faces.

The stars she photographed were stars already, overexposed personalities. But somehow Deena made them hipper and more human and more radiant. She always managed to find some original angle, using her camera to psychoanalyze them, strip away their public shields, find their core, capture it, and magnify her own star power in the process. A symbiotic thing: the stars using Deena, and Deena using the hell out of them.

In her early twenties, Deena had learned her craft as a stringer for *Rolling Stone*, starting out as a groupie with a Nikon. After a couple of years on the road, her breakthrough came with a single black and white of Mick Jagger, shirtless, his jeans hanging so low on his skinny hips that pubic hair boiled above the waistband.

The hotel room was in shambles, bedside lamp broken, a painting above the headboard askew. On Mick's face, his usual insouciance was replaced by a lewd stare, his lips twisted into a snarl so vulgar and ghastly it verged on the pornographic, as if she'd caught the rock star in the feverish aftermath of a thwarted rape.

Maybe Deena had led Mick on, seduced him, brought him to the brink, then cut off his advances with her camera. How she managed that shot, she never said. One of her many secrets.

That *Rolling Stone* cover was the start. More followed, then spreads in *Vogue*, *Vanity Fair*, *Life*, and *Look*—the slicks, the big time—and critics started taking her work seriously. These weren't glamour shots or paparazzi hackwork. This was virtuoso fine art, and it wasn't long before her covers were hanging on the walls of galleries in Manhattan. That's when the stars began to court her en masse.

Deena was their entrée into the holy high culture. Their uptown validation. Reputations made in Hollywood or on the political stage or concert tour couldn't rival the status of having their faces appear in a classy Manhattan gallery.

By her midtwenties, Deena had produced iconic portraits of Springsteen, Madonna, Pacino, Newman, Streisand, McCartney, Michael Jackson. She would go on to add to her list: brother and sister Fonda, Nicholson, Bon Jovi, Liz Taylor, Woody Allen, as well as dozens of frank and unsettling shots of world leaders, saints and sinners, and swaggering tyrants.

Deena's work was mounted in an exhibition at the National Portrait Gallery. Only the second woman to be so honored. Her first book, a collection of eighty-six photos, put Deena Roberts on the short list of major American portrait photographers. The second volume, *The Last Bloom*, came thirty years later, revisiting twenty-five of those same celebrities.

In the three-decade interval, some had transcended their superstar status, becoming legendary characters, while others swooned into anonymity. A few faces had deteriorated beyond recognition, and others were so surgically enhanced their features had become rigid masks, sad, freakish reproductions of their younger selves. The side-by-side shots were frank and melancholy and achingly honest. The grim power of thirty years.

As Deena's apprentice, Harper loaded and processed film, set up lights, did meter readings, and shot test Polaroids. Little more than a lackey. And though Harper had taken only three of the twenty-five new photos herself, Deena insisted on listing Harper as the coauthor of *The Last Bloom*, nudging her to follow in the career that had consumed Deena for four decades. Though Deena claimed she saw in Harper's work a unique and delicate sensibility, an artist in the making, Harper decided she wanted a family. A rooted life, a stable, durable marriage. Those simple, ordinary pleasures that Deena had so thoroughly disdained.

After Deena's death, Harper refused all requests to stand in for her at book signings and gallery showings around the country. But when Deena's old friend, Dolly Grimes, former first lady of the state of Florida, pleaded with Harper to take Deena's place as the headliner at a fundraiser for Doctors Without Borders, Deena's beloved charity, she could find no graceful way to decline.

At nine thirty, Harper's host, the patrician Dolly Grimes, herded the crowd off the putting-green lawn and into the mansion's library for Harper's dog-and-pony show. As her audience settled in the half circle of padded chairs, Harper chatted with Manuel Vega, the video assistant sent along by the publisher. A dozen signed copies of *The Last Bloom* stacked on the nearby dining table were to be auctioned off later in the evening.

Dolly made a brief introduction. Harper thanked everyone for coming, then nodded to Manuel to kill the lights. Behind her on the screen appeared a portrait of the young, brash Cassius Clay, his elegantly structured face, his eyes afire with wicked humor, and on the facing page was the white-haired version, bloated and unfocused, yet somehow Deena had captured a glimmer of wisdom radiating from his fading presence.

"Never liked the guy," a man called from the shadows.

A woman shushed him, called him George, then apologized to the assembly.

But George was just warming up.

"Goddamn Muslim draft dodger."

His wife shushed him again amid the uneasy murmurs.

"Did you meet him, Harper?" a woman asked from the front row.

"Several times, yes."

"What was he like?"

"Like that." Harper motioned at the screen. "Exactly like that."

Harper nodded at Manuel Vega, and Ali's twin selves dissolved, replaced by the young and old versions of Jamal Fakhri.

Harper stiffened, her mouth suddenly dry. She cast a panicky look across the shadowed room, as if one of Jamal's jackals might have infiltrated the gathering to avenge the ruler's murder. But of course that wasn't possible. She quieted her breath. Tried to calm herself.

Only Harper's handler knew her role in Fakhri's last moments—no one else, not Ross, not Deena, not even her brother, Nick. She'd made a clean escape. No . . . the reason Jamal's image floated on the screen beside her had to be something more prosaic. She'd given Manuel Vega a list of tonight's portraits, but he must have decided to use the most notorious subject in Deena's book, as any good promoter would do.

On facing pages, both shots of Jamal showed him in a starched white shirt buttoned to his throat. He'd aged little in thirty years. Only subtle differences—his nose and ears were fractionally larger in the second, but the most telling change was his eyes. Young Jamal looked into the lens with the haughty snarl of self-assurance, a man who saw his rise to absolute power as an easy-glide path stretching out before him. The elder Jamal's eyes were hooded and as grim and lightless as those of the thousands he'd butchered to retain that power.

"Wasn't he assassinated?" asked a woman from the front row. "Beheaded or something."

"Good riddance," called George from the back. "Why the hell waste film on a shit-heel like that?"

"Did he seem evil when you met him?" another woman asked.

Harper couldn't form an answer.

"He was murdered right after this was taken. That's what I read. A couple of days later." George again.

The room rustled with whispers. Harper was still too rattled to speak, the scene brutally fresh in her mind. A hotel suite in Rome with a balcony view of the Spanish Steps. Jamal was wearing another starched white shirt. Everything glaring on that fiercely sunny day. Deena was five stories down on the sidewalk below, hailing a cab to the airport, heading off to Paris and her next shoot. Jamal was gliding around the room, plying Harper with risqué talk and a chilled Masseto merlot. Two bodyguards posted outside in the hallway, two more in the lobby, several down below on Via dei Condotti. Harper sweating, a fast clock ticking in her breast. All the rehearsals, the months of training leading to this small window, this rare chance. Working up her nerve, choosing the moment. Reminding herself of the mass killings, the carnage, the atrocities Jamal was guilty of. Her heart flailing.

As it flailed now. Harper gathered a breath, blinked away the memory of that blinding sunlight, that plush hotel suite, the rug flecked with blood. She raised her hand, signaling Manuel Vega to move to the next photos.

Behind her, Jamal's face vanished, and on the screen a familiar Hollywood scowl materialized. Ben Westfield, gaunt and defiant, already a superstar at forty, he stood shoulder to shoulder beside his seventy-year-old self, a mythic presence now, twice as lean and ten times as cool.

"Now you're talking," George said. "Westfield's my kind of guy. Man's man. Hairy-chested son of a bitch."

Harper cleared her throat and was finding her voice when the overhead lights came on.

At the rear of the crowd, Nick appeared. His dark mane slicked back, his bulky shoulders looming, no longer the skinny runt he'd been as a kid. These days he radiated a force field of vitality.

How he'd located her, and why he was here, she had no idea, but a wave of chills lit up her back.

He held her eyes, sending an old message, one they'd telegraphed each other since their early days of hand-to-hand combat on the practice mats of various dojos.

This is going to hurt. Dig deep.

Nick came forward through the crowd, his face tight. Discreetly, he held up a cell phone and motioned for Harper to follow him. The guests whispered as she moved away from the screen, and, together, Harper and Nick headed to a parlor just off the library.

"What's wrong?"

"It's bad," Nick said and held out the phone.

Harper took it, pressed it to her ear, and heard a man's voice she didn't recognize. Official, impassive. Giving his name. Identifying himself as Detective Joe Alvarez, City of Miami police, asking if this was Harper McDaniel. Wife of Ross, mother of Leo.

FOUR

Five of the eleven engines housed at Fire Station 8 on Oak Avenue in central Coconut Grove were dispatched just after 8:30 p.m. to the three-bedroom wooden cottage that occupied a corner lot five blocks northeast of the station house. Teresa Wallace, a neighbor, called in the alarm after hearing two pops she believed at first were firecrackers, followed a half minute later by an explosion that knocked dishes from her cupboard and sent her spice rack clattering to the floor.

When Teresa stepped onto her front porch, she saw what she later described to the arson investigators as a white fireball erupting from the shingle roof of the house two doors down and across the street. The flames quickly turned orange and red and whooshed through the dwelling from front to back. Streamers, they were called, lines of accelerant that led from one room to another.

Two minutes after her call to 911, the three engines arrived and tapped into a hydrant a half block away. With such a rapid response, they were able to contain the fire to that single house and a nearby oak tree, but even after twenty minutes with all hoses working, the cottage was a total loss, and by the time Harper McDaniel arrived home at nine forty-five, driven by Nick, only the brick chimney and portions of a back wall still stood amid the smoldering wreckage.

Harper pulled away from Nick's restraining arm and plunged into the crowd assembled on the sidewalk across from her home.

She called out for Ross and called his name again.

She searched the crowd for his face and for Leo still strapped to his chest. She marched down the row of onlookers. Recognizing neighbors, some teenage boys from three doors down, and Amos, the homeless man who pushed a grocery cart up and down their street.

"Ross?" she called into the darkness.

Nick was beside her, hand on her shoulder, slowing her.

"Help me," she said to him. "I can't find them."

"They're not here, Harper."

"Where are they? The hospital? Where, damn it!"

Nick turned toward the smoking rubble. Men in orange turnout gear were moving around the edge of the wreckage, hosing down the remains. A couple of police officers strung yellow tape around the perimeter of their lot. A female crime-scene tech took photos, stepping off the outer boundary of the house's foundation, her strobe flashing and flashing.

Rising from the cinders was their refrigerator and, clinging to its door, the magnets that spelled out silly messages to each other. Coils of smoke rose into the night sky, and a shower of sparks exploded upward as a portion of the last wall collapsed.

"We have smoke detectors," Harper said. "Ross changed the batteries last week."

"You need to talk to Alvarez, the detective. He has some questions. Can you do that, Harper? Can you speak to the police?"

And though she knew, she heard herself ask again in a quieter voice, "Where's Ross? Where's Leo? I want to see them." She marched across the street, tore apart the yellow tape, and walked into her front yard.

Two officers moved in to block her way. "I'm the owner, I live here. My husband and son, where are they?"

"No, ma'am, you can't go any farther," one of the cops said, taking a grip on her upper arm. "You need to stand back. Someone will come speak to you shortly."

A short chopping blow to the side of his throat sent the cop stumbling backward. She dispatched his partner with a knee. Coughing, the first cop fumbled for his weapon, and Harper slung him to the ground.

Nick was yelling at her to stop. More officers were sprinting in her direction. But Harper marched on. It was her house, her loved ones. No one could stop her from confronting this, seeing what was there.

"Let her through," someone called, and the phalanx of firemen and cops parted.

The hoses shut down. A few swirls of smoke rose from the old green couch where she and Ross had first made love on a cool December evening two years ago. Leo's crib was collapsed on its side, his collection of dump trucks and stuffed lions somehow spared from the flames. She walked around the side of the house to what had been their bedroom, where a man in a white protective suit, surgical gloves, and a paper mask was kneeling beside a white sheet.

"She's the wife," Nick called from somewhere behind her.

"Show me," she said to the kneeling man.

He shook his head.

"This is a crime scene, lady. You can't be here."

"Show me, goddamn it."

She shouldered in beside him, stooped over the sheet, ripped it back. Ross was dressed in a pair of red running shorts and a long-sleeve white T-shirt. Leo, wearing his *Lion King* pajamas, was strapped to Ross's chest.

Leo's face was untouched, as though Ross managed to spare him from the ravages of the fire. Only a smudge of soot marked his cheek. Leo's eyes were half-open and his mouth pulled wide into a dreamy grin, as if this were some fresh prank his parents had staged for his amusement.

On his pajama top, there was a ragged perforation through Simba's left ear. Leo's heart had shielded Ross's heart. It had taken a second bullet to bring down both father and son. That other slug had entered Ross's forehead, dead center, a neat puncture that hardly bled. Just a smudge, as if someone had dabbed a bloody fingertip against his flesh.

Harper sank to her knees in the ash and laid her body across the two of them. Father and son.

Blue lights pulsed around her. She heard a wail, maybe her own.

Hands drew her upright, brought her to her feet. She struggled for balance as the neighborhood spun. The sirens shook the trees, trembled the darkness. The whirl of emergency lights, her own howl of anguish, the scream of a mother and wife. This wasn't possible. This was not real.

Someone led her to a gray unmarked police car. Eased her down in the backseat, leaving the door open. Nick stood nearby while Harper sobbed.

When the weeping subsided, she lifted her head and looked around to find that most of the crowd had wandered off; only a few stragglers remained. The fire was extinguished. Bright lights were being erected on metal stands to illuminate the scene.

A detective came to speak to Harper, but she had nothing to say. He was paunchy, wearing a white short-sleeve shirt and dark trousers. His gut hung over his black belt. She stared into his face, uncomprehending. He asked her a couple of questions, and when she didn't respond, he left to walk the scene, taking notes, speaking to his colleagues.

"I'm okay," she said to Nick. "I'm okay."

"Shall I call Alvarez back? Get this over with?"

"Not yet."

In the distance, she saw Ross's body laid out on a stretcher. Two attendants were bumping the gurney across the yard toward an emergency vehicle. Under the sheet was the bulge of Leo still in the sling, as if Ross were pregnant and being rolled away to the maternity ward to deliver their son. All this happening without her, as though she were watching from the sidelines of a dream, paralyzed by sleep, knowing this was wrong, unacceptable, but unable to move, unable to speak or affect the outcome. Her husband was going into labor, suffering the terrible pains of childbirth without her.

As they opened the rear doors of the ambulance and cranked the stretcher higher, Harper pushed herself upright, stepped out of the car, shrugged off Nick's hand, and jogged across the street, the policemen stepping aside for her this time, cautiously watching her go, Harper yelling for the paramedics to stop, don't leave her behind, she needed to be in the operating room, needed to hold Ross's hand, help him breathe and push, help him survive the hours of travail, be there for the delivery of their smiling boy, Leo, who embraced every new thing, including the trauma of being born, a yip of joy at the sight of the operating room lights. A bright, happy yip.

FIVE

February, Coconut Grove, Florida

Harper was back in the car, numb, dizzy. The door was open, and the detective stood in front of her, smoothing a hand over the swell of his belly as if it had just appeared there and he was becoming familiar with it.

He asked her questions, several in a row, which Harper only half heard, until he asked, "Know anyone who would want to do harm to your husband?"

She shook her head, keeping her eyes on Nick, who stood behind the dark-haired cop.

"Did you have video surveillance on the property?"

"Why would we?"

"These days a lot of people do."

"No cameras, no."

"Ross, your husband, he was a reporter?"

"An excellent reporter."

"I'm sure he was. Know if he'd had any recent disagreements or hostile encounters? Perhaps on the job, a colleague, someone he'd written about."

Harper shook her head, saying nothing.

"Look, I'm sorry for your loss," the detective said.

She brought her eyes to his, this cop whose voice was flat, devoid of sentiment, his eyes dulled by too many nights like this.

"Spare me," she said.

"The sooner we do this, the more helpful your answers might be. You want us to catch this guy, don't you?"

She choked on her response, made a noise like a child's hiccup.

"Okay, okay," the detective said. "Tomorrow we'll talk, when you've had a chance to compose yourself."

"Agreed," Nick said.

The detective asked Nick if he was a friend or relative.

"Brother."

"You'll see she has somewhere to sleep tonight?"

"I want to get Leo's stuffed animals and his trucks," she said.

Alvarez told her she couldn't do that. There'd been enough contamination of the crime scene. Maybe by tomorrow afternoon their work would be done and she could see what items she might salvage. The site would be well protected. Nothing would get stolen.

"This was arson," Nick said. "I smell accelerant from over here. Gasoline, kerosene, something. You don't smell it?"

"Doesn't work that way. We process the scene, find the origin of the fire, do lab work on the materials, canvass the neighborhood. We don't sniff the air."

"It was an execution," Harper said. "Fire was to destroy evidence. It's not complicated."

"Possibly," the detective said. "We'll know soon enough."

"Why? Who would kill a child and set him on fire?"

The detective looked away. "I need a phone number, sir, where I can reach Ms. McDaniel, then you're free to go."

Alvarez handed Nick his business card and a pad and pen. Nick scribbled on the pad and handed it over.

"What part of town you in?"

"Condo on Brickell, the Aqua. You need an address?"

"I know the place. I'll call in the morning, see if she's ready. Come by when it's convenient, but the sooner I get a statement the better."

"That's it?" Harper said. "Exchange phone numbers, send us home?"

"Look, Ms. McDaniel. Considering you assaulted two of my men, I'm being pretty patient. Somebody else running this crime scene, you'd be downtown now."

"No need to threaten her," Nick said.

"You're her brother," Alvarez said. "And her lawyer too?"

"I'm her bodyguard," Nick said. "And she's mine."

They had a brief stare-down until the cop looked back at Harper.

"Moments like this," the cop said, "sure, I've seen people lose it. But putting two officers on the ground, that's a first. I'm giving you a pass, but honestly, you're straining my goodwill. Both of you."

The capillaries threading the cop's nose and cheeks were engorged. His eyes flickered as if Harper's rage and grief had roused in this man some dormant fury of his own, not directed at her but toward some larger failure of humanity he'd witnessed too often. This was probably as close to empathy as the detective could muster. Repressed by his training, calloused from other gruesome nights, he'd acquired the survival techniques he needed to keep going.

"I'm sorry," Harper said. "Please ask the officers to forgive me for blindsiding them. I'll try to get ready for your questions tomorrow."

With a curt nod, Alvarez paced back to the rubble, rejoining a couple of other men dressed in white short-sleeve shirts and dark trousers.

Nick helped Harper out of the car, led her down the row of emergency vehicles and patrol cars to his red Mercedes. He held the passenger door for her and took her elbow as though she were an invalid. She looked back at what was left of her home, the house Ross had occupied for a decade before they met, the house where they fell in love, had their first candlelight dinners, where she became pregnant, the charming cottage they were going to share till they were old.

Someone called her name, someone hustling down the street.

Nick stepped in front of Harper to shield her from this new intrusion. Out of the smoky gloom, Geneva Carlson came huffing toward her.

Senior editor at the *Miami News*, Ross's boss, wearing a black tracksuit and running shoes, holding some rolled-up papers like a baton. Geneva was in her late sixties with a silver cloud of hair. Though she was short and delicately boned, she was a dynamo in the news business, a relentless broad whose decades of covering the Miami crime beat had earned her the unwavering support of the most cynical of her stable of reporters. Ross had loved her.

"Tell me it's not true," Geneva said. "Ross and Leo."

Yes, it was true, Nick told her, giving her the outline. Gunshots, arson. A two-sentence summary.

She rocked forward, bowed at the waist, hands on her knees, a silent yawp of pain. Harper put her arm around Geneva's shoulders and raised her upright.

Geneva stared into Harper's eyes. "This is my fault," she said.

Harper stepped away. "How could it be your fault?"

Geneva walked over to the Mercedes and unrolled the newsprint on the hood of the car.

"Tomorrow's edition, it's just out. I should've said no. It felt risky, a violation. But it was such a great story. Ross didn't tell you, did he?"

In the murky light, Harper and Nick leaned close to the page.

Ross's byline.

The Mobster Living Next Door

She scanned the first paragraph, and the name leaped from the page: *Sal Leonardi*, the gangster. Deena's father. Harper's cold-blooded granddad.

SIX

Sal Leonardi was born of immigrant parents in Newark during the Great Depression. When Sal was still a child, his father, Giuseppe Antonio Leonardi, was drafted, sent overseas to fight against the Nazis, and damn if he wasn't among the 160,000 Allied troops storming the beaches of Normandy. Along with four thousand other unlucky Americans, Giuseppe Leonardi lost his life that day, leaving young Sal as the eldest male in the family. That was how Ross's article began.

Harper knew every heartbeat of her grandfather's story. She'd told Ross some of it herself. As it turned out, Giuseppe was no war hero. He died a coward. Executed by his own commander as he raced back to the landing vehicles through the bloody waves and bobbing corpses. Running for his life, a deserter, struck down as an example to the others.

After he lost his father, Sal devoted himself to the church, an altar boy, drugging himself on the incense of piety. For the next few years, he was a priest in training, until one August night when Sal was fifteen.

Sal's mother, Margaret, a modest, religious woman who bore a resemblance to a slimmed-down Sophia Loren, was walking home late at night from her second job as a barmaid at an Irish alehouse when she was waylaid by a gang of punks she'd been serving earlier that evening. They dragged her into their automobile, and for the next few hours they worked her over, used her and used her again in every way those hoodlums could imagine, then tossed her out on a desolate highway like trash.

The next day, Sal—the apprentice priest, Sal, the fifteen-year-old boy with angelic features, a soft voice, and a deep religious fervor—marched out of the church and never returned.

The first corpse was discovered in the weeds beside a school yard. The Irish punk was castrated, his eyeballs scooped out, testicles jammed into the sockets. His penis was missing.

All this, each grisly detail, Harper first heard at the age of six. Portioned out, one grim anecdote after another, night after night, as Deena used her family's dark history for Harper's bedtime fairy tales.

Harper had shut her eyes and squirmed, but even so, she was enthralled. One night at the conclusion of the latest installment, Harper admitted she was confused about the moral of these bedtime stories.

"This is what's in us, darling," Deena said. "You should know, this is what's swimming in our veins."

Harper couldn't tell by Deena's tone: was this a warning or a boast?

After a second castrated body appeared, Sal's priest appeared at the Leonardis' door and took Sal into a room alone and commanded that he stop what the priest and everyone else in the neighborhood knew full well he was doing.

A few days after the priest's visit, the third corpse was discovered. Again, the testicles were replanted in the eye sockets, the penis gone.

Michael Tessalini, the boss of Newark's leading crime family, was the next to arrive at the Leonardis' door. Like the priest before him, he sat with Sal alone in their parlor. He asked after Sal's mother. Convalescing upstairs, Sal told him. All right, Tessalini said, what you're doing, these killings, this is not good, not good for business. The Irish coppers are seething, some are harassing my men.

The mobster understood Sal's anger, of course, for who could not understand such a thing, an eldest son protecting the honor of his mother. But this had to cease. Sal said nothing but nodded as if he understood. When Tessalini was finished, Sal walked him back to his fancy sedan and watched him drive away.

A week went by before another of the Irish punks was found mutilated like the others. Which left only one, the leader of the group, a loud and reckless lout named Patrick Mulligan. In a panic, Mulligan left Newark, running to Boston, where some of his cousins promised to protect him. He spent every waking hour in their presence, slept in the gang house with his door bolted, a gun at his side.

Two months after Sal's mother's savage violation, on that same desolate roadway where Margaret Leonardi was found bleeding and unconscious, Mulligan's body was discovered sprawled on the shoulder of the road, eyes gone, replaced by his gonads. A collection of withered penises lay on his chest.

Soon afterward, Tessalini paid another visit to the Leonardi home and sat with Sal in silence. The mobster gazed in wonderment across the room into the eyes of the fifteen-year-old boy, amazed that a child whose only knowledge of the world until a few weeks before had been acquired in the hushed sanctuary of the Church of the Little Flower on Fowler Street could have transformed himself into a killer who inspired awe throughout the hard-bitten neighborhood and the respect of men as cold and depraved as Tessalini.

Finally, Tessalini asked him if he was done, if he'd had his justice.

"No more killing," Sal said. "I'm finished."

"No matter," Tessalini said. "There's other uses for a young man like you."

Thus began Sal's career. And that was the lede of Ross McDaniel's story. Everything Harper had heard of her grandfather was contained in Ross's article. Each element fully faithful to the facts that Deena had long ago relayed to her.

But Ross McDaniel had clearly gleaned the details from other sources, since Harper had always been guarded in what she revealed to him about Sal. Only the broad outlines. She'd never mentioned Tessalini, never told him about the Boston gang of toughs that hid Mulligan and failed to protect him. All that and more, Ross uncovered on his own. Somewhere, somehow.

———

In the haze of days that followed, Nick looked in on her at intervals, offered homemade chicken soup, scrambled eggs and bacon, sandwiches, meatloaf, mashed potatoes, comfort food, Harper shaking her head, no, no, she couldn't eat, she could barely breathe, even when Warren Roberts, her work-obsessed, cosmically distant father, and Willow, his shiny new wife, came for a visit and stood stiffly in the doorway, mouthing banalities: If there's anything we can do please let us know, do you need anything, anything at all? Help in planning the memorial service maybe?

I want my child back and my husband, she told them. Can you do that, can you bring them back to life? I want to hold Ross in my arms, cradle my son, my spunky kid. Can you do that, Dad? You have some special powers I don't know about? All your money, your high-powered connections, can they buy back my family?

You don't mean that, Harper, said Willow.

Oh yes, she did. She damn well meant it. She wanted them back, she wanted her world back, her lucky life that was snatched away. Slinging her anger, her bottomless despair into her father's pale, round face.

A runty man, five foot eight, Warren Roberts sighed with what sounded like relief, turned, and left. Failing again to muster a simple comforting word or touch. He seemed forever confounded by the language of empathy. A deficiency that was only magnified by his marriage to Deena, whose personality and success so dwarfed his own that Harper never understood what strange alchemy drew them together in the first place and kept Deena returning home from her far-flung travels.

Harper rose and shut her door and wept and writhed on Nick's guest bed. She paced. She read Ross's article again, a detailed accounting of her grandfather's appalling life, his growing power in the mob, his brushes with the law, multiple indictments for racketeering, tax evasion, conspiracy to commit murder, all dismissals or hung juries. Photos of Sal at a nightclub, showgirls on each arm, always surrounded by squat, flat-eyed gangsters, politicians, and Hollywood types. Another shot of him leaving a Manhattan courthouse, smiling, giving a thumbs-up. In the latter stages of his Mafia career, he became an elder statesman to his young compatriots, brokering disputes among warring families, gliding above the fray with a newfound authority. Last, Ross described Sal's final transition, his quiet withdrawal to South Beach, just another old fart, crab-walking the sunbaked avenues in his plaid Bermudas. He quoted one of Sal's neighbors: "That Sal is a sweet old guy, quick with the joke. All the kids on the street love him."

Living among the naïve, a wolf among lambs.

Harper never warned Ross away from Sal. Never thought it necessary to tell him that Sal was off-limits. It was so obvious. Sal was their family's private disgrace, the mob's paymaster, a man who'd overseen dozens of hired killers.

She'd not seen or spoken to him in years. But she remembered him vividly. Vital and twinkling with wit. An irresistible charmer. Everyone loved him. Shoeshine boys, mayors, jockeys, cops, Hollywood femme fatales swinging their perfect hips in tight sparkling gowns just to catch Sal's eye. High, low, it didn't matter. Everyone knew Sal. Everyone perked up when he entered the room, arrived at the track, sat in a barber's chair. Harper had loved him too, when she was a kid. Before she knew who he truly was—the fearsome ogre of Deena's fairy tales.

SEVEN

February, Brickell Avenue, City of Miami

The morning memorial service was held at Coconut Grove Congregational, and dozens of Ross's colleagues from the paper filled the pews. When Harper couldn't manage the eulogy, Geneva stepped in, told a string of anecdotes about Ross, his lighter side. His love of practical jokes, poignant stories about his early years as a street reporter before he discovered his investigative skills. Stories from the years before Harper knew him.

Harper sat dazed and half hearing, the sanctuary filled with a woozy fog. Her breasts were swollen and aching. Engorged with Leo's untapped milk. She'd put cabbage leaves inside her bra to soothe them, a remedy Deena had shared in Harper's early days of pregnancy. So typical of Deena. Before Leo was even born, she was already coaching Harper on how to push her child away, excommunicate him, tear him from her breasts so she might return to more serious matters.

Early that afternoon, Nick filled the doorway. Detective Alvarez had arrived. Was she finally up to answering some questions? She shrugged. She'd already put him off for four days.

"Want me to stay?"

She told Nick no, that wasn't necessary.

"Then I'm going for a run. Back in an hour."

Alvarez fitted himself into a bedside chair, laid a manila folder in his lap, and clicked his cop's eyes around the room as if taking an inventory of Nick's decorating taste.

Harper was propped against pillows on the bed across from the TV with the sound off. She thought the television might blunt the pain. The twenty-four-hour news channel with its incessant churn of horrors, mass executions, beheadings, tsunamis sweeping away towns.

It hadn't worked.

"What do you want?"

"Anything you know that might help. Like some longstanding feud Ross had with somebody at work or some other area of his life. Was he worried about some person or situation? Did you have the kind of marriage where he'd confide his troubles with you?"

"We shared everything."

"Geneva Carlson says Ross never talked about his works in progress, even with Ms. Carlson. Does that apply to you? Like, did you know about this article he was writing about your granddad Sal? Or what he was working on next?"

"That was the only thing he kept to himself," she said. "The only solitary thing."

"Far as you know it was. I mean, if he was keeping secrets, then they were secret, right? So did he seem bothered by anything, something going on in his world and he didn't want to talk about it. Like you could tell from his mood that he was being pensive or brooding?"

"All right," she said. "There was something wrong. Ross was concerned. The last time I saw him, the last time we talked."

"And what was that?"

"The story he was working on next."

"How do you know he was worried? He say something?"

"He didn't need to. It was in his eyes."

Alvarez nodded, but he seemed disappointed. "He wrote his stuff at home, right? Used a laptop."

She said yes, at home.

"Didn't go into the office, maybe type on the paper's computers?"

"He went to the office for editorial meetings, that's all."

"That's too bad," Alvarez said. "Arson guys combed the scene. Everything's burned to cinders. Notebooks, laptop, it's all gone."

"I'm giving you the key," she said. "Chocolate."

"Chocolate?"

"The article he was writing. It was about chocolate. The history of it, the chocolate industry."

Alvarez shook his head as if to clear it. "Pretty far afield from his usual racket—politics, public corruption. Chocolate? You know this how?"

"He told me the night he died. The subject of his article: chocolate. That's it. I saw something in his eyes that night, so I asked him about it."

"Look, I understand this is rough, you're having a hard time. You say you saw something in his eyes, okay, fine. But I need something solid. Maybe you could tell me what else you recall in the days leading up to the event. Phone calls, a suspicious person wandering the neighborhood, an odd piece of mail, anything out of the ordinary."

"I think Ross was giving me a hint in case something happened. Like he saw it coming, knew he might be in danger."

"I'm sorry. This isn't computing for me."

"Then screw you. Quit harassing me, go do some real police work."

She hated how she sounded. Snotty, privileged. The surge of rage strangling her voice, making it tight and shrill.

"Police work," Alvarez said softly, as if trying out the phrase. With an awkward smile, he looked past her at the curtains pulled across a window, staring at the material, summoning patience. "Let me tell you a little something about police work, okay? What I've been doing these past few days. Would that interest you?"

Harper took the TV remote from the side table and snapped off the set.

Alvarez drew a pad from his shirt pocket and paged through it. He found the note he wanted, studied it, then looked back at her.

"What I read was your husband's byline for the last eight years. Very prolific, a real bulldog. He averaged ten articles a year, nearly one a month. Add in the follow-ups, comes to one hundred four separate articles. As I was reading, I was making a list. Each and every person your husband went after. Want to know the results?"

She waited. Staring at the blank screen.

"I couldn't lump everyone together, the targets of his pieces, too varied. Politicians, cops, real estate developers, lawyers, judges, sports guys, Miami Heat, Dolphins. Quite a list. So I broke them down. Ones did actual jail time. Those still in prison, those that were released, paroled, served their time, whatever. These are people who were indicted as a direct result of your husband's work. Things he uncovered the state's attorney couldn't ignore that went to the grand jury.

"It's an impressive roll call of sleazewads. Eleven wound up serving time. Three still inside, two dead already, which leaves six who are out, still living in South Florida. There's half a dozen people with strong motivation to seek revenge against Ross for causing their downfall.

"But see, I'm just getting started, because after those convicted felons, you got the loved ones of those six, relatives, spouses, kids. People close to the ones in jail, some of them, they could be harboring hard feelings, think your husband did them dirty. Their breadwinner's locked up, maybe they had to sell their houses, pay lawyers' fees, make ends meet. Serious lifestyle adjustments. These people could be pissed.

"So there's seventeen of those, more if you count kids who grew up without Daddy or Mama, every one a possible time bomb ticking and ticking until one day, that's it, they can't take it anymore. They have to strike out. And who do they blame? Maybe it's Ross McDaniel."

"This is meaningless," she said.

Alvarez consulted his notebook again, flipped a page. "In addition to those two groups of suspects, you got your run-of-the-mill-public-humiliations, fifteen-minutes-of-infamy crowd. They didn't serve jail time; then again, you never know with high-profile folks how they're going to react to public shaming. Your husband digs up some dirt on a guy, suddenly that guy loses his country club privileges, his favorite tee times, head waiter at Joe's Stone Crab doesn't give him his favorite table anymore, he's got to stand in line with the rest of the bozos, bouncers suddenly don't know his name, won't unsnap the velvet rope at his favorite club.

"Different people, little slights like that, it could hit them hard. They simmer a few years or months or whatever, then pop and decide everything started going south when Ross McDaniel published his article.

"So that's what I've been doing, making my lists, tracking down the people on my suspect list, interviewing those I've found. I'm up to nine so far. Does that qualify as police work?"

Harper said nothing, fighting off a bitter comeback. She had to calm down, remind herself this guy wasn't the enemy.

He tucked the notebook back in his shirt pocket, rose from the chair, unfastened the folder, drew out several eight-by-ten glossies, and offered them to her.

"What's this?"

"Crowd scenes, night of the fire. Standard procedure with suspicious fires, a crime-scene tech shoots the crowd. Firebugs like to be there, up close, watch the results of their work. It gets them off."

"Firebugs? This isn't arson, it's murder. The fire's a cover-up."

"Take a look, see who you see. Maybe something'll jump out."

She took the photos, paged through them. Neighbors and bystanders she didn't know, their faces brightened by the strobe's flash, squinting at the horror before them, the wood cottage destroyed, two bodies rolling away. She went face by face down the rows, saw a couple of them chatting to each other, a smiling woman, a smug man, a guy in the back talking on his cell. It wasn't their catastrophe. They could go on living as before. Be grateful their own houses were still standing, their loved ones intact, an undercurrent of relief in most of the faces.

"Look for someone who doesn't fit. Maybe somebody from another part of your life, it's weird they'd be in a crowd of onlookers, anything hinky, out of place."

She slid the photos back in the folder and held it out.

"Keep them," he said. "If it's too hard to look at them right now, do it later. Put some names to faces if you can. It might be helpful. Okay? Humor me."

"Are we done?"

Alvarez wasn't done. He was on his feet, prowling the room. Stopped in front of the bookshelves, took one of the trophies down and examined it. Put it back, took down another one and another, fascinated.

"Judo, karate, tae kwon do, jujitsu, these others I never heard of. These are yours? Your name inscribed right there. Harper Roberts. How many? Fifteen, twenty? Man, you kicked some serious ass. So these are the moves you used on my guys? You were holding back, huh?"

She didn't answer.

"What's your brother doing with your trophies?"

"He pulled them from the garbage."

"Yeah? You threw them out? Really?"

"Is that a crime?"

"Myself, I never won a trophy, not for anything. If I had, I think I'd keep it forever, pass it on to my kids if I had kids."

"I travel light."

"On the road with your mother, taking photos, globe-trotting."

"My mother took the photos. I was along for the ride."

"I heard she was training you to take her place."

"I was her assistant. No one could take Deena Roberts's place."

He picked up another trophy, a gold figure on the top, a woman in a fighting robe executing a hip throw.

"You were seriously into this martial arts thing. Mind saying why?"

She sighed. The guy was bullheaded.

"For Nick's sake."

"How's that?"

"He was a skinny kid, looked different, his accent stood out."

"So he got bullied."

"Relentlessly," she said. "He was too shy to go alone to training classes, so I went along."

"You stuck with it for a good while."

She nodded to herself. A good while, yes.

"Tell me about Nick. He's not a blood relation I take it."

"Adopted," she said.

"He's what, Serbian, Polish, one of those?"

"Russian," she said.

"I was close. Got those Slavic cheekbones. A handsome guy. How'd he wind up an orphan?"

"How is that relevant?"

"Probably isn't, but in this business, you never know."

She sighed and said, "Nick's father was an engineer helping build a power plant in Turkey along the Syrian border. A terrorist group attacked the compound where the foreign workers lived, both his parents were killed. Nick got sent back to a Russian orphanage."

"That's a rough start."

She was silent, staring at the empty TV screen.

"And Nick does what? Business card he gave me says he's a banker."

"He works for the World Bank, but he's not a banker."

"What? Like a loan advisor or something?"

"He's a resettlement specialist."

"That's a new one on me. What is it?"

"World Bank loans money to build a road or a dam in some country, Nick figures how much to compensate the farmers who lost their land. Helps them find a new home."

"I should know what the World Bank is, but I don't. I thought it was, you know, like a big bank."

"You might want to look it up."

"Okay, yeah, I'll do that."

"Is that all?"

"Well, about that accelerant your brother smelled at the scene. It was charcoal lighter, a big can sitting on a shelf in the back pantry."

"What?"

"That shelf survived the fire, there was a rust outline matching the bottom of the charcoal lighter can. So it's like the killer saw the lighter fluid, sprinkled it around, and set the blaze. Crime of opportunity. Guy operating on high emotion, angry, impetuous. He kills, then, Oh my god, what the hell did I do? I have to cover it up. He finds the can, and bingo."

Harper shook her head. Too painful to follow the logic, too harrowing to picture.

"You two close, you and Nick?"

"What's that got to do with anything?"

"I don't know. Way he was acting the night of the fire, that thing he said about being your bodyguard. That struck me funny."

"What're you saying?"

"It's part of the process, ruling things out. Start close to home."

"Like what? Nick's a suspect?"

"I'm just trying to fit the pieces together is all."

"So how's that work?" She leaned forward, burned him with a look. "Nick and I are lovers, he killed Ross out of jealousy? Are you crazy?"

"Your words, not mine."

Alvarez set the photos on her side table along with his business card, his cell phone scribbled on the back, told her good-bye, went back to the bookshelf, examined the trophies again, and left.

Harper pushed herself off the bed, picked up Alvarez's card, wadded it into a tight ball.

She drew her cell phone from her purse, stared at it for several moments, then punched in a number. A familiar voice answered before she even heard a ring.

"Hey, Harper. I thought you might call."

"So tell me what you know."

"Nothing to tell."

"It wasn't Jamal's son?"

"No. Jamal Junior didn't kill your husband."

"You're sure of that? A hundred percent?"

"It wasn't him or any of his people. Jamal is too busy destroying his country. Fending off coup attempts every other week. Unlikely he knows you exist. Even if he did, he doesn't have time for a stunt like that."

"A stunt?"

"Sorry. Wrong word."

She drew a breath, looking out the window at the silver sunlight flickering on the bay.

"So, tell me, Harper. You considering coming back in?"

"That an official invitation?"

"Someone with your skills, door's always open."

She didn't reply.

"Had to ask. So tell me, you need help? As you know, we've got resources your local cops never dreamed of."

She crushed Alvarez's business card into a tighter ball and tossed it into a wastebasket.

"No thanks," she said. "This is mine to do. All mine."

"In case you change your mind, don't lose this number."

After the line clicked off, she kept the phone to her ear, listening to the stillness. Finally, she drew a long breath and set it aside.

She got up, showered, put on fresh clothes from Nick's closet. Baggy jeans, a black T-shirt, and a red flannel shirt. Tall, lean Nick. She had to roll up the cuffs of the jeans, but otherwise his clothes fit.

She marched to the front door, stepped into the hall. Waited till her heart settled, then she shut it behind her and set off down the carpeted corridor.

Outside at the valet station, she told a uniformed young man she needed a cab.

"Where to?" he said.

"Is that any of your business?"

The valet straightened, gave her a quick look, then turned to the line of cabs and waved one forward.

EIGHT

It was stupid what Spider was doing. Parked in the guest lot outside the Aqua, a fancy-ass condo a mile or two from downtown Miami, twenty stories of white stucco with splashes and stripes of rainbow trim, trying for a hip art deco feel.

He'd been out there off and on for four days, windows down, watching the comings and goings of the residents and maids and delivery guys. A steady stream of Mercedes and Jags and low-slung whatevers. Hot Latinas in tight clothes and stilettos, carrying shiny shopping bags inside the building. Studs handing over their fancy cars to the valets. All the guys looked younger than Spider, no apparent jobs, but lots of cash for their wheels and clothes and their haircuts.

He was nursing a bad attitude toward the residents of the Aqua. Developing an itch to hurt somebody, break a car window, piss on their soft leather bucket seats.

After the killings, he'd followed Harper and the wavy-haired guy over here. Waited around for a while, then headed back to the Marriott, where he was staying, got some sleep, did some Internet work, and learned the dark-haired guy was her brother, Nicholas Roberts. Crack of dawn, he stopped at a convenience store, bought a morning paper with Harper's photo on the front page. He filled his ice chest with Gatorade and beef jerky and Ritz Crackers, and came back over and found a parking spot in the guest zone, excellent vantage point to watch the entrance.

Stupid, stupid, stupid. He'd never behaved like this before. Always the consummate pro, same routine each time, doing his due diligence, scoping out his target, choosing the most advantageous time, then executing the job. Afterward, he'd pick up his envelope of cash and move the hell on, put a thousand miles between himself and the scene of the crime.

The plain fact was he missed his daily dose of Harper. Spying on her routines, shower, dress, making meals in the tiny kitchen, kissing her husband, playing silly games with her kid, all the trivial things. The woman had snuck into Spider's central nervous system, taken up residency. Harper, the virus.

Four days and no sign of her. He was starting to think she'd left the condo when he was back at the motel, but then early that afternoon the same fat cop who'd questioned her at the fire showed up, same dumpy clothes and gray Mercury four-door. Which meant she had to still be in there, probably grieving, immobilized.

Ten minutes after the cop arrived, brother Nick headed out for a jog. In the valet area, a couple of Latina chicks stopped and watched Nick run past. That kind of guy.

A half hour after that, the slobby cop left.

Brother not back yet, Harper all alone in there.

Spider was jittery, feeling like he was building up to doing something he wasn't sure what.

He got out of the car without a plan.

Spider always had a plan. But look at him now, walking across the parking lot, heading to a side door that someone left propped open. He was going inside that building, heading upstairs to the eleventh floor,

1101, where Nick Roberts lived, where Harper was shacked up. Crazy Spider. Out-of-control Spider.

Halfway to that side door, goddamn if Harper didn't emerge from the front entrance. So close he could see the coffee brown of her eyes, but she didn't glance his way. She was wearing a red plaid lumberjack shirt, baggy jeans, getting into a taxi. A strained look on her face. Not the serene woman he'd been watching on his iPad. This Harper was gaunt, dead eyed, stiff, walking with a delicate tread, like someone wearing a bomb strapped to her chest.

Spider hustled back to his rental.

Stupid, stupid, stupid.

———

On the sidewalk outside Sal's apartment, Harper paid the cabbie and sent him on. When she was done with Sal Leonardi, she had no exit strategy, no picture of the future, only a blank, endless wasteland stretching into a hazy forever.

Sal's apartment was on the first floor of a two-story building on the corner of Lennox and Fourteenth, west of Flamingo Park. Ten blocks east was the beach, four west the bay. The windblown stench of low tide and rotting seaweed filled the air. Inhaling that heavy breeze, Harper fought back a sharp-edged memory of her last beach outing with her family. But the harder she pushed it away, the more insistently it returned.

At Crandon Park on Key Biscayne, Leo gurgling with delight. Coated in sunscreen, half-hidden under a floppy hat, waving at the seagulls. Ross was hugging his bare knees, staring out at the water, at the bright streamers of Sunday sunlight ricocheting off the flat sea.

It was just over a week ago. Ross must've been finished with his piece about Sal and was working on the chocolate story. Maybe at that moment he was debating whether to confess to Harper what he was so worried about, and when his eyes strayed off to the flat sea and went vague and unfocused, he was struggling to reconcile his longstanding habit of hiding his story subject against his growing concern.

Or maybe he was oblivious to all that and was just fiddling with the prose. Rewriting in his head. She didn't know that part of Ross. As she stood outside Sal's apartment on the empty sidewalk, she grappled with this recognition: that she'd never fully known that vast quadrant of Ross's interior. His work, his compulsion to expose.

She pushed open the iron gate, walked down a narrow sidewalk, and turned right at the first apartment. Sal's place. A year ago, this same season of the year, Deena had pointed it out. Driving past, on the way to a photo shoot on South Beach, she'd said, "That's where he lives. Right there. Apartment 101. Like a normal citizen. Like everybody else."

Without another word, Deena had braked hard, swerved into a parking space, staring at the white building with the green trim.

"What're you doing?" Harper said.

"The son of a bitch. He's in there watching TV, jerking off, or whatever the hell he does with his time."

Deena threw open her door, staggered into the middle of the street, and halted, the traffic easing around her. She screamed out his name. She screamed it again and again until faces appeared at windows of the neighboring buildings. Deena howled some long syllable of pain until Harper got out and quieted her, getting her back into the car.

"He's in there," Deena said as Harper drove them away. "The son of a bitch is in there smiling."

"Did he do something to you? Is that what this is about?"

"He never touched me," her mother had said. "But he tainted everything. He stank of cigars, stolen money, and fresh blood."

Harper went to the door of 101, her mother's howls echoing between the buildings like a tortured spirit riding an ancient wind. Overhead, a gull squealed. Cars passed on the street. Twenty years since she'd seen the old man. A Christmas visit unannounced, Sal arriving at the front door with an armload of gifts. Deena blocked his way. Ordered him to leave. Still in her pj's, Harper stood a few feet away. Sal looked past Deena, his eyes on Harper. He had shrugged his helpless apology to her, turned, and walked back to his black Cadillac.

Now she gripped the aluminum doorknob. Twisted it, found it unlocked, pushed the door open, and stepped inside.

Sal was sitting at a small desk, typing on a laptop. He wore a blue terry cloth beach robe. Beneath the desk, his legs were spindly and hairless, white flip-flops on his feet. His bulky body had dwindled in the years since that Christmas morning. He'd acquired a hunch, a forward tilt of the neck and shoulders, as if the burdens he carried were deforming him.

Peering over Sal's shoulder was a young Asian man in swim trunks and a tie-dyed T-shirt.

They both noticed Harper at the same moment, and Sal reached out quickly and shut the lid of the laptop and stood.

He spoke quietly to the Asian man. Bowing to Harper several times, the young man edged past her and exited.

"My neighbor," Sal said, rising to his feet. "No social skills, but a good kid. Been teaching me some computer tricks."

Harper hadn't prepared a speech, hadn't prepared anything. She stood in Nick's clothes. Out of body, out of mind.

Sal studied her for a long moment, then drew a breath, his face looking suddenly tired.

"Come in, come in. Good to see you, kiddo, even at a bad time like this. My sympathies, by the way."

Harper broke free of her paralysis and shut the door. She stepped closer to him. Maybe she appeared menacing to the old gangster, or maybe Sal felt a pang of modesty, because he tightened the belt on his beach robe, pulled the lapels together across his pelt of white chest hair.

"You're mortified. Your grandfather, the mobster. The newspaper article, it blindsided you."

"Mortified? Like I didn't know all that already?"

"Your mother tried to poison you against me."

"That's not why I'm here." She took two steps toward him. Sal holding his ground. "People are saying you murdered Ross because he exposed you. This was your retribution."

"You believe that?"

She blew out a breath. "Not even you are coldhearted enough to kill your great-grandson."

"I appreciate your high regard for me. So what brings you?"

"I need to know something."

"For you, doll, I'm an open book."

"Ross interviewed you for that piece, didn't he? You two talked face-to-face."

"A half dozen times, yeah. A good kid."

"And in all that time, did he ever mention chocolate?"

"What?"

"You heard me."

"I don't know from chocolate. But yeah, we talked, I told him my story. He took notes. But no, I don't know anything about any chocolate."

"It's what he was working on next, a story related to chocolate, cacao beans. You're sure he didn't mention anything?"

"That why you came to see me? You playing detective?"

"Somebody has to."

"Well, hey, glad to hear it." He looked away, running something through his head, then coming back to her. "Look, since you're poking into things, something maybe you should see."

He moved to an ancient TV cabinet and plucked out a small object.

"Know what this is? Ever see one before?"

He held it out: a white disk the size of a shirt button.

"Recognize it?"

Harper came forward, took the object from his hand. A piece of electronics, charred on the edges and partially melted.

"That little piece of shit was in your house," Sal said.

"What're you talking about?"

"It's a spy cam, that's what I'm told. See that little aerial, like a cat whisker? It's a 1080p HD. Twenty feet away, it can read the time on your wristwatch. The shit they can do these days, it's scary."

"In my house?"

"In the rubble. My guess is there're more in there. This one, it's from the master bedroom, the master bath, one of those."

"How'd you get it?"

"Contacts I got."

Harper shook her head, trying to focus through a sudden whirl of light-headedness. She set the spy cam back on the TV cabinet.

"Contacts in the Miami police department?"

"There, yeah, other places too. Should see my Christmas card list."

"Somebody in the police department gave you a camera they found in the remains of my house."

"It's not like anybody volunteered. But, yeah, I called around, talked to some people, let them know my granddaughter was the one who lost her husband and her little baby, and was there anything they could do behind the scenes, a courtesy to an old friend. Maybe later on I could assist in some capacity, use my resources.

"Guy shows up yesterday, stands where you are, hands me this. Says the camera was up on a wall, in a corner. Sent video and sound to your Wi-Fi."

"I don't understand."

"Maybe Ross put it in, like a security thing. Didn't tell you."

Harper held to the back of a chair as the floor swayed. "He wouldn't do something like that without consulting with me."

"Just so you know, that newspaper article, it was my idea. I called Ross, invited him over, laid out my deal. Made him lunch. We talked over pastrami on rye. Took a while to convert him, show I was serious. He thought I was scamming him. I liked that young man. A smart kid. Skeptical, a nose for bullshit. Knew what he believed, had values. You picked a good one, Harper. A good, solid man."

"And why'd you do that, call Ross?"

"I'm getting old. Got some medical bullshit going on, so I know the clock is speeding up. I wanted to come clean, see if there was a possibility of a second chance."

She shook her head, not getting it.

"Second chance with you. What's left of my family. Your mother, shooting herself the way she did, it was a kick in the gut. Made me start thinking about things. Like it might be nice to see my great-grandson from time to time." He raised a preemptive hand. "Oh, I'm not crazy, I knew you weren't going to invite me over for Thanksgiving, nothing like that. But I thought, I don't know, maybe you and me could come to an understanding, reconcile. If I put my ugly past out there, it might get things rolling. A public confession like they do in AA and that bullshit. Stand up, ask for forgiveness. Ross thought it might do the trick."

Sal went over to the TV cabinet, picked up the camera, studied it.

"I'm not sure there'll ever be another Thanksgiving," she said. "But if there is, sure, you're on the list."

He looked at her, his face softening, and he nodded his thanks.

"I keep thinking about this thing," he said. "Somebody wanted to kill Ross, okay, maybe it was some dirt he dug up on a cop, some guy on the take, I get that. The boy was a hard-ass. He knocked over some hornet nests, made enemies. But when I run it through, I keep getting stuck on this little camera.

"A hit man, now there's a trade I know about, but I never knew a pro hiding cameras around the house of his target. Why'd he do that?

51

What's he trying to find out? That's where to start. That little piece of plastic. Where it came from, why it's there. Anything it could tell us."

Harper took a measured breath and looked into Sal's eyes. The old man was smiling at her.

"You follow? I think that little camera is where to start."

"The camera."

"Where you start digging. I got no confidence in the cops. I mean, sure, plenty of times I been the beneficiary of their ineptitude, yeah, yeah, lucky me. But this time's different, this killer, I want this asshole. So what I'm doing, I'm making it my project to nail the guy's ass to the wall. It's how I got started in this business in the first place, things coming around full circle, personal vengeance, pure and simple. You interested?"

Though she knew the answer, Harper asked the question anyway, wanting to hear the words spoken aloud, complete the choral response, this chilling ceremony they were performing.

"Interested in what?"

"You and me join forces, find the lowlife that did this. You want in?"

NINE

On the sidewalk outside Sal's apartment, Harper tried to catch her breath. The old man had offered to drive her back to Nick's condo, at least call a cab, but she wanted to walk, burn off the manic shivers.

She set off fast, a block, another block, steering east toward the beach. Minutes later, when she arrived at the water's edge, crossing Collins over to the white stretch of sand and the boardwalk and the breezy palms, she found the ocean still as a lake.

She crossed the boardwalk and slogged through the soft dune sand and kept walking toward the water's edge. Her heart had lost traction, skipping and wallowing without rhythm.

At Sal's apartment she'd come looking for information. A long shot that Ross let something slip about his chocolate story. A few minutes later, Harper made a pact with the old man. Partners now, they would track the killer, uncover the motive, and when they found him, they would execute whatever grim justice they decided on.

At the end of their meeting, Harper had shaken Sal's dry, bony hand, agreed to speak later, to share what evidence she could obtain from Alvarez, with Sal doing the same. He'd activate his network of cronies and former associates, call in more favors. Between the two, it might take a week or a month or a year, but they'd succeed.

The foamy surf curled around her ankles, soaked her shoes. She waded forward, up to her shins. The sand loosened around her feet. She could feel the alluring undertow calling out the names of the weak and willing.

She thought of Deena in the palatial Crillon Hotel, the slug blasting apart the muscles of her heart.

She looked out at the spread of the ocean and imagined disappearing into the blue foam, taking a long pull of the brine and being finished with the pain. Join Deena and sweet Leo and Ross in the darkness, in the vast empty room on the other side.

"Good god," came a voice behind her. "You're her. You're Harper."

She halted, turned to look into the face of a tall, red-haired man with pale-blue eyes. He wore white slacks and a loose Cuban guayabera and was holding out the front page of the *Miami News*, the issue from three days ago with her photograph on the front page.

"Look, I hate to intrude," he said. "But this is you, right? Harper?"

She stared at him a moment, then nodded.

"Oh, man, I'm so sorry. My deepest sympathies. I was just reading what happened, these crimes, and I look around and there you are. I couldn't help saying something. I can't imagine your pain."

"Thank you. But I'm okay."

He took a long, worried look at her.

"Well, I'm sorry, but you don't look okay. You seem a little, I don't know, you seem lost. I don't want to be forward, but is there anything I can do? Call a friend. Maybe give you a ride somewhere."

"I said I'm okay."

She turned from the waves, mounted the hard-packed slope, passing by the man. He was silent, staring down at the newspaper in his hand, at her photo. He seemed flustered by his own forwardness, holding himself stiffly, an awkward grip on the paper.

Back on the powdery sand with the sunbathers and vacation revelers, Frisbees in the air, jarring music, the scent of coconut oil, she plodded across the boardwalk, found an empty bench beneath a cluster of palms and could go no farther. She sat.

The man had tagged along and was standing a few feet away at the far end of the green bench.

"My name is Harry, by the way. Though my friends call me Spider."

She nodded, giving the man a longer look. His pale-blue eyes seemed tranquil and faraway. A poet's eyes. A mystic's.

"Look, I'm sorry I bothered you. I apologize."

He folded the paper, tucked it under his arm. She'd registered something about him, an echo of another face, one she'd seen before, one she'd seen recently. She couldn't remember the context, couldn't pluck that single image from the harrowing flurry of the last few days.

"You're sure you're okay?"

"I'm sure," she said. "Thank you for your concern."

He told her good-bye and started off. He'd gone a few feet when Harper called after him. He halted, turned slowly, and returned. She thought she knew where she'd seen the face. Not certain, but if she was right, she couldn't let this man simply walk away.

"If it's not any trouble," she said, coming to her feet. "I guess I *could* use a ride."

TEN

February, Brickell Avenue, Miami

The man called Spider drove in silence, following Harper's directions back across the causeway and onto the mainland. Out her window, there was a sad shimmer on the palms and roadside greenery, and though the sky was powder blue and cloudless, the light seemed oppressive, as though the sun were being suffocated by some universal force that only she could see.

Maybe this was to be the feel of the world from now on. Maybe her grief would permanently alter her vision the way a concussion can recalibrate the brain, cause a subtle slippage of gears, a new microscopic tremor in every frame of the film. Where even breathing becomes the solemn and tedious labor of someone trapped in an iron lung.

Spider turned into the Aqua parking lot and found a space in the guest area, turned the engine off.

"How did you know where I lived?"

He turned to her and gave her an anxious smile.

"You told me a while ago. You steered me here, turn by turn."

"Did I?"

"I'm afraid you're not thinking straight," he said. "I mean, I'm a complete stranger. We just met at random. I could be anybody, I could mean you harm. You got in my car, let me drive you home. You're muddled. It's understandable, what you've been through. But still."

"Do you mean me harm?"

He smiled, a nervous twitch in his lips. "Of course not. It's just that because of your heartache, your loss, you're confused and vulnerable. You need to be careful. You need to protect yourself. This is Miami, for god's sake. Not the safest city."

"Does this mean you don't want to come up to my apartment?"

Spider looked out the windshield at the high-rise. In the afternoon sunlight Harper studied his profile. He had long, feminine lashes, and the angle of his long nose smoothly continued the slope of his forehead. From that angle and in that slant of light, his pale eyes seemed to have iced over, giving them a thin, foggy coating like cataracts.

On the back of her neck a set of cold fingers trilled a warning. She was no longer sure she recognized this face. Maybe he was right and this impulsive act of hers was a grave mistake.

"If you want me to, I'll come up," he said. "Only to make sure you get home safely. Nothing more than that."

"I'll make us some coffee."

"No, I won't come inside. Just ride up, see you to the door. Only that much." He said it in an odd singsong as if making a vow to himself.

In the elevator he stood apart from her, cut his eyes to the stainless steel panel next to him.

On the seventh floor, Spider hung a few feet behind Harper, following her down the carpeted hallway to her door.

She fitted her key into the door and swung it open. In the kitchen, the blender was snarling at high speed.

"Come in," she said. "I insist. Just for a minute."

Maybe she was crazy, but after dragging the stranger this far, she had to double-check her hunch.

She called out a hello. The Cuisinart stopped, and a second later Nick appeared at the kitchen doorway, holding the glass jar of the blender.

"Nick, this gentleman was kind enough to drive me home from Sal's."

Nick nodded and said hello, but she could see from the subtle stiffening in his shoulders that Spider had tripped some alarm.

The two of them shook hands awkwardly.

"All this time you were at Sal's? I was starting to worry."

"Give him some of your protein shake, Nick. I need to take care of something."

Spider cleared his throat and glanced around the foyer, his gaze settling on the bronze Buddha perched on the teak console table, then tracking across Nick's collection of Asian watercolors, Japanese castles rising from mountain mists, two women in lavish kimonos standing shyly side by side, heads bowed, a landscape of Mount Fuji, a single owl on a branch printed on silk. Art from the Far East was one of Nick's passions, rooted in his martial arts training and collected during his world travels.

As he stood engrossed before the wall of paintings, Spider withdrew into himself like one determined to memorize every detail laid out before him so he might recount them later.

Harper stepped down the hallway to the guest room, shut the door behind her, and went to the side table where Alvarez's stack of photos lay facedown.

She fanned them out on the bedspread, eight shots from the night of the murders, most of her neighbors and a collection of strangers gawking from the sidewalk. She bent close and studied them, going from face to face until finally one stopped her. She took that photo to the sliding door that opened onto her balcony and drew open the shades and tilted the photo to the light and peered at the assembled spectators.

He was standing in the back row next to Teresa Wallace, who lived directly across the street. That night, Spider had been wearing a different guayabera, and his forehead gleamed in the rippling light. He seemed transfixed, more focused on the tragic event than any of the others around him. There was the blur of movement in the crowd, people speaking in whispers to the ones beside them. She could almost hear the murmur of empathy, a cringing sadness for the horror of what was unfolding before them. But there was no compassion in Spider's face, only a stark, rigid focus, a narrowing of the eyes, not unlike the look she'd seen a few moments ago as he drank in every fabric, every shape and color and material in Nick's apartment. A man mesmerized.

Nick sat at the kitchen table, drinking his blueberry-and-kale concoction, the same one he made every day, the morning paper open before him.

"Where is he?"

"Your friend left," Nick said.

"Just now?"

"A minute ago." Nick put down his glass. "What's wrong?"

"We need to catch him. He's involved."

"Involved?"

Harper hustled to the door and stepped into the hallway. It was empty. Nick followed her to the elevators. The lighted panel showed both cars were in the lobby.

"You going to tell me what's going on?"

"The guy was standing outside the house on Margaret Street the night of the murders. He was in the crowd shots Alvarez left. Bumping into him this morning, that wasn't an accident. At the very least, the guy's stalking me."

Harper mashed the "Down" button once, twice, three times, but both elevator cars remained on the ground floor.

"The stairs," she said.

Seven floors, rubber legged, Nick passing her halfway down. Out the front door, past the valet stand, trotting at half speed while they scanned the parking lot.

"In the guest lot," she called to him, "second, third row."

A moment later she spotted a man with his profile, same hair, same shirt, slipping between a row of cars. Not in a particular hurry, not looking back. A guy with nothing to hide. A few steps farther, she lost sight of him as he rounded the back of a parked UPS truck.

"Come on. That's him."

Harper broke into a sprint. After a few strides she could hear Nick breathing evenly a step or two behind.

At a shoulder-high hedge, she came to a halt. She'd lost him again. Nick stopped beside her. "Maybe he saw us, he's hiding."

"There."

Twenty yards away, Spider appeared from behind an oversize SUV with darkened windows. Still sauntering. He didn't look over. Stopped at the driver-side door of the car he'd been driving and dug out his keys.

Harper pushed through the hedge, shifting into a brisk walk, no hurry now; she was well within range and didn't want to spook him.

Ten yards away, as Spider fit a key to the lock, the windshield of the car beside him exploded. More slugs peppered the adjacent cars.

"Down, down." Nick grabbed Harper and dragged her to her knees in the aisle of parked cars. She heard the scream of tires and the thuds of a dozen more rounds slamming into fenders and doors and trunks. Then everything was quiet again.

PART TWO

ELEVEN

February, Coral Gables, Florida

Alvarez said, "The shots came from that building, you're sure of it? The yellow-and-white one?"

Harper said yes, as sure as she could be with it happening so fast.

Alvarez asked what floor the shooter was on.

Nick said, "How many times do you need to hear it? We didn't see the shooter. We were hiding. We stayed down for five minutes, maybe longer."

"You heard the actual shots?"

"No."

"How do you know for sure the guy was in that building, not the next one over?"

Nick said, "We saw what we saw."

"I think he was hit," Harper said, "maybe a couple of times."

"Yeah, yeah," said Alvarez. "From the blood trail, looks like he was winged pretty good. He'll be lying low somewhere unless he's stupid enough to show up at a hospital."

"He didn't seem stupid. Brazen, maybe. Not stupid."

"Before he was shot, while he was with you, Ms. McDaniel, driving over from the beach, he do anything physical? Touch you?"

"No."

"Why?" Nick said. "You think he was planning to hurt her?"

Alvarez shrugged. "He was at the fire, and we've also spotted a man resembling him on two neighbors' security videos, walking toward the McDaniel residence earlier that same evening, just after nine, a minute or two after Ms. McDaniel leaves for her fundraising party. They missed each other by a hair. Few days later, same guy shows up on Miami Beach, bumps into her, clearly no accident.

"What's he up to? I see two possibilities. He wants to pick her brain, see what she might know about the investigation. Find out if he's in danger, needs to run. So he's insinuated himself in her life for information purposes. Second possibility, not one I like, maybe the guy's not finished. Ms. McDaniel is his target. Maybe she was the primary target all along."

"Harper the target? Why?"

"Can't say for sure."

"Then who shot him?"

"Don't know yet, but look, I'll put some men on you, Ms. McDaniel. Twenty-four-hour watch, a week or two until we sort this out."

"Not necessary," said Nick. "She has protection already."

Harper asked him what protection he was talking about, but Nick said nothing more.

———

The next morning, Friday, Harper forced herself out of bed. Had silent coffee with Nick, read the morning paper, a front-page account of the mysterious shooting in the Aqua parking lot. No one hurt, several cars damaged by gunfire. Shell casings found in a ten-story empty condo next door. Miami PD had no comment on the incident at this time.

Harper sent Nick on his jog. She didn't need around-the-clock babysitting. When he was gone, she took a seat at his Mac, logged on to her e-mail account, and read through dozens of notes of condolence, friends she hadn't heard from in years. Answered most in a sentence or two.

She watched the cursor pulse, then on impulse, she tapped Ross's name into the search window,

Thinking maybe she could bring alive some memory, some tangible scrap of him. She'd already exhausted the photos on her phone. Scrolled through them again and again, wept over each one, mined them for every association, every hour surrounding the split second when the image was captured.

Luckily, the Leica R8 she'd used to snap those final photos of Ross and Leo playing with shaving cream was still in the backseat of her car. For no good reason, she'd carried that old camera out of the house last week when she'd left for the charity event. Thank god for that. But those images of Ross shaving, Leo strapped to his chest, would have to wait until Harper was strong enough. And that could be a long while.

Every other scrap of their life together was lost. Albums, snapshots she'd developed herself, dozens of framed photos, even Ross and Leo babbling a recorded message to callers on their antiquated answering machine was lost in the fire.

She clicked on their joint bank account, knowing this was pointless masochism, but Harper found herself looking at the images of Ross's checks, his handwriting, his signature, the wild inconsistent scrawl of a man dashing headlong through a chore he hated. Caught in a mindless pattern, she clicked and clicked. Phone bills, Florida Power & Light, the check for his credit card, their cable bill, their Internet bill.

Telling herself to stop but unable to, looking at just one more, and another. The hot pressure of tears building behind her eyes. Water bill, online movie streaming service, and then with a jolt, she realized what she was really doing.

Her heart rolled. She closed her eyes, settled her breath as the weight of this exercise became clear. For days she'd been feeling her way through the haze of anguish and confusion, fending off despair, thinking she was lost when all along she'd known this one thing was lurking just below the surface of her thoughts: a key.

She blinked away the mist in her eyes, straightened her shoulders.

She moved cautiously through the checks, one by one discarding them and moving on. She knew exactly what she was searching for, even knew the amount they paid once a year. But she couldn't allow the word to take shape in her mind, as though it might somehow jinx this process.

She paged through the months until she reached the previous July, and there it was, the due date for their yearly bill. Eighty-nine dollars paid to Epic Enterprises. She stared at the image of the check.

For years, Ross used Epic as his cloud backup service. Any article he was writing was automatically saved and would still be alive on Epic's server, flickering somewhere in cyberspace.

She navigated to Epic's website, typed in Ross's e-mail address, then tried his most common password. *LovelyLeo#1.*

Access denied.

She tried their landline number, another password they'd used off and on. Same thing, no access.

Their bank account password failed, as did the one they used for shopping websites.

She tried the oddball mixture of numbers, letters, capital and lowercase, with four asterisks in a row at the end. It was their top-level password for their single credit card. Same deal, access denied.

She scrolled through the company's web page, located the customer-service number, and used her cell to call. She worked her way through Epic's automated obstacle course and finally heard a human voice, a curt older woman.

Harper explained her dilemma, trying to access her husband's account, didn't know the password, tried several with no luck.

"The e-mail associated with the account?"

Harper gave it to her. The woman was clearly reading from a script.

"Your name?"

"Harper McDaniel."

"No such name listed on the account."

"It's in my husband's name. Ross McDaniel."

"Unless your name is attached to the account, you're not permitted access."

"My husband's dead. Murdered a week ago."

There was a lengthy pause. This wasn't on her script.

"Sorry for your loss," she said, not sounding at all sorry. "But if the person on the account is deceased, I'll need an official death certificate to release the password. Are you ready? I'll give you the fax number."

"Give me your supervisor, please."

Without another word, the woman broke the connection and the empty line buzzed in her ear. She tamped down her fury and redialed.

It took her four more tries before she found someone with enough daring to bend the rules. The employee sent the password to Ross's e-mail. Harper got it and unlocked the Epic account, and there, filling the screen, was every file on Ross's hard drive.

Pages and pages of JPEG icons, his collection of snapshots, more pages of music files, and, at the tail end, a single movie file.

On the final page were two folders of Word documents. One held all of Ross's finished articles arranged by date. She ticked through them and saw the final one was titled "The Mobster Living Next Door."

There was no rough draft of whatever he'd been working on next.

The other folder had its own password protection. But it opened on the first try. *LovelyLeo#1.*

Inside was a single document many pages long.

Leaning close to the computer screen, she scrolled quickly till she reached the end. Just over fifty pages. Most of it seemed to be notes about chocolate. Research on the history of cacao beans, methods of agriculture, names of manufacturers and chocolatiers.

At the very end of the file, Ross had made a short list. He'd labeled it *Contacts*. And he'd numbered the items, one to four. A person's name, location, and contact information.

The first two were Jean Luc Diallo and Moussa Kouacou, both with addresses in the Ivory Coast.

The third was Adrian Naff with a Zurich, Switzerland, address.

And last was Jackson Sharp, living in South Florida.

She scanned the pages again, and her eye lit on a section set apart from the notes on chocolate. Ten pages, dialogue, scene, action. A different font and double-spaced. It looked like a short story embedded in the center of his research notes. It was dated early December, two months back. She read the first few pages. A scene set in a Denny's restaurant in downtown Miami, told in the first person, as though the material was too raw to be handled in his detached newspaper-journalist voice.

TWELVE

Miami, Florida

"Know anything about chocolate?"

I didn't care for Jackson Sharp's pissy tone, but, hey, I'd agreed to meet the guy, listen to his tale, see if there was a story worth telling. So I was straining to be patient.

"I like my Cadburys like anyone else."

"Might help if you read up on the subject."

"Listen, Jackson, don't get ahead of yourself. I haven't signed on for this. I'm just listening."

"Okay, let me tell you how she got involved."

"Maybe we should cut to the finish."

"You need to hear the whole deal. It won't make sense otherwise."

I sighed, said fine, the whole deal.

"Rachel had this idea, a short documentary film about chocolate. The way cacao was grown, harvested, manufactured, then focus on the high-end gourmet stuff. Nothing controversial, a demo, really, show her skills, her camera work. That's all she wanted, enter some film festivals, a foot in the door. She loved chocolate, a total chocaholic, so it was a natural. She was

researching, looking for a catchy angle, when she stumbled on something, started tugging on this thread, and the more she tugged, the scarier it got."

"When did she discover this scary thing?"

"Two months before she was murdered."

"I'm sorry? Your wife was murdered?"

"That's right."

"And when did this alleged murder take place?"

"Not alleged, it happened."

"Okay, when did it happen?"

"October, same time as the harvest on the cacao plantations in Africa."

"And you reported this murder to the police?"

Jackson slumped against the padded booth. Wiry guy in his late thirties with ostentatious sideburns, a neck tat of a fancy crucifix.

"Sure, I talked to the cops and some idiots at the State Department, for all the good it did." He stared glumly out the plate glass at the midmorning traffic. "No one could be bothered. They didn't take me seriously. A murder all the way over in Africa. What proof did I even have? Maybe she ran away. Was your marriage solid? Insulting shit like that.

"After a while I thought, Christ, I keep going the official route, I'll ring somebody's alarm, put myself in the crosshairs of the people who killed Rachel. These guys have spies all over. Then I started thinking of other ways to go, and I remembered you, the stuff you write, what a bulldog you are. And I thought, yeah, put it out in public so the law would have to take notice."

I was silent, worried Jackson Sharp might be a total whack job. Spies all over—made him sound like a conspiracy nut. Wouldn't be my first.

"What kind of work you in, Jackson?"

"High school teacher. History."

"Here in Miami?"

"Gables High. Look, come on. Let me show you the film so you see what's what."

"I don't know. This isn't exactly what I do."

"You need to see the goddamn film, okay? Do that, then you can walk away. This whole thing might be too hot for you. These are dangerous assholes, they do whatever it takes to keep their secrets. They've got more money than the pope. They killed Rachel; they'd come after you if they knew what you're doing."

Like he was searching for eavesdroppers, Jackson made a show of scanning the restaurant, looking over the late-breakfast crowd, mostly retirees and, three booths away, huddled over pancakes, some party-dressed kids trying to quell their South Beach hangovers.

I knew Jackson was baiting me with the danger bit, but I couldn't help myself and said, "Listen, just so we're clear, risk is not an issue for me. My subjects have to meet certain criteria. So far, this one doesn't."

"Yeah, yeah. You need a Miami connection, well, this has one. Rachel was born and raised here. I've been here for twenty years."

"This isn't what I do, Jackson. I go after corruption, political issues."

I raised a hand, motioned for the waitress.

She made a U-turn and came over. I asked for the check, and the woman looked down at my half-empty coffee cup and Jackson's water glass, shook her head at the big spenders. Jackson stared out the window. I mustered a smile for the woman. She tore off a slip from her pad and let it flutter to the table between us. Miami manners.

When she left, Jackson planted his forearms on the table, leaned forward, and spoke in a rush: "Film's only two minutes long, watch it, that's all I'm asking, the soundtrack is muffled, but I'll narrate."

He picked up the iPad, held it out, eyes pleading.

I sighed, said fine, two minutes.

"Okay, so, Yacou's the one they're rescuing, he's far left. Nine years old. Snatched from his village, dragged two hundred miles to this plantation where the video is shot."

"I'm listening."

"So, Yacou, he's been working on the plantation for years, a slave like the rest of these kids. All of them abducted. So why rescue just Yacou, why *didn't this guy liberate all the kids? I asked Rachel that before she went out there. Answer he gave her, it was too dangerous. One at a time is all Charlie was willing to do. Nothing she could say, it was his show, Rachel just along for the ride, filming over his shoulder."*

"So the guy she was with, his name was Charlie?"

"Charlie, yeah, worked for International Global Relief, setting up water-purifying systems, infrastructure out in the boonies. This rescue was like a hobby, 'his calling' is how he described it to Rachel."

"How'd she hook up with this Charlie fellow?"

"They started talking in a bar at the Sofitel where she was staying, and she said the magic word, cacao, and I don't know exactly what went on after that, but she called me before she shot this footage to tell me she was going with this guy Charlie into the jungle, going to film him while he rescued Yacou."

"Charlie have a last name?"

"Don't know it. I spent hours on the Global Relief website, went over the list of employees. Not a single 'Charles' posted in Côte d'Ivoire."

"All right. Your wife is tramping around the West African jungle with a guy with no last name who may or may not work for an international relief agency. And then?"

Jackson Sharp drew a breath and started the video, cocking the tablet so we both could watch.

Several boys in frayed T-shirts and baggy shorts were squatting in a circle on the ground. Working in a mechanical daze, they held the cacao pods lengthwise in one hand, gave them two sharp whacks with the machete, snapped them open to expose the milky cocoa beans, and shook them out onto the growing pile in the center of the circle.

"Two years Yacou is chopping pods, spilling out seeds, other risky work, you name it, spraying pesticide, no mask, zero protection. Never been to school, no future, all without any idea what chocolate is."

I nodded, warming a little.

"See those?"

Jackson tapped the screen and I leaned forward.

Crosshatching the kids' arms and legs were shiny scars like the engravings of some horrific tribal ritual.

Jackson said, "All the kids have them. One wrong swing of the machete. No doctor on the plantation, no medics, these kids are on their own. Disposable."

Palm fronds framed the image of the boys. Apparently Rachel and Charlie were hiding in a thicket around thirty feet from where the boys worked. As far as I could tell, the kids were unsupervised.

"Yacou knows this is the day. Charlie's been prepping him. Sneaking into this same spot in the jungle, somehow getting Yacou alone and working on him. Kid's homesick as hell. Finally Yacou builds up his courage, says okay. Plan's simple. He makes like he has to piss, walks into the bushes where Charlie will be hiding, they make a run for it. Not exactly Mission Impossible, *what could go wrong? But watch."*

Yacou was scrawny. His face narrow and bony, cheeks sunken, and he had a high, wide forehead. On his feet were yellow plastic flip-flops.

Rachel kept the focus on him as he glanced around the group, then gazed off in the direction of the camera and coughed.

"That's the signal," Jackson said.

The boy rose, said something to the others and headed toward the camera position. In a smooth arc the camera panned to the right and focused on a slender pathway into the dense, green foliage.

A few seconds later the bushes parted and Yacou appeared. He stood there for several seconds, then winced as if he'd felt a stab of pain.

A man's voice said, "What is it? What's wrong, Yacou?"

"That's Charlie talking," Jackson said.

The boy raised his hand slowly and pointed at them, swung around and called out in French.

"Ils sont ici." Here they are.

Two Africans in khaki uniforms crashed out of the brush behind him. Following them was a tall man whose blond hair was barbered short and oiled in place. With his blue button-down shirt, striped tie, and pair of black square-framed glasses, he looked ridiculously out of place, like an accounting professor had parachuted into the center of a jungle. There was a fourth man, a white man who showed up at the edge of the frame, a split-second flash of his face, then gone.

Yacou scrambled off into the bushes.

The African man in the lead snatched the camera and hurled it. It toppled through the bushes and landed on a patch of earth, still running, still capturing a cockeyed ground-level view past the base of a shrub.

The next few moments were chaotic with a lot of high-pitched talk I couldn't decipher. A half minute later when the film ended, I winced and looked across at Sharp.

He was nodding his head, see, what'd I tell you?

I said, "How'd you get this film?"

"That's part of the story."

I drew a breath and said, "Play it again."

"So you'll do it? You'll take it on?"

More slowly this time, I said, "Play it again."

Maybe with some computer enhancement the voices would clarify, but the tones were clear enough. At first Rachel and Charlie lashed out at their captors, then their indignation melted into hopeless groans. A man whose accent was tinged by inflections that might be German countered the two Americans' protests with a series of cool, clipped replies.

After more muffled exchanges, the woman, Rachel, made what sounded like a plea for mercy, followed by a series of desperate noes.

Though I knew it was coming, the final slanted image captured by the lucky positioning of the camera took my breath away a second time.

Only a foot from the lens of her own camera, a dark-haired woman slammed to the ground. Flat on her back, she stared up at the sky with wide and empty eyes. Her throat slit, blood pulsing in sync with her final heartbeats, pouring down her neck, puddling onto the brown earth.

Harper sat unmoving, waiting for the chills to fade. After she drew a decent breath, she tapped the keys, sent Ross's document to Nick's printer. When the job was done, she paged through the hard copy until she found the "Contacts" page and settled that on top of the stack.

She packed the printout into a manila envelope and tore off a page from Nick's pad to jot him a note, let him know where she'd gone. But a few words in, she stopped, balled up the paper, and threw it in the trash.

She would just drive by Sharp's place, check it out. Nothing more than that. She didn't need backup.

She had to scroll through a long list of contacts on her phone to find the name of the travel agent Ross had used for years. It was typical of her old-school husband to still be hanging in there with Johnny Parker, Happy-Go-Lucky Travel.

She asked to speak to Johnny, gave the receptionist her name.

He came on the line with a flood of apologies. For not coming to the funeral, for not sending a card, for—

Harper interrupted him. "I need to know something."

"Anything."

"Did Ross make travel plans with you in the last few weeks?"

"Don't worry, I canceled them when I read about what happened."

"Tell me his itinerary."

"He didn't tell you about it?"

"Just read me the list, okay?"

"I don't even need to look it up. It was such a weird trip. He never said what it was about, just gave me the cities and dates."

"The list, Johnny."

"Starts in Africa, Ivory Coast, capital city, Abidjan. From there he flies to Zurich. After that, back home."

"You canceled everything?"

"I did."

"How long was he planning to be gone?"

"I can't believe he didn't tell you."

"How long was the trip, Johnny?"

"With layovers, six days."

"When was he planning to depart?"

"Today, tomorrow, I can look it up," he said. "I'm sorry, but is this about his . . . you know, his murder?"

She closed her eyes. "From now on, Johnny," she said, "everything is about his murder."

He was quiet for a moment, then: "I'll do whatever I can. Ross and I go way back."

"Thanks. I'll get back to you."

She looked again at the list of addresses.

Number 1. Jackson Sharp. Edgewater Apt, 3-C, CG

If CG meant Coral Gables, as she believed, then she knew exactly where Edgewater Apartments was. At this time of day, with any luck, she'd be there in five minutes.

THIRTEEN

February, Coral Gables, Florida

It took seven.

She circled the block twice to make sure no one was following her, then parked on the street across from the three-story apartment complex. It was a twelve-unit holdout from the fifties, a grubby concrete-block building with rusty window air conditioners and mildew-streaked walls. The Edgewater was surrounded by posh condo towers that put it in perpetual shade. The street empty in both directions.

Across the street between the high-rises, she could see the iridescent shimmer of Biscayne Bay, smell the sea breeze sifting between the buildings, and hear the wild hilarity of seagulls.

On the bottom floor each unit at the Edgewater had a small patio. Some were decorated with ferns, bicycles crowded others, charcoal grills, mismatched furniture. Code violations for the Gables good-taste police.

She decided on a closer look. A quick walk by, nothing more.

She took the stairs on the north end. Met no one. Smelled meat cooking, a stew. 3-C was on the far end. Rap music thudded from 3-B next door. Beneath her feet, the walkway vibrated to the beat. She ran her hand along the concrete parapet.

Cold waves prickled across her shoulders. Not fear, not alarm. But a growing certainty that she was precisely where she was supposed to be, doing what she was meant to do. A resolve she hadn't felt in ages.

The door to 3-C was shut. The single window was cranked open, but its blinds were closed. A breeze off the bay rattled the aluminum slats, and she saw that a couple of them were bent inward around the hand crank. She stooped, and through the gap she made out a sliver of a tiny kitchenette, countertops littered with pizza boxes and take-out Chinese, dishes piled in the sink, a couple of glossy roaches reconnoitering. On a flimsy table sat a half-empty jug of wine.

She leaned closer, peered in, and saw a man in the kitchen, opening and shutting drawers, rifling through cabinets, pulling out cereal boxes and spices and bags of rice, letting them fall to the floor. He was around six feet tall, rugged with sandy hair. He had long, thick-wristed arms and a supple physique accentuated by a tight yellow polo shirt, skinny blue jeans. He drew open the oven door, stared inside, slammed it shut.

Was this Jackson Sharp? He looked too buff to be the same guy who'd eaten all those pizzas and egg rolls and left the boxes for feasting roaches.

The man turned her way.

Harper swung back, pressed her shoulders against the wall, waited to a count of five, then took a deep breath and stooped and peeked from that slanted angle. The man had his back to her now, and as he moved deeper into the kitchen, she saw past him into the living room, a lamp fallen to the floor, the glitter of broken glass on the tile, a lounge chair cocked all the way back, a man in gym shorts and white T-shirt sprawled in the recliner. Muttonchop sideburns, a gaudy crucifix tattooed on his neck.

It had to be Jackson Sharp. His eyes were shut, his head thrown back, arms clutched to his gut. His hands coated in blood.

The rapper from the apartment next door continued to throb through the cement walls. "Every day I'm muscling, every day I'm muscling . . ."

Another breeze clattered the blinds and swelled them inward. Harper took a backward step. Legs soft, uncertain.

As she turned to get the hell out of there, the blinds snapped open and the man stared at her. Blondish flattop, face impassive.

She ran. Heard the apartment door slam. Ran faster.

At the end of the landing, the stairway a few feet ahead, an iron hand caught her by the collar and yanked her to a stop. A hard, unmistakable object nudged her spine.

"Easy now, Harper. We're walking back to the apartment."

No. Never let your enemy choose the field of battle.

It was a simple move, one she'd practiced hundreds of times, rehearsing it daily on sweat-stained mats—a compact torso swivel, a windmill swing, and a chopping blow, the blade of her hand cracking against his wrist.

His pistol clattered to the cement as she continued the move, straightening and coming up with a fast, hard elbow. The blow glanced his cheekbone, knocked his glasses over the balcony rail.

It stunned him, left him open to two fast chops to his nose then throat. Which sent him backpedaling, coughing. The guy had dropped his guard. Maybe he was a fighter, maybe not, but he'd mistaken Harper for a pushover, and that would cost him.

It surprised her that she retained the choreography of the junkyard aikido that used to be her specialty. She was stiffer now, less polished. And she'd forgotten the required speed. Way faster than she'd revved her body for years.

The man was slumped over, dazed, hands on his knees, panting. As she stepped forward, he grunted and cut to the right and his hand flashed out, a blur, and landed a crushing blow to her right breast, emptied her lungs and staggered her against the apartment wall. Hands gripping her shoulders, he spun her around, got her by the right wrist, yanked her arm up, pressuring hard against the elbow. Over her shoulder she slashed at his face with her free hand, but he pulled away.

He held her there for a moment, then slammed his body against hers, flattening her against the wall, his breath fast and hot against her neck. In seconds her arm was numb. She couldn't breathe. She saw smoke filtering in from the edges of her vision. It was then that the chant came back to her, the one Rocky Garcia, her last sensei, used to make all his students repeat: *Don't forget your legs, your legs, your legs, your legs.*

She went slack. A moment passed, his hold still firm. She was weak, close to fainting, when finally the man bought her deception and backed off the stress on her arm, giving her room to move her hip from the wall, find leverage.

"Now we're going to walk very quietly back to the apartment. You're going to be a good girl, aren't you?"

Brit accent with a Germanic inflection. It was him, the throat slitter.

She groaned as though signaling her submission.

As he drew her away from the wall, she faked a stumble, and he went forward with her. She set her feet and swept her right leg knee-high, hooked his legs, and toppled him against the cement railing. She lowered her shoulder, bulled him against the low rail, kept grinding into his chest until he tipped backward, then thrust harder, shouldering him over.

Three stories down, he thumped on his back, half in grass and half on the sidewalk. A woman walking her Lab halted, and her dog sniffed the man's shoe. She tugged the dog away and stepped around the body and continued down the walkway without a backward look, as if men regularly fell from the sky in this neighborhood.

Harper nabbed the man's pistol and headed down the steps. She'd always hated guns. Since Deena's death, she hated them even more.

On the sidewalk, she halted, scanned the area to fix her bearings. Felt a swoon of bewilderment.

The man was gone.

A second later when she heard footsteps slapping fast down the sidewalk, she tossed the pistol away, pivoted, set her feet, lifted her hands. Ready position. But as the runner came into focus, she lowered her fists, relaxed her stance, and drew a long, ravenous breath.

FOURTEEN

February, Coral Gables, Florida

"What the hell happened, Harper? You're trembling."

Nick looped an arm around her shoulder, held her tight.

"How did you get here? Were you following me?"

"I saw you leaving the condo. We were worried, so we tagged along."

"We?"

Nick lowered his arm, stepped away, and motioned toward the street where a yellow Prius was double-parked. The darkened driver's window slid down, and Sal Leonardi gave her a cheerful wave.

"What's going on, Nick? You and Sal?"

"He called me, told me you'd been to see him, the two of you were going to join forces, poke around on your own. I invited myself in. Sal thought it would be okay with you. Now what the hell happened?"

Sal U-turned and eased into a parking spot across the street.

"Nick," she said. "This is some scary shit. You sure you want a part of this?"

"Do you even need to ask?"

They walked across the street to Sal's car. Harper climbed into the front seat, Nick folded into the rear, and she told them what she'd learned, leaving out nothing. Finishing with, "The guy who attacked me knew my name. He recognized me."

"So tell me about the dead guy," Sal said, "this Jackson Smith."

"Sharp," Harper said. "Jackson Sharp."

"Okay," Sal said. "And if you don't mind me asking, what the hell were you going to say to this guy? You have any kind of plan?"

"Hold on a minute," she said. "What're we doing here? What about the cops? Somebody attacked me, probably the same guy that killed Sharp and maybe Ross and Leo, and he's getting away. We need to call Alvarez, throw a net over the area."

Sal turned and shot Nick a look. "You tell her or do I?"

"Sal thinks we should cut loose from Alvarez," Nick said. "Go our own way."

"What's that supposed to mean?"

She turned around to read his face, but Nick was staring out his side window.

"Like I told you," Sal said. "I got good contacts. One of them, her name's Connie Woods, she's a secretary, high up in the chief's office at Miami PD, so most things at that level, they get channeled through her, messages, face-to-face meetings, things of that nature. The woman knows what's going on, got her ear to the pulse. Me and Connie, we go back. So she calls me up, heard I had feelers out about Ross's murder; she's suspicious, thinks there might be a leak in the office, information about the case going to a third party, a private individual outside law enforcement, messages back and forth to and from this party. Says there might be orders coming in by phone from the same individual."

"What kind of orders?"

"What Connie thinks, she believes somebody might be having a say in the investigation, an outsider. Do this, don't do that. Steering the bus."

"Who in god's name would that be?"

"Don't know the answer to that yet," Sal said.

"So the thing is," said Nick, "with this other agenda going on, the cops aren't kosher. From here on, we don't trust Alvarez."

Harper was silent.

"What I'm thinking," Sal said. "You tell us there's a corpse in that apartment, okay, say we leave it for Alvarez and his friends. Well, good chance things'll get murky after that. Maybe we don't ever find out what it all means. How it pertains to you and Ross and Leo. And now with this guy Spider whatshisname getting shot at, and this other guy showing up, knowing your name, jamming a gun in your ribs, that seals it: too many wild cards stacking up. We gotta go our own way."

"Just walk away from the body?"

"Hell, no," Sal said. "Process the scene ourselves."

"Since when do you process crime scenes?"

"Everything the cops do, I got guys with similar capabilities." Sal smiled at her and gave her a sorry-but-that's-how-it-is shrug. "DNA, ballistics, fingerprints, you name it, all the ID stuff. My boys can handle all of it. Even clean the scene afterward, no traces."

Harper cursed under her breath.

"It's true," Sal said. "My associates, they got labs, they got the skills, same equipment, sometimes even better. This way, see, you got no chance of a leak. It's a hundred percent safe and secure."

"Sal has lots of friends. Why not use them?"

"Sal's private CSI crew."

"My guys are good," Sal said. "I'm not bragging, but, hey, lots of times they get better results doing it their way than the cops."

"I don't see the problem," Nick said. "Given the investigation is compromised."

She turned in her seat to face Nick.

"You're sure about this, Nick? Being a part of this."

"You can't do this alone."

"Can't I?"

"Nobody doubts you. But you can depend on me. In case you haven't noticed, I'm not a sickly kid anymore."

She held his fierce gaze. He wasn't squirming, wasn't trying to dodge. Eyes she'd looked into thousands of times, eyes she'd always been able to read, even from the first day they met, a puny child who spoke only a word or two of English.

A boy whose earliest memories were of a dismal orphanage in Zelenogorsk, a town of shacks clustered around a single uranium-enrichment plant. That boy had dreamed madly of the bright, amazing world beyond the boundaries of his village on the desolate Kan River, warming himself with an improbable fairy tale that improbably came true as Deena Roberts appeared one January afternoon, scanning the room full of frail kids, and fell in love with young Nicholas's dark, haunting eyes, two weeks later liberating him from the bitter gloom of Russian winter and whisking him away to a fanciful tropical city on the edge of the sea, and that was only the start of the fantasy, for year after year when she circled the globe, Nick and Harper were in tow, Deena shooting her photos in Paris, in Rome, in London and Berlin, Singapore, Rio, Beijing, introducing the two kids to monarchs, dukes, heads of state and billionaires, rock legends and dazzling movie stars. By fifteen, Nick and Harper had become as inseparable as conjoined twins. They'd filled the pages of a half dozen passports and could finish each other's sentences in seven languages.

All that togetherness ended when they left high school. Nick flew off to Providence, spent four years at Brown, Harper staying home at the University of Miami. After all those years of travel with Deena, Harper hungered for roots, for constancy. Not Nick. Still simmering with wanderlust, after graduation, he found his dream job.

Working for the World Bank let him continue his peregrinations, but more than that, it gave him a chance to bring some measure of fairness to rice farmers in Laos, provide fair compensation for being displaced from the land they and their families had tilled for generations, land destined to become a national highway. Or indigents exiled from their homes by a dam built in Tanzania or a power plant in Almaty, Kazakhstan. That became Nick's work. Traveling the globe, striking a balance, as best he could, between the public good and private needs, paying fair value, giving power and voice to people exactly like the dispossessed kid he'd once been.

Harper stared ahead out the windshield at the breeze sifting through the palm fronds, its shadows trickling along the sidewalk like the dark, twisty tongues of serpents.

"Okay," she said. "Here's what we'll do. Sal, call in your CSI guys, find out whatever you can about Jackson Sharp. And that man in the apartment, he wasn't wearing gloves. His pistol is in the grass over near the sidewalk. There have to be prints. Find out everything you can about who that man was."

Sal smiled and gave her a quick salute. "So you're gonna pilot the ship? Hand out the jobs?"

"You know anybody better?" she said.

"And how about you?" Nick said. "What's your assignment?"

Harper looked at the slit of horizon showing between the two bayside condos.

"I'm going to the mall," she said. "I need some traveling clothes."

FIFTEEN

Early March, Côte d'Ivoire, Africa

After searching to no avail for information on Jean Luc Diallo, the first name on Ross's contacts, she sent a brief e-mail to the address Ross had included. The second name on his list was Moussa Kouacou, a name so unique it took her only a few minutes of Googling to learn that Moussa was an agricultural minister in Abidjan, capital city of the Ivory Coast. She wrote him an e-mail, explaining that she was continuing Ross McDaniel's research because Ross had fallen ill. Fishing for hints about what Ross had turned up.

The next afternoon she received the reply she was after.

Moussa Kouacou was most sorry to hear of Mr. McDaniel's unfortunate sickness and would be quite delighted to meet with Harper McDaniel and escort her to the Royale Plantation, as planned, where she would interview Mr. Jean Luc Diallo, the foreman of the plantation. As previously agreed, Mr. Diallo was fully prepared to discuss grave matters that had transpired on the plantation. But Mr. Diallo insisted that such discussion occur face-to-face.

A search of Ross's notes turned up a single reference to Royale Plantation, a cacao farm of formidable size. Jackson Sharp had told Ross that the plantation was the location where Rachel Sharp was killed. So apparently Kouacou was to be Ross's guide and lead him to Diallo, the whistle-blower.

An exposé of child slavery, chocolate, and murder.

"You trust this guy Moussa?" Nick asked her. "Some stranger on the other side of the globe."

"Ross trusted him."

"And look what happened to him."

"What do you suggest? Step away, let Alvarez take over?"

Nick continued to campaign to go along to Africa, but Harper refused. This was a fact-finding trip, nothing more. If anything looked the least bit dodgy, she'd summon Nick and wait for him before proceeding. He didn't like it, and neither did Sal.

"Because I'm a girl, I need a strong man at my side?"

"It's not like that. We have no idea what's going on. You've been attacked already. The guy knew your name, for god's sake."

Sal said, "And that spy camera in your house. I been thinking about that. Only thing I can come up with is whoever took out Ross was trying to find out if he'd talked to anyone else about what he was investigating. If he told them anything, they'd be a target too. You know, like mentioning chocolate, like he did with you."

She closed her eyes and was silent for a while, then blew out a hard breath. "I don't care, Sal. If I'm in danger, if I'm a target, fine. Let them come for me, let them try."

Sal nodded and winked at her. Right answer.

———

Moses Chonen, president of Coconut Grove Bank and longtime friend of Deena and the Roberts family, summoned the bank's locksmith to drill open the safety deposit box that Harper and Ross kept there. There was no other choice since Harper's own key had been lost in the fire.

She hadn't expected to find any of Ross's research documents stashed in the box, and there were none. But she needed her passport, and after a long moment staring into the open box, she picked up the entire stack of hundreds. A small part of her inheritance from Deena. She'd never had the heart to count it, but it was plenty. Between the cash and her credit cards, Harper could travel for weeks. Or even longer if justice was slow in coming.

——

Bone-tired from eighteen hours of air travel, Harper was in no mood for this get-acquainted dinner date or whatever it was Moussa Kouacou had in mind, but she agreed to it because, damn it, she needed this guy.

On the endless flight she'd been racked with doubts and misgivings. So far from home on a quest with such a vague target, so unlike anything she'd ever attempted before. She considered turning back, going home, letting the professionals handle it. But in the cab from the airport to the hotel, in a sudden rush of recognition, the doubts fell away.

She was traveling in Ross's footsteps, taking over the task he'd set for himself. Completing his arc, making it her own. In this way, giving his death some kind of meaning, and her own journey a purpose beyond mere revenge.

She checked into her room, took a quick shower, arrived at the hotel restaurant at nine thirty, their agreed-upon hour, then waited with growing impatience for thirty minutes before a man appeared at the entrance and the maître d' pointed him toward Harper's table.

He was tall, narrow-shouldered, in his middle thirties, with a long face and a shaved head that gleamed in the honeyed light. He wore a pale-blue caftan and matching pants embroidered in reds and greens.

He halted at her table and introduced himself in French.

Harper gestured at the seat across from her. With old-world formality, he half bowed and settled into the chair, then reached out, a large box of burgundy and gold in his hand. Chocolates.

She smiled her thanks and set it beside her glass.

Moussa's caramel eyes matched his skin, and despite his smile, in the depths of those eyes, Harper detected the same mix of sadness and distress she'd witnessed in many eyes since she'd arrived in this West African nation, as if he and his countrymen shared a communal dread that their homeland was about to slip into chaos.

The restaurant, however, Le Toit d'Abidjan, on the twenty-third floor of the Sofitel Hotel, with its sweeping views of the Ébrié Lagoon and the chic Cocody district of Abidjan, seemed far removed from the strife in the streets below. Lights set romantically low, quiet piano music filtering in.

Harper had traveled to Africa a dozen times, but this was her first time in the Ivory Coast. Moussa had offered to be her driver and guide. Though she disliked being dependent on anyone, especially a stranger, she'd agreed to the arrangement because navigating the back roads of this country had grown increasingly risky since the failed coup and the rise in extremist terror groups. And by god, she wasn't about to let some regional political turmoil derail her mission.

Harper took a breath and tried out her rusty French.

"Mon français est délicat. Il a été de nombreuses années."

"No, no. I understand you most perfectly." Moussa smiled, showing brilliant teeth. "But we can converse in your language if it pleases you."

"Either way is fine with me," Harper said.

"Is that a Parisian accent I detect?"

"Paris, yes," she said. "When I was young I spent time there."

"With your mother," he said. "The world traveler. The rock star."

"Ross told you that?"

"Oh, no. I have been a great admirer of your mother's work for many years, you see."

"Well, my mother . . . ," Harper began, then decided to soften her reply. "My mother photographed rock stars, but she wasn't one herself."

"But notorious, yes?"

"I suppose. Notorious in some circles."

The waiter appeared, distributed menus, and Moussa ordered a local beer. With a flourish the waiter topped off Harper's glass of sparkling water. All very civilized.

Looking out at the harbor lights and the twinkle of boats moving across the lagoon, she imagined she was home in Miami, not this bedraggled port city in a small tortured country on the Gulf of Guinea. Liberia to the west, Ghana on the east, and Burkina Faso and Mali closing off the northern border.

"You shouldn't have bothered," Harper said, touching a fingertip to the box of chocolates.

"Something for later. I believe you will find this item alone worth your journey. A Belgian product made of Valrhona cocoa, blended into a creamy ganache, then hand rolled with a dark truffle on the inside and finished with a dusting of cocoa powder."

She thanked him again.

"Ah, it is my pleasure. But please save it for a private moment."

"Of course," she said. "Now, we need to talk."

Moussa said, "Perhaps we should order our meal first. While we still have a happy appetite."

Harper flinched.

"And what does that mean?"

Ducking his eyes, Moussa was silent.

"You've changed your mind? You're going to refuse me?"

He looked around them, and though their closest neighbors were several tables distant, he lowered his voice.

"This man you wish to meet, Jean Luc Diallo. What do you know of him? Are you close?"

"I'm sorry, but I don't see how that's your concern. You've agreed to be my driver. I don't need a guardian."

He stiffened, looked off with a pained smile as if she'd badly offended him. When he turned back and spoke, his voice was a whisper.

"There's grave danger. There are military checkpoints everywhere. Rebel forces set up blockades at will. Kidnapping is common. You could be held for ransom, or a fate much worse."

"But you go back and forth into the countryside, don't you? Others do. There's a way."

"This is my home. I know the customs, the rates of extortion. But even then it is dangerous for me. But for you, a woman with your appearance, and a Westerner, no, it would be *trop dangereux*. Foolhardy and a reckless escapade."

"I've come this far. And now you tell me this."

"As a politeness to your husband, I agreed to assist you, and it grieves me to disappoint you at this late moment. But the events of recent days have made the journey you have in mind simply too treacherous. I have made other arrangements."

"What arrangements?"

"Let us please order our dinners first."

"Someone got to you. They made threats and now you're afraid."

He looked up from his menu and gave her a rueful smile. "I understand the walnut Saint-Jacques with sweet potatoes is most excellent."

"With or without you, I'm going."

"The hot foie gras and pickled beets is supposed to be quite great, yes, and I'm also told the chocolate sorbet is a sheer delight."

She pushed back her chair and rose.

"I'll be leaving at midnight. If you're going along, be in the lobby."

"Please stay. There are vital matters still to discuss."

"Midnight," Harper said. "With or without you."

"And how would you manage? No trustworthy driver will take you to Akoupé at that time of night. It is one hundred forty kilometers, well over two hours by car. Bad roads, desolate terrain, no highway lighting."

"I'll find a way," she said. "That's what I do."

Without another word she left him there with his box of chocolates.

SIXTEEN

Early March, Côte d'Ivoire, Africa

Back in her room, Harper stripped off the black cocktail dress—the only fancy outfit she'd packed for her journey—and flung it back into her bag. Though she'd bathed an hour earlier, she showered again to rinse away the perfume and makeup and returned to normal. With the hot water blasting, she scrubbed herself hard, then harder still to fend off the swell of frustration pressuring her chest.

Afterward she wrapped herself in a towel and unpinned her hair, brushed it out and fastened it into a ponytail, and stared at the fogged-over mirror. She didn't need to rub away the mist. She knew all too well what she'd see. In these last few days the woman she'd become was nearly a stranger, a face hardened and severe. Her brown eyes had grown shadowy and guarded, and seemed almost to have changed colors as if dimmed by a layer of mist. Her cheekbones had always been prominent, but now, with the weight loss, the flesh had cinched tight around them, giving her a haunted and menacing edge. Even her jet-black hair, parted on the side and falling beyond her shoulders, had lost its luster.

Several times lately she'd raised a pair of scissors to that mane. But she always lost her nerve. It seemed so pathetic, so trite. A ritual that grieving women succumbed to. Hacking away the years of growth as if such a renunciation could obliterate the past, wipe away her pain.

She changed into her travel gear: olive trousers, battered hiking boots, a dark top, and a Bush Poplin safari jacket.

From her cosmetic kit, she withdrew the silver perfume atomizer Sal had presented to her just before she left. He'd even insisted on giving her a lesson on the use of the silly device. Take it, it could come in handy, he assured her. And you can sneak it through airport security, no sweat.

She slipped it into a lower pocket of her jacket. Easy access.

Fully dressed, she sat on the edge of the bed, folded her hands in her lap. She stared at the wall and listened to the hum of the bedside clock and felt the grind of minutes mounting and tried to compose herself. And though she had resisted the urge during the long airline flights, she could not stop herself any longer.

She rose and took the three black-and-white photos from her carry-on bag and sat back on the side of the bed and studied them. Her final photos of her husband and son. Ross shaving with Leo strapped to his chest. The lucky slant of light zinging off the blade of the straight razor poised against his throat. Leo grinning, a hand out before him pointing at his mirrored image and the dollop of shaving foam on his cheek.

Until now, she'd refrained from looking at the photos, afraid they might weaken her resolve, send her into an emotional tailspin.

She'd been wrong. They did the opposite.

At midnight she took the elevator to the lobby, stood for a moment surveying the spacious area. It was empty. Moussa had been true to his word. He'd been scared off. Or bribed.

Behind the check-in desk, a grandfatherly man in a scarlet-and-gold dashiki and matching skullcap saw Harper crossing the lobby and hurried out from behind the counter and caught her at the automatic doors.

"Oh, no, miss, it is not safe. At this hour the city is shut down, even the dancing clubs are closed. There is no walking around. Unsavory youth roam the streets, some of them drunken, capable of rowdy behavior. Atrocities are not unheard of. At this hour, there are sometimes crocodiles climbing from the sewers. Most dangerous."

She assured him she wasn't going far. Just needed a breath of air.

"For your air may I suggest you attend the pool and patio. Please, miss. Not on the streets at this hour. Even here in this good district, things cannot be predicted."

She thanked him for his concern and stepped past him through the doors and out on the sidewalk. The night was sticky and airless, exhaust fumes seasoning a sluggish breeze. Bats flickered above a streetlight on Boulevard Hassan. A half block away, she saw a white Mercedes sedan stopped in the middle of the street, surrounded by a band of youths straddling mopeds. Out of the driver's window, a man waved his arm, shaking his fist at the gang of boys who hooted and jeered back at him.

She headed in the other direction, west along Hassan, a wide street lined with coconut palms, government buildings, banks, and office towers with clothing shops along the thoroughfare. Ahead of her, the avenue was empty. A ghost town.

Her arrangement was to meet Jean Luc Diallo at his home two hours past midnight. He'd promised to tell her the sordid tale Ross had wanted to hear. But Harper must come in secret, speak to no one about her mission. She must be prepared to turn back immediately from their scheduled meeting if even the smallest detail seemed suspicious.

In their e-mail exchange, she'd assured him she would follow his directions faithfully. Then, a few days ago, he'd e-mailed her and begged her not to come. He'd changed his mind about revealing what he knew. Radical changes were taking place on the plantation. Without warning his bosses had become hypervigilant. New security regimes were being strictly enforced. In recent days several workers had disappeared. Others, terrified by the new threats, were fleeing into the jungle, heading back to their villages. With cash rewards offered for anyone unmasking a traitor, everyone was snooping on everyone else. He feared that even his e-mail was being monitored.

Harper sent him a terse reply. She was to arrive as scheduled on Thursday and would appear at his home around two in the morning, and if he were to renege on their arrangement for any reason, she, herself, would expose him as a spy to the owner of Royale Plantation. She had no intention of going through with the threat, but it accomplished her goal.

The next day Jean Luc Diallo responded.

> Comme convenu. Je vais être en attente pour vous.

As we agreed. I will be waiting.

Harper headed north down the empty streets. She figured it was roughly a dozen blocks to the spot on Boulevard des Martyrs where she'd seen a taxi station on her drive in from the airport, a cluster of orange cabs waiting to be called into action. Surely Abidjan was enough of an international city and economic center to warrant keeping a few taxis operational through the night. Now that Moussa Kouacou had abandoned her, this was all the plan she had.

It was when she was passing by Mairie de Cocody, the district's town hall, with only a few more blocks left to the taxi station, that she heard the low rumble of an automobile idling behind her. She didn't turn to confront the driver shadowing her, but as she walked on, she slipped her hand into the pocket of her jacket and fingered the atomizer.

In another half block, the car caught up. Harper turned to face it, an older white Mercedes, the same car she'd seen earlier. Its headlights were extinguished, but a rear door hung open, and a yellow map light illuminated the car's interior.

The man behind the steering wheel was slumped in his seat, and as the car pulled abreast of Harper, she saw the long, narrow face of Moussa Kouacou, his head lolling.

The car swerved two steps in front, bumped onto the sidewalk, and collided with the safety cage across a storefront.

Harper hurried to his door. The front windshield was cracked in several places as if it was pelted by stones.

Moussa's electric window lowered.

In a frail voice, he said, "Get in. They're coming for you."

"Are you all right? What happened?"

"I was waylaid. When I saw you exit the hotel, I managed to break away and follow."

"Who are they? Do you know them?"

"Get in the car. It's you they want. They mean you harm."

He winced and turned his face away, and it was then she saw the pearlescent handle of a pocketknife, its blade sunk deep into Moussa's left shoulder, blood darkening his blue caftan.

"Not a mortal blow," he said. "Get in."

"Move over," she said. "I'm taking you to a hospital."

As she was easing Moussa across the bench seat into the passenger side, she heard the snarl of small engines, and when she looked back down the Avenue of the Martyrs, she saw a pack of mopeds tearing up the empty boulevard toward them.

SEVENTEEN

Early March, Côte d'Ivoire, Africa

Four bikes, six riders.

"Moussa, hold on."

He shook his head, eyes growing sleepy. "No, I will help you. These are . . . depraved men."

"Stay put. I'll handle this."

She stepped from the car, chose an open space, and positioned herself as they roared up. They formed a half circle around her. Five guys and a girl.

The largest of the young men, the one with the girl behind him, had long Medusa dreads, a few of them dyed blond. He wore a black tank top, aviator sunglasses, ragged blue jeans, and an ugly grin. The others glanced at him as if awaiting orders.

He motioned at Harper and spoke in a harsh dialect to his boys.

The two closest to Harper gunned their engines, then killed the motors, set their kickstands, and dismounted. Those two weren't grinning. The others stayed astride their bikes, engines muttering, watching the thugs approach her. The one in the lead was chunky. His skintight

T-shirt showed off big, smooth muscles. He was a few inches taller than Harper. The enforcer.

He stepped within an arm's length of her while his scrawny partner stayed a few feet behind like a waiter in training.

"You the American?" the leader called out. "Name Harper?"

"Tell your goon to back off. Do it now while he still can."

Muscle Boy stretched out his neck, bared his teeth at her, and clacked them together several times like one of those windup chattering dentures from a toy store.

The others laughed.

Muscle Boy's first strike was tentative, more of a lazy slap than a punch, as though he was mocking Harper or testing her reflexes.

She slipped sideways, blending with the trajectory of the swipe, grabbing his wrist, and steering him as a dance instructor might correct the errant move of a bumbling student, stretching him out until Muscle Boy was teetering on one foot. In the next instant she stabilized his open hand, found a thumb lock, and halted his momentum, wrenching his wrist backward and forcing the hooligan to his knees.

She held him in place one-handed, tightened the backward pressure against his wrist until he gasped and tried to swing away. Again, she went in the direction of his move, then rocked back against the grain, cocked the wrist joint at a more severe angle, widened her stance, bracing herself, feeling the crackle of the man's cartilage beneath her fingers.

His pals were yipping and laughing at the sight of their muscled-up brother-in-arms shamed by this lightweight woman.

"It's kung fu fighter Missus Bruce Lee," the leader called out.

His gang members chuckled.

The leader dismounted, lifted his shades, and settled them high on his forehead.

"Get back on your bikes and go," Harper said, "all of you, or I'll break his wrist. He'll never ride again."

Muscle Boy groaned and hunched down as she cranked the grip tighter, clamping his thumb closer to his wrist. There were countermoves he could try. A seasoned fighter would have twisted in line with the pressure, or swept a foot at her ankles, broken loose, forced her to find a new joint lock. But this young man relied on brute force, pushing, shoving, undisciplined punches. Crude, bullyboy skills that had won him his position in the gang. But he'd never been tested. He'd crumpled at the first jolt of pain and would not be a threat again on this night.

The leader, however, was another matter.

Still grinning, not cowed, he seemed intrigued by her.

Which meant one of two things: either he was more skilled at hand to hand than his flunky or he was armed. She decided it was the latter. She hadn't seen the gun yet, but she suspected, from the way his tank top fell off-line around his waist, that the pistol was holstered at the small of his back.

"How do you know my name?"

"I know many things," the leader said.

"Someone paid you to rough me up. Frighten me."

"What is this? Rough up?"

"Hurt me."

"Oh, no, we want to be very, very nice to you, sweet lady."

The leader's girlfriend dismounted the bike and sauntered over.

A bulky girl with buzzed hair, heavy breasted, and thick at the waist. A snarl growing on her lips as if she didn't like Harper chatting up her man.

"Who paid you?" Harper applied more torsion to Muscle Boy's wrist, and he yelped. "His name, or your friend will be left-handed from now on."

"This punk is worthless," the leader said. "Kill him all you like."

Muscle Boy groaned long and low, and his body went slack. Passed out or faking, she wasn't sure. She released her grip and took a step back. Muscle Boy wilted facedown against the pavement.

Harper turned to the side to shield the move, her right hand dipping into her pocket, retrieving the silver atomizer. Palming it.

When she turned back, as she'd expected, the leader had drawn a stubby revolver and had it trained on Harper's face. He kicked the shoulder of the fallen man and ordered him to get up. The young man groaned and staggered to his knees. He cradled his right wrist in his other hand and blinked at Harper.

"Shoot her, Jules. She fucked my arm."

"Hands up, Missus Bruce Lee," Jules said. "You coming with us."

"One final chance," she said. "Who sent you? What's his name?"

The leader barked an order to his girlfriend, and she pulled a white plastic strip from the pocket of her jeans. Flex-cuffs. She handed them over, and when the leader's head was turned to take them, Harper raised the canister of pressurized CS military gas, pepper spray on steroids, the nozzle set to fire in a shotgun pattern rather than a pin stream. Sal claimed it was excellent for crowd control. No marksmanship required. Bless the old man's heart.

With a sweep of her hand, she sent a cloud of gas across the gang. Jules saw it coming and ducked and waved a hand in front of his face. Too late. His sunglasses fell to the sidewalk. He retched and scrubbed one-handed at his eyes, the gun waving, directionless. The others choked and scattered blindly. Motorbikes clattered to the ground.

Staying beyond the noxious mist, Harper watched the gang boys thrash and cough until the cloud began to break up. She held her breath, stepped forward, and grabbed Jules by a dreadlock, then yanked him backward, chopped the gun from his hand, and kicked it down the street. She hauled him to the car while he gasped and huffed and flailed his arms in an awkward backstroke. She moved fast, kept him staggering.

Moussa slid across the bloody seat, settled against the passenger door. He looked feverish, his face glossy with sweat. Somehow he'd managed to extract the blade from the meat of his shoulder and was gripping it overhand, ready to stab.

"We're taking this one along," she told Moussa and whacked Jules's forehead hard against the doorpost. When he continued to resist, she slammed his head again. He shivered and sagged, blacking out long enough for Harper to fold him into the car and shove him across the seat alongside Moussa.

She started the car, squealed onto the street, and sped down the empty avenue. After a few blocks, Moussa relented, admitting he was in distress. Directing her to the nearest hospital, Hôpital de Port-Bouet, guiding her back toward the hotel, then onto Boulevard de Gaulle. A fifteen-minute ride this time of night, he told her.

Jules knuckled his eyes, muttered. A halo of marijuana clung to him.

"Listen to me, kid. You tell me who hired you, and I let you go. Give me his name, and there'll be no police."

"Fuck you, Missus Bruce Lee. Fuck you, you fucking fuck."

Moussa shook his head sadly. "Your American movies, they have shameful encouragement on our national youth."

Moussa touched the knifepoint to Jules's cheek and demanded in slow, precise French that he reveal the identity of the man who sent him.

Jules's sight was coming back. He leaned away from the blade, turned his head carefully, and squinted at Moussa.

"Who sent you?" Harper said.

Jules faced forward.

"One thousand American dollar," he said. "I tell you what you want."

"Get serious."

Jules was sniffling, eyes raw. "Okay, tough American lady want to bargain. Then here we go. Eight hundred dollar and you teach me Bruce Lee trick you did to my boy. Teach me this, and eight hundred, I tell you name you want."

"Forget it. You talk to me or go to jail. No bargaining."

Jules was silent as Moussa directed her through the remaining turns.

As they approached the hospital, Harper eased into a parking space behind an ambulance near the emergency entrance.

"All of us are going inside together," she said. "We get Moussa medical attention, then you and I are going to talk, Jules."

"No, Missus Bruce Lee. Not tonight." Jules grunted and shouldered hard into her, swung his leg over the transmission hump, and stamped the accelerator.

Lurching forward, the Mercedes slammed the rear bumper of the ambulance. Jules twisted and threw himself on Moussa, seized his knife hand, and slammed it against the dashboard, breaking the weapon loose.

Harper grabbed for a dreadlock but missed. Shoving Moussa out of his way, Jules jumped from the car and bent down to speak to her, eye to eye.

"Big people want you dead, real big people, Missus Bruce Lee. You in bad trouble, plenty bad trouble." Then he bolted into the darkness.

EIGHTEEN

Early March, Côte d'Ivoire, Africa

Harper helped Moussa shuffle into the emergency room. He spoke at length with the admitting nurse, then they took their seats. The room was full of the bloody and broken and the sick, citizens of a country tilting toward anarchy. She would not be driving north to Akoupé tonight.

"I spoke to him." Moussa shivered, his voice delicate.

"Spoke to who?"

"Jean Luc Diallo."

"You did? When?"

"Two days ago on the telephone, then I drove to the plantation to meet face-to-face. To be certain the journey you were undertaking was safe, that I would not be exposing you to danger."

"You didn't need to do that."

"Listen to me, please. You speak a great deal but are not highly proficient in listening."

Harper nodded. She knew Moussa's reprimand was on the mark.

"When I reached the Royale Plantation outside of Akoupé, Jean Luc was the source of a great uproar. Murdered only hours before my arrival."

Harper closed her eyes and groaned.

"Stabbed repeatedly, body discovered in the weeds outside his office. The authorities claim his killing was because he had spoken out against the army's ruthless attempts to stifle dissent. This is what we are now calling justice, these lies, this violence. But Jean Luc's wife is certain her husband was killed not for his political words but for other reasons, murdered by his own employers, the bosses where he works, the cacao plantation. She believes they learned of his disloyalty, that he was about to expose their wrongdoings."

"Because of me. To shut him up."

Moussa dismissed her guilt with a feeble wave. "Jean Luc's wife is a good woman. She believes the owners of the plantation are dishonorable and dangerous. For that reason she presented to me a gift that she believed might assist you. Lead you to what you seek."

"What gift?"

"I don't know what it is. I did not open the gift."

"Where is it?"

"I tried to give it to you already. The box of chocolates at dinner. But you would not let me explain and walked away angry."

"Oh, Moussa, I'm sorry."

"You are in danger, miss, and should leave our country at once and return to the safety of your own land."

In the far doorway a nurse with a clipboard appeared and called Moussa's name.

Harper helped him stand and limp across the room, but at the entrance the nurse would not allow her to go farther.

"I'll wait out here," she said.

"No need," Moussa said. "My wife is to come soon, they telephoned her on my behalf. Back at the hotel, the desk clerk is holding your gift. Please leave my automobile keys with him. And when you return to America, tell Mr. Ross McDaniel I wish him great health and speedy happiness in all his future endeavors."

Twenty minutes later back at the Sofitel, Harper approached the main desk, and the clerk rose from an easy chair and smiled broadly.

"Ah, yes, good lady, you have returned safely. I am so pleased of it."

"Do you have something for me?"

"Oh yes, oh yes. A most lovely gift."

He hurried into the office and returned with the gold box of chocolates. With a merry smile he handed it over. "I understand these are splendid delicacies, these candies. I was very tempted to thieve one for myself."

Back in her room, she settled the box on the desk.

After staring at it for several moments, she leaned over and sniffed it. No scent of chocolate. No scent of explosives either. Not that she would have recognized such a smell. But it felt like a trick, a gift sent from the wife of a dead man. A man who'd died while trying to relay some grim secret to Ross and through him to the outside world.

Was the box truly a gift from Jean Luc's wife or a booby trap? She nudged it away and stood. The flesh on her shoulders was rippling with chills. Someone at the plantation knew she had arrived in Abidjan, and they'd sent a gang of thugs to kidnap her. Would they also have sent an explosive device? A backup plan in case the thugs failed?

Whoever they were, they'd sent a man to murder Jackson Sharp and ransack his apartment. Maybe the man was searching for the film Jackson showed to Ross at the Denny's back before Christmas. Evidence of a crime, the faces of the guilty.

Was the blond guy in Sharp's apartment the man from the film, and the same one behind this box of chocolates? Not ready for another go at her, he'd hired henchmen for his dirty work, sent along explosives in case his punks botched the job?

Or was Harper simply feeling the cold itch of paranoia?

She sat across the room from the box and dialed Nick's number.

"I can be there tomorrow late afternoon. Say the word."

"No," she said. "Not yet. I'm making progress."

"Tell me."

"Actually, I'm not sure that's wise."

"People listening?"

"Christ, I don't know. They planted spy cameras in our house. Whoever they are, they're devious shits."

"You don't sound good. You sure you're okay?"

"I'm staring at a box of chocolates. Afraid to open it. Does that sound okay?"

"What box?"

She told him about her night, softening her encounter with Jules and his half-assed gang and leaving out Moussa's knife wound. If she'd told him the full story, he'd be on the next flight. As much as she loved him and trusted him, she'd begun to relish her independence. She was nimbler without him alongside second-guessing.

"Trust your intuition, Harper. If you sense something's wrong, then leave the box and get the hell out of there."

"It's too heavy to be chocolate truffles."

"Leave it. Go back to the airport. Get out of that room."

She rose from the chair, walked to the desk, looked down at the gold box. She switched the phone to speaker and set it on the desk.

"Did you hear me, Harper?"

She told him yes, she heard him clearly.

"Well? What's going on?"

She picked up the box, felt its contents shift, something solid. She set it down, stepped away.

"What're you doing? Talk to me."

She came back to the table, tugged on the bow, unfastened the red ribbon, loosened the ties.

Maybe she was more like Deena than she wanted to believe. Taking suicidal risks, plunging ahead into this reckless quest. Not courage at all, but simply nothing left to lose.

She closed her eyes for a moment, bracing herself, then lifted an edge of the lid.

No explosion.

She took a quick look inside, stiffened, let the lid fall back.

"Talk to me, Harper."

It wasn't a bomb. But it wasn't chocolate truffles.

"I'm going to send you a photo, Nick. Hold on, I'm taking it now. Tell me what you see."

"Goddamn it, stop playing games."

"It's coming now."

After she sent the JPEG, Harper walked to her window and looked out at the dim lights beyond the Ébrié Lagoon. A single small boat slicing across the black sheen, on some lonely mission.

Across the room, Nick spoke her name. She returned to the phone.

"Is that a mask?" he said.

"It is. It's carved from wood. Mirrors for eyes."

"I don't get it," he said. "The wife of the man Ross was going to interview sent you a wooden mask."

"The Internet here is spotty," she said. "Could you research this? Give me somewhere to start. Who makes this sort of mask, what it might mean. Anything. Can you do that?"

"I'll try."

"Call me back when you have something."

It was two hours later, Harper dozing on the bed, still dressed, lights glaring, when Nick called back.

"Doctor Henri Bakayoko, professor of anthropology at the university in Abidjan."

"Why him?"

"I believe it's a Mossi mask. The Mossi are an ethnic group from Burkina Faso originally, but they've spread through Ghana and the Ivory Coast."

"You've been busy."

"Just a search of Google images, row after row of African masks. I think this one is for a girl child. The mirrored eyes mean female, the two vertical horns indicate it's a child."

"And this Henri character?"

"It's his area of specialization. The university where he teaches isn't far from your hotel."

NINETEEN

Early March, Côte d'Ivoire, Africa

Nine the next morning, she took a taxi to the university. Fifteen minutes, north then west into the Cocody district. The Université Félix Houphouët-Boigny was composed of several three-story brick-and-glass structures scattered across wide lawns and connected by covered walkways. No ivy-covered campus, this place had a stark industrial feel and was filled with neatly dressed men and women, solemn and quiet as if their studies were a grave undertaking, far from the frivolous collegiate spirit Harper was familiar with.

She located Professor Bakayoko's office, was told by his young female secretary that the professor would appear within the hour. Harper sat in a guest chair with the chocolate box on her lap and tried to tune out the pounding of a pile driver operating nearby, close enough to rattle the diplomas on the office walls at ten-second intervals.

The professor arrived with an armload of books and a sweaty face. He was short and round, and his red tie was askew. White shirt rumpled, dark suit shiny with age. He was in his seventies, a fringe of white hair rimming his scalp. He had bulging eyes and a glower that looked like a permanent fixture.

He spoke to his secretary in brusque French that Harper couldn't follow. Then he turned on her and asked her in the same growling French what she wanted with him.

She rose and held out the box of chocolates, and his face relaxed momentarily, then hardened again.

"You are American?"

"I am."

"Bringing me chocolates? For what do I owe this gift?"

"Can we speak in your office?"

He huffed at her and plodded away, nudging open his office door with his hip. Harper looked questioningly at his assistant, and she shrugged and waved go-go-go, follow the professor.

His office was tiny with barely room for the desk and his high-backed leather chair. Nowhere for visiting students to sit. She stood waiting till he had unloaded his books on his desk and was seated. He dabbed his face with a handkerchief, then stuffed it back in the breast pocket of his coat.

"My name is Harper McDaniel. I'm investigating a crime back in my homeland, and I think you may be able to help me."

"You are police?"

"No, this is unofficial. My husband was killed and my child."

"And this has what to do with me?"

She set the box on the desk in front of him and stepped back.

He opened it, took a long look, lifted the mask out of the box, and held it close to his face.

"What is this?"

"I was hoping you could tell me."

"You are testing me? You question my knowledge? My expertise."

"No. I came for your help."

"You insult me with this."

"What are you talking about?"

"You are spy, come to mock me, take my job. I know what you are doing. I understand. Go, get out of here. I will not play this ugly game."

He placed the mask back in the box and gave her a backhanded wave.

She picked up the box. "There's some kind of misunderstanding."

He rose from his chair and stalked around the desk, his glower tightening into an even uglier scowl. "Go!"

On Harper's way back to the lobby, the young woman who'd sat outside the professor's office caught up to her. She was Harper's height, painfully slim, with dark, eager eyes.

"I'm sorry, miss. Forgive my granddad. He's not well."

The girl glanced nervously back down the empty hall, as if expecting the old man to appear. She put a light hand on Harper's back and guided her down the stairs.

"I'm Henriette, I watch out for *grandpère*. No one else has patience for it. In these recent years, he's very stubborn and difficult with people. Last year he was made to retire but refuses to leave. Out of respect, the university allows me to keep his office open. So I watch after him and make sure he causes no trouble."

At the lobby, the young woman peered up the stairway, then edged Harper into an alcove and lowered her voice.

"You want to know about a Mossi mask. I hear you speaking through the office wall."

"That's right."

"My auntie, she can tell you what you need to know. I will write you a map, how to find her. She is Mossi and knows many people. She's a minister. Her English is much superior to mine."

———

When the taxi driver read the slip of paper, he demanded his payment in advance. Five thousand West African francs, less than ten dollars.

He drove her west out of the city, beyond several miles of decaying office buildings and empty storefronts. A half hour later, the asphalt turned to gravel, then to a muddy track. Lining the roadway were one-story shacks with corrugated siding and plywood roofs. Throngs of children played by the roadside, three- and four-year-olds in diapers, older boys in Day-Glo tee tops, kicking balls and rolling car tires.

The auntie's name was Fatou. She was settled in a chair, cooking a yellow mush on a covered grate that occupied the center of an open courtyard next to the single concrete structure in the village. Around her, a dozen children squatted in the dirt, watching the steam rise from the soup. An orphanage, the taxi driver explained, giving a melancholy sigh.

"Too much war," he said.

Fatou was speaking on a cell phone while she stirred the mush. Seeing Harper, she snapped it shut. The children eyed Harper with a mix of curiosity and dread. As Harper passed by them, two girls around seven clutched each other in a desperate hug, as if she might be there to tear them apart.

Harper halted in front of the steaming kettle and introduced herself in French. Fatou looked at her with interest and replied in husky English.

"Henriette says you possess a Mossi mask and come with questions."

"That's true."

"How did this mask arrive to you?"

"Someone on the Royale Plantation sent it. I think she meant for the mask to lead me somewhere."

"Lead you where?"

"I don't know. Maybe here."

"Let me see it, this mask."

Harper slid the box from her shoulder bag, opened it, and held out the mask.

Fatou stared up at her, eyes unreadable.

114

"Your purpose here is what?"

Harper had to consider that for a long moment. "I'm seeking the truth," she said at last.

Fatou drew in a deep breath. "What you are seeking, the truth, this is easy to attain."

"Is it?"

"What you do next, after you have this truth, that is not so simple."

Fatou raised her ladle and chimed it against the side of the kettle.

The children rose and formed a ragged line. Another woman in a red, flowered dress arrived with wooden bowls and handed them to the children as they passed by for their dipper of soup.

"Some of these children, the ones you see before you, some of them once lived in Soko, the village where this mask was made. It is carved from *Ceiba pentandra*, the false kapok. It was made to honor the deceased and allow their spirits admission into the world of their ancestors. Without this mask, the dead cannot enter the afterworld and instead make trouble for the survivors."

"Where is this village?"

"Soko is across the border in Burkina Faso. But Soko no longer exists."

"What happened to it?"

Fatou gave Harper a searching look, then turned and shouted something toward the open door. A moment later, a young man in his twenties with sleepy eyes came stumbling into the gray sunshine. He wore faded blue jeans that hung dangerously low and a white polo shirt with the collar cocked up.

"This is Desmond. If you want, he can take you to Soko to see the truth. What comes after truth, that you will have to discover on your own."

TWENTY

Early March, Côte d'Ivoire, Africa

In the car, Desmond said, "You have pretty hair."

Harper thanked him.

"You look like romantic movie star, no? To my eyes."

Harper didn't reply. She settled back, watched the scenery roll by, a woeful slum of narrow alleys cutting between makeshift dwellings of large wooden crates, some thatched roofs, and plywood and corrugated tin. A smoky haze hung low over the shanties.

"So, miss, you like African men?" Desmond was smiling at her with one eyebrow cocked.

"So far I have no reason not to."

He smiled wider as if they were sharing some intimate joke.

"But that could change," she said.

He was quiet for the next mile, as if trying to unravel the meaning of her words. When he spoke again, it was clear he'd arrived at the wrong interpretation.

"I never been together with a white woman. Not in the pleasure way. Maybe someday I will get so lucky."

"Maybe you will," she said. "But it won't be today."

Desmond drew a breath and his smile faltered. She wasn't sure if he was dangerous or simply inept at flirtation.

"How long is our journey?" she asked.

"How long would you like it to be?"

"How long?"

"You are a serious woman, you. No joking with you."

"Yes, I am doing serious business. How long?"

"Hours, yes. We arrive before darkness. Return by morning if nothing happen on the way."

She shifted on the seat, gave her full attention to the vista out her window. The water in a nearby canal was at the brim, lapping through scraggly grass and seeping into the road. The sky was low and gloomy, a warm, breathless breeze fluttering palm fronds, and in the distance she could see low hills, treeless and scarred by erosion. The smell of sewage and decaying meat, which had grown more potent in the last half hour, was finally beginning to fade.

The road was rutted, potholed, and littered with fist-size rocks, and the old car, whose make she couldn't identify, had long ago lost the spring in its suspension. Every jarring mile they traveled north, they lost more contact with humankind, until the villages grew smaller and scarcer and finally disappeared altogether as they entered a forest where the road meandered like an ancient deer trail, one lane, then less than one, the branches scratching at Desmond's window and her own.

Another hour on that torturous road through more forest, then open stretches where the timber had been clear-cut, leaving barren plains and an oasis here and there of palms that somehow had escaped the butchery.

It was late afternoon, the sun dissolving behind a range of low hills. They were entering another wooded area, the trees so tightly packed sunlight barely filtered to the forest floor.

"Soko is close," Desmond said. "Some more minutes ahead."

Three men appeared from the woods, closing ranks until they stood shoulder to shoulder in the center of the road. Two in red berets, the third in a camo ball cap, all wearing sporty sunglasses. Their uniforms were dark green, sleeves rolled up, leather belts holding an arsenal of small arms. Automatic weapons in their hands. They were blocking the path about fifty yards ahead.

Desmond said, "Oh, lord. These are guerillas."

"Out in the middle of nowhere?"

"Deserters, *charognards*. This is bad trouble."

"Turn around. Get out of here. Go."

"Trop tard."

He pointed at the rearview mirror, and Harper turned in her seat to see two more soldiers blockading the road behind them.

"What do they want? I have some money."

"There is no bargaining with rebels. They will have what they want."

One of the men in front called out to his rear guard, and both groups broke into a trot. In seconds, the five men surrounded them.

The man outside Harper's window was stocky with dark wraparounds and a collection of wooden bangles cinching his impressive biceps. He rapped his gold ring on her glass and waved for her to get out. The last of the day's sunlight was trapped in the overcast sky behind his head.

The men on Desmond's side stood back a few feet and aimed their automatic rifles in his direction. A tall, thin man in light-blue camo with three ammo belts draped over his shoulder stepped away from his group and leaned close to Desmond's window and yelled an order at him.

Desmond reached for the ignition key, but his hand was shaking so badly he fumbled it, and fumbled again before he managed to shut the engine off.

Blue Camo Man wrenched Desmond's door open, grabbed him by his shirt, and hauled him out of the car. The stocky wraparound man on

Harper's side was more placid. He opened the door, stepped back, gave a slight nod, and in a flourish he waved his hand for Harper to step out.

She did.

Desmond was chattering with the blue camo man, gesturing at Harper and chattering some more.

"Your friend say you American," the stocky man said.

"Yes."

"You long away from home."

She didn't answer.

"Why come here? Jungle is not safe for woman."

"I'm studying," she said.

"Study? What you study?"

"Your country, its resources, trees, cacao beans."

Stocky Wraparound yelled across the car's roof to Blue Camo. Blue Camo glared at Harper and said, "Journalist?"

"No," Harper said. "Student."

Blue Camo shoved Desmond toward the other two soldiers and gave them a terse order. They gripped Desmond's arms and marched him into the roadside trees. He shot a backward look at Harper, eyes wild with panic.

Across the roof of the car, Blue Camo spoke to Wraparound. Harper caught a phrase in French. *Search her.* Then another burst of French she couldn't follow, and both men laughed. Then Blue Camo headed off toward Desmond and his captors.

Wraparound gripped her upper arm and swung her toward the nearby woods. She jerked her arm loose.

"Wait a minute. What the hell do you want?"

Blue Camo grinned. "Soon enough you will know."

Stocky Man glanced at his comrade and said something guttural that was unmistakably foul.

It had all been too easy. The blond guy at the Edgewater Apartments who she'd caught off guard and sent over the balcony rail, Jules and his stumblebum street gang. Even the cops she'd blindsided the night Ross and Leo were killed. So much combat in these last few weeks, but all of it so unchallenged she'd lost touch with her limitations as a fighter. She hadn't been tested.

So when Stocky Man's head was turned, Harper saw an opening that wasn't there, not crediting the soldier's reflexes or his wariness or his strength as she snatched at his automatic rifle, twisted it against his thumb, tried to tear it loose from his grip. She'd pictured it, once she broke the rifle free, finishing the move by ramming the butt into his groin. He'd gasp, double over, and she'd slash upward, crack the hand-guard against his nose, send his wraparounds flying.

But it didn't go that way. The man kept his steel grip on his weapon, and with a casual smile he brushed aside her move, levered his arm upward, hammering the stock against her temple.

She knew she should duck and parry a second strike, but the world was gray and wobbly, and her arms useless, and when he smacked the rifle against her head again, a yellow flare filled the sky, and her vision shrunk to a pinhole. Then that shut.

She fell backward, smacked hard, and that was all she knew for five minutes or five hours before her head began to clear.

Layer by layer, she surfaced through the nauseating haze and spin, a vast weight holding her in place. Trapped in a cocoon of numbness. Her chest empty, mind blank. Struggling to remember where she was and why.

There was blood in her mouth. A molar felt loose. Her tongue swollen. Something sticky sealing her eyelids shut. There was an insect tracking along the rim of her nostril. Voices. Men speaking a language she didn't recognize.

She peeled open one eye, then the other.

In the dusky light, a flickering nimbus hovered around the trees. She couldn't lift her head but she could turn it. She saw them. The stocky one with his back to her. He was pissing. His comrade stood beside him doing the same. High glistening arcs into the brush. A schoolboy contest.

Her bag lay on the ground nearby. Its contents strewn. Hotel key, wallet, the atomizer. Ten feet off, their rifles were propped against a tree.

She felt a breeze spilling across her bare breasts. Her shirt was open, bra torn loose. Trousers tugged to her thighs.

Holding very still, she toured her body, clenched herself down there, a long Kegel, as she'd done before Leo's birth to strengthen the pelvic floor. Another clench and she felt no burn, no wetness, nothing leaking from her.

They hadn't raped her. What then? Just had a look? A feel?

She lifted her head. Wiped her eyes, caught the chlorine smell of sperm. Looked down at her exposed body. A sprinkle of fluid on her breasts, gray droplets going clear.

They'd had a circle jerk and left their drizzle on her belly and breasts and face.

To humiliate her? Degrade the American.

Or was this foreplay? Waiting for Blue Camo and the others to finish their work with Desmond and form a line to begin the real assault.

She rolled onto her side, pushed to her knees. Groaned against the headache spiking behind her left eye. Felt the lump above her ear.

She staggered to the tree as the two were zipping up. She grabbed the closest weapon, fit the butt to her shoulder, fingered the trigger. Swung around.

It was a Type 56 assault rifle, a cheap Chinese knockoff of the Kalashnikov AK-47. She couldn't be sure how many rounds were in the magazine. She believed it maxed at thirty. She hadn't trained on the Type 56, but she was well acquainted with the AK. Close enough.

Stocky Wraparound was the first to turn.

Harper's vision was blurry, knees unsteady, a burn in the back of her throat like the prelude to vomit. Her shirt was still open, their cum crusty on her flesh.

"What an idiot you are," the stocky man said. "Give my rifle."

He held out his hand and took two steps toward her.

The automatic bucked hard, spraying a burst of fire in the dirt at his feet. It wasn't as earsplitting as the AK, but loud.

Wraparound lowered his hand, and his mouth hardened.

He cursed her in French and lowered his head and reset his feet as if he meant to rush her. She emptied the clip. Tore his legs from under him, kicked him sideways. He landed hard on his back and thrashed his arms above his head as if he were trying to backstroke into the bush. Alive but going nowhere.

His buddy had disappeared into the trees.

Harper tossed the rifle into the grass, seized the second one and headed in the direction that the others had taken Desmond.

She met them as they were sprinting out of the woods, no doubt summoned by the gunfire. Blue Camo Man was bringing up the rear, a cigarette hanging jauntily from the corner of his lips. His two fighters froze when they saw her. Ten feet away. So close she could shred all three of them with a single trigger pull.

Instead she barked at them in French.

"Déposez vos armes."

Giving them a chance to drop their weapons.

Blue Camo Man waited behind his crew with an amused look, as if he were observing some painfully amateurish performance.

She repeated her order quietly and firmly so there was no mistake.

Blue Camo Man hissed something only his men could hear, and after a moment's hesitancy both soldiers raised their weapons. Harper swept the assault rifle at their legs. One screamed and fell writhing to the ground, the other slammed the earth with solid finality.

Coolly, Blue Camo Man said, "And what now for you?"

She told him again to drop his gun. And when he'd set it lightly at his feet, she said, "Take me to Desmond."

"Ah, Desmond," he said. "Your friend is much changed."

"Lead me."

In a clearing thirty feet from the jeep trail, Desmond sat propped against a palm tree. He was weeping into his hands.

She called out his name, and Desmond wiped tears from his face and stared at her, stunned for a moment, then his eyes widened, and he called out her name with something like reverence.

She wheeled and, with the rifle's stock, clubbed Blue Camo Man in the skull. He wobbled but managed to turn his head and give her a sulky look as if to disparage the strength of her blow. She clipped him a second time, and without further mockery he shut his eyes and finished his collapse.

"Can you walk?" she said to Desmond.

Desmond pushed himself to his feet, groaned, and straightened upright in painful stages.

"We go in hurry back to city, yes."

"No," she said. "Finish what we started. We're going to Soko."

"These men, they have camp close by," Desmond said. "Other guerillas there. Must go back to city. Go now before others come."

"You said Soko was near. We see that first, then the city."

She drove the old car with Desmond sunk low in his seat, eyelids heavy, flirting with sleep.

"Did they hurt you?"

Desmond closed his eyes and turned away. She asked him again.

He looked at her grimly and pulled up his shirt and presented the welts and blisters, at least a dozen of them.

"Cigarette?"

Desmond nodded.

"Man say I am spy, come to send military after them. They make me confess to what I do not do."

The village was another ten minutes down the jeep trail. She parked, got out. Desmond led her down a short pathway to a clearing of about an acre.

There were the remains of a few dozen huts, thatched roofs, mud walls. They'd been burned a few months back; most had caved in and were almost hidden in vines and weeds. Circling the perimeter of the village was a rock wall that had been partially dismantled, its large stones assembled into dozens of neat piles scattered around the open spaces.

"Graves," Desmond said. "Mossi people return to bury the dead."

There were at least fifty grave markers, clustered in groups of three or four. Families.

"And there," Desmond said. "In the tree."

He pointed to the frayed remains of a half dozen ropes knotted to several heavy branches. Below the ropes in the dust were a collection of moon-white skulls, rib cages, leg bones, and arms.

"Mossi men return to Soko for burying children. They captured and hung by necks."

"Who did this? The guerillas? Like the men we just saw."

Desmond closed his eyes and opened them again. "Officials in government say yes, guerillas do this."

"Is that true?"

"Children at Fatou's, they say no. Not rebels."

"Fatou's orphans, they escaped this massacre."

"A few from here, yes."

"What happened?"

"Ran into woods," he said. "Hid for days. Many starved."

"Who did this?"

"The children may tell you. You must speak to them."

"You tell me."

Desmond turned his back on her and headed to the car, calling over his shoulder. "We must hurry before more soldiers arrive."

She caught up to him, gripped his shoulder, and stopped him. Twilight birds swooped over the highest branches of the forest like the ragged remnants of the dead—the spirits of villagers unable to depart this blood-soaked ground. Circling and circling.

"Who, Desmond? Who's behind this slaughter?"

Desmond looked down and muttered under his breath.

She put a finger below his chin and lifted his head so he was looking into her eyes. "Say it."

In his dark, opaque eyes she saw him frame the words. He swallowed, touched his tongue to his upper lip. His face shone with sweat.

"It was revolt. The Soko people rise up against men who come steal their children and make them slaves. Go on that way for many years. They say no more, no more stealing children. All finished."

"Who stole the children, Desmond?"

She knew the answer but needed to hear the words.

"You are strong woman," he said. "And brave, but you cannot win against these men. They have too much muscle even for you."

"Tell me, Desmond."

He sighed and looked off.

"Chocolate people," he said. "This what children say. The chocolate people do this."

TWENTY-ONE

Early March, Zurich, Switzerland, Paradeplatz

"You wanted to see me?" asked Adrian.

Larissa Bixel didn't look up from her engorged right biceps. Wearing a low-cut purple bodysuit with serious cleavage showing, the sturdy, thick-limbed woman perched on the edge of a weight bench in the corporate gym, elbow on knee, curling what looked like forty pounds of iron.

"I have some queries for you, Mr. Naff."

She stayed focused on the bulge, didn't make eye contact with Adrian Naff. Hell, she rarely looked anyone in the eye. It was some kind of neurological disorder, Adrian believed. Asperger's syndrome or one of its cousins.

She must have been closing in on forty years old but had the thickly muscled body of a compulsive gym rat half that age. Almost Adrian's height, she was an intimidating presence, a woman whose twenty-year rise through the ranks of the Albion Corporation was rumored to have been a bloody gladiatorial affair. Some said the hallways of the Albion building were littered with the ghostly remains of the men who'd briefly blocked her passage.

Behind Larissa Bixel, with his blond crew cut glinting in the sunlight, stood Helmut Mullen. Dressed impeccably as always. Versace, Dolce & Gabbana, or was it Prada? It was beyond Adrian's expertise, but somehow Mullen's almost scruffy look radiated high-culture affluence. A black bomber jacket in a soft leather. Tailored jeans that hung just so and a mustard-colored turtleneck sweater. The jacket and sweater couldn't quite disguise his build: slim waist, wide shoulders, long and sturdy arms, and thick wrists. At this moment, Helmut's hands were clasped behind his back, but Adrian had seen the man's knuckles. They were defaced by scars. Either years of harsh blue-collar work or plenty of bare-fisted brawls. Adrian's money was on the latter.

Adrian had never been formally introduced to the man, and though he'd combed the corporation's worldwide directory, he'd never found Mullen's name anywhere in the vast chain of command. The man seemed to float on the periphery of Larissa Bixel's inner circle like her ethereal bodyguard or perhaps her gigolo.

Unlike Larissa Bixel, Mullen had no problem with eye contact, a sly smile on his lips as his dark, appraising eyes locked to Adrian's. His chin and right cheek were scuffed, and the edge of a compression bandage peeked out of the cuff of his right sleeve. Apparently, the boy had been tangling with someone at least his equal.

Bixel continued to study the swollen veins in her biceps for a long, irritating moment, then looked up and briefly met Adrian's gaze. It was only the second time their eyes had touched. The first had been a year earlier, when Bixel grilled him for two hours in this same gym. His final interview before being hired as security chief for Albion International.

"Happy to be of service. What can I help you with?"

Larissa allowed herself a dry chuckle. "Well, let's see. Do you think I might consult you about the derivatives market? Or perhaps you have expertise in commodities trading, arbitrage, cocoa bean futures? Skills I'm not familiar with?"

Adrian waited several seconds to let Bixel's scorn wither in the silence. She cut a look up at Helmut Mullen. The humorless smile was still in place, cool disinterest in his eyes.

"No, ma'am. My expertise is security."

"I'm so pleased to hear that. That is, after all, what we're paying you for."

While Bixel concentrated on her opposite biceps, Adrian's gaze drifted past her close-cropped bronze hair and Helmut Mullen's shoulders, out the floor-to-ceiling window with its distant view across the slate rooftops of the international banks strung along Poststrasse, a vista that stretched all the way to the blue shimmer of Lake Zurich. It was a crisp March afternoon, so clear and fine that even Larissa Bixel's condescension couldn't sully it.

Adrian wasn't impressed by bullying bosses. He'd served alongside men and women who'd survived decades of back-alley combat and all-out war. No petty slights dished out by the VP of global affairs in a sterile Swiss office building could rival the tests of his previous life.

"This man you referred to me, this Spider person, didn't you realize he was incompetent?"

"Harry Combs?"

"Combs, Spider, whatever you call him. You vouched for him. You gave him your highest endorsement."

"I worked with Combs on several operations. He's battle-tested, a pro. Highly skilled, methodical. Why do you ask? You're not satisfied with his work?"

While she cranked the weight, her empty gaze was directed a foot above Adrian's head. Clearly, she'd reached her monthly quota for eye contact.

"This pro, as you call him, this methodical, highly skilled man, yes, he completed his task, then afterward, when he should have left the area immediately, he stayed put and began to behave recklessly. And in so doing, he put Albion's best interests at risk."

Adrian waited as Larissa set down the weights. Helmut handed her a hand towel, and she patted her glistening face, then tossed the towel away.

"I can't help you," Adrian said. "I don't know the details of the work he did, and I suspect it's best it remains that way. As for your grave concerns, well, that's between you and Spider."

"Spider is missing," Helmut said.

"What?"

"Your friend," Helmut said, "or whatever he was, your associate, he has disappeared."

"Why would Spider disappear?"

"Because," Bixel said, "Helmut is apparently a very poor marksman."

Mullen drew his chin in a few inches and squared his shoulders as if preparing for Adrian to take a swing.

"You tried to kill Spider?"

"He's badly wounded, I believe." Mullen looked off at a window. "In all likelihood, he's no longer alive."

Adrian stared at Mullen. He wouldn't have called Spider a friend, but they'd had each other's backs in more than a few critical situations in the not-so-distant past.

"You and Spider were both contractors for the Aegis Group."

Adrian managed a nod.

"What exactly did you do for Aegis?" Bixel said. "Last year at your interview, you were tenaciously vague about the specifics of your work."

"I've told you what I could."

"But surely whatever allegiance you swore to your previous employer is no longer in effect."

"I collected intelligence and ran covert ops. That's all I can say."

"Were you an assassin?"

"Why do you ask?"

"Spider admitted he had done contract work as an assassin, so I assume you did similar work, taking men off the battlefield. And thus you know sometimes blood must be shed for the greater good."

Adrian waited, trying to keep a deferential look on his face, not let them see how disgusted he was, how close to stripping off his ID badge and walking away from all this. But then he wasn't sure if he still had that option. This wasn't a job you quit capriciously. He'd been given too much access to the company's inner workings and knew too many corporate secrets to be allowed to casually sever the connection. Meaning this seemingly cushy corporate job resembled the kind of work he'd thought he'd left behind.

"Tell me," said Bixel, "that you aren't bored with simply bodyguarding Albion executives, carrying briefcases in and out of interchangeable banks and five-star hotels, sitting in risk management meetings, and overseeing software heads and techies?"

"What exactly do you want?"

She picked up the barbell again, thought better of it, and held it out for Adrian to dispose of. He took it from her, turned, and let the weights clang to the floor. Then he wiped her sweat on his trouser leg.

She read the mutinous gesture, and all her haughtiness evaporated. She slitted her eyes and focused their dark venom on Adrian. "I want to send you into the field for some hands-on work. But I need to know you are capable of any action necessary."

"You want me track down Spider?"

"That would be a start."

"Then remove him?"

"I'd like to know you're capable, if it came to that."

"Commit murder, is that what you're asking?"

"Do you have a problem with that?"

"Mullen can fix his own fuckup."

Mullen shifted, hands rising. About to try his luck with Adrian.

"That's enough," said Bixel.

Mullen glared at Adrian a moment longer, then drew a tight breath and took a half step to the side. Conceding the round.

Bixel took a beseeching look at the far wall. "You remember the second man on the list you gave me, your other former associate from the Aegis Group?"

"Jackson Sharp. Yes, I remember."

"Another of your highly recommended, battle-tested comrades."

"You wanted names. I never said Sharp was the greatest soldier."

"Here's the issue: Some months ago in the Ivory Coast, a series of very poor decisions were made. Your friend, Mr. Sharp, was a participant in those events. That misadventure resulted in an unholy mess that Helmut and I have been trying to clean up ever since.

"Then, a few months after those events took place, I received a demand from Sharp, threatening to expose these unfortunate actions. In his effort to blackmail Albion, he went so far as to contact an investigative journalist at a large American newspaper and encouraged him to dig into the matter to increase the pressure on Albion. Rather than give in to these demands, I engaged Spider to remove the threat."

"Instead," Mullen said, "your buddy Spider made matters worse."

"So you tried to kill him. Now you want me to patch things up."

"Helmut removed Jackson Sharp as an immediate threat, but in the process, Helmut's identity was compromised. His face is known to certain parties. Therefore, I have summoned you to complete the mission. It was your former associates who have brought us to this situation, so it seems only reasonable for you to resolve it."

"Too many euphemisms for me," Adrian said.

"I'm being as explicit as I can be."

"That's not how it works, Ms. Bixel. Not in my business. If I clean up a mess, I have to know exactly what the mess is."

"You know all you need to know."

"This African fuckup, it happened on Albion's cacao plantation."

Bixel drew a slow breath. "Where did you get that idea?"

"Cacao is Albion's major holding in the Ivory Coast. What happened? Child slavery again? Afraid of more bad press?"

"It's a bit more complex than that."

"Is Mr. Albion aware of this misadventure?"

"What Lester Albion knows doesn't concern you."

"He doesn't know," Adrian said, "or the two of you would be gone."

"Don't be so sure of that."

Larissa Bixel sighed and rose from the bench. Her shoulders and arms were flushed from her workout, a cloud of earthy musk overwhelming her toiletries. She craned forward a few inches and peered into Adrian's eyes, moving so close he felt a sudden tidal pull in his chest, as if he'd been drawn inside her dark, magnetic field.

He dropped his eyes from hers and briefly watched a ribbon of sweat unfurl from a hollow in Larissa's throat and roll toward her shadowy cleavage. He averted his gaze from its downward track, turning his eyes to the far window.

Bixel took note of his restraint, and her smile was bitter. Adrian had foiled her. She was used to men like Helmut, who could not rein in their appetites. She played on their proclivities, their automatic responses. All that was in her unpleasant smile as her eyes held his once more. "I have two jobs for you, Mr. Naff. First, find out if Spider is still alive. If he is, I want you to reach out to him. Bring him in safely if you can so we might talk to him. If he resists these efforts, you can finish the job Helmut began. Either way works for us."

"And the second?"

"Her name is Harper McDaniel. She lives in Miami, Florida, and is the wife of the journalist I mentioned. We believe her late husband confided in her certain details of the African mishap."

Helmut said, "And the bitch saw my face."

"We believe," Bixel said, "Ms. McDaniel poses a danger to Albion's reputation and therefore to the health of our business. I want you to defuse that danger by removing her. Can you handle these two items?"

"Kill a civilian? A woman?"

Bixel's nod was almost but not quite imperceptible.

"And if I refuse?"

"Then I believe you should update your resume at once."

"I'll think about it," Adrian said.

"I'll have your answer now," Bixel said. "Yes or no?"

Adrian looked past her out the window at the Zurich skyline. With Bixel, a no would be final. He'd be packing his office this afternoon. While a yes would at least buy him time to find out what the hell was going on. So he gave her what she wanted, told her yes, he'd do it.

"Excellent," she said. "I knew we could count on you."

"A word of warning," Helmut said, brushing his hand against his damaged cheek. "Don't underestimate this McDaniel woman. She has skills. Fighting skills."

———

When Naff was gone, Larissa Bixel turned to Helmut.

"Are you angry I'm involving Naff?"

"He's competent enough, I suppose."

"Do you know the real reason I'm doing that, using Naff in place of you? It's not just because the McDaniel woman saw your face."

"I can guess the other reason," Mullen said.

"Go ahead."

"It's a reprimand," Helmut Mullen said. "For my gross mishandling of the Ivory Coast affair. For not tying up the loose ends properly."

"You made a complete botch of that, yes. Leaving behind the video camera, that was an idiotic error. And you and Jackson Sharp, your actions at Soko, they were barbaric, far beyond what the situation required."

"I agree. We lost control."

"Well, be that as it may," Larissa said, "there's another, more critical reason I've put Naff on this."

Larissa motioned at the stack of white towels; Helmut Mullen handed her another one, and she patted the fresh sweat off her throat and upper breasts.

"Naff is expendable," she said. "You're not."

"Thank you."

"You'll shadow him as you did Spider. Mr. Naff troubles me. Despite his assurances, I find his allegiance questionable. In short, if and when he completes his missions, I want him gone. Am I clear? Can you take care of this?"

"Certainly," he said. "It will be my pleasure."

TWENTY-TWO

Early March, Zurich, Switzerland, Paradeplatz

"Can I tell Mr. Albion what this is about?"

Adrian told her no, it was a security matter, boss's ears only.

The young woman produced an icy smile and rose from her desk and entered Lester Albion's office. A minute later, she opened the teak door and stood beside it and motioned for him to enter.

Lester Albion sat behind his desk, studying a color-coded pamphlet that lay open before him. All Adrian could make out on the pages were columns of six- and seven-digit numbers. Beside the prospectus, or whatever the hell it was, sat a glass jar filled with foil-wrapped candies.

Behind Lester, a wide plate-glass window showed the same view as the gym five floors below, only this vista was superior by a hundred feet, a spectacular view of the lake and, beyond it, the mountains. The Albion building wasn't a skyscraper, but it was as close to one as Zurich permitted.

In a nearby chair, Bonnie, Lester Albion's seven-year-old daughter, was perched with an electronic tablet in her lap.

"I'm out of school today," she said. "I had a stomachache, but I'm better now. Daddy, it's your friend, Mr. Naff."

Lester removed his reading glasses and set them aside.

"Daddy doesn't have many friends," she said. "You might be his only one. He likes you because you're a tough guy. You remind him of Ben Westfield, the movie star. He's Daddy's favorite actor because of how tough he is. Daddy's not tough. He's a soft man. A pushover. Aren't you, Daddy?"

"According to your mother."

Lester was small boned, a couple of inches over five feet, balding, with a receding chin and deep-blue eyes that smoldered with an intensity at odds with his diminutive stature. He was wearing his usual costume, a khaki short-sleeve shirt with epaulets and faded blue jeans, more fitting for an African safari than the presidential suite where he spent his days. A silly aping of Hemingway.

"Tell me, Adrian, you're not going to cancel our shooting date. I do so want to try out the new Glock."

"No, we're still on. Wouldn't miss it."

"Daddy's mother, she's my granny, she wouldn't allow Daddy to have toy guns when he was little. She was domineering. Now she doesn't talk, just sits in a chair all day. She had a stroke. So Daddy can do whatever he wants. Guns or anything."

"Bonnie," Albion said. "Mr. Naff isn't interested in our private lives."

"All Swiss men of fighting age are issued rifles or pistols," Bonnie said. "But Granny kept that gun away from Daddy too. She doesn't like guns because her husband killed himself with one. That's called suicide."

Lester sighed and gave Adrian a rueful smile.

Shortly after Adrian was hired, Lester had appeared in his office to question him about his experience with handguns. He'd read Adrian's file and was hopeful Adrian might become his mentor. Now, six months later, after a dozen sessions at a local indoor range, the two of them had formed a bond that was almost but not quite a friendship.

Adrian stepped to the near wall that was decorated with promotional posters of Albion's more successful food products. Chips and soft drinks, crackers, cookies, ice creams, cereals, toaster pastries, breads, frozen fruits and vegetables, olive oils, and a variety of butters. A large portion of the wall was dedicated to Albion's candies and chocolate bars, which came in dozens of shapes. On the adjacent wall, hanging by itself, was a framed photo of the Hollywood star Ben Westfield. The guy was wearing a cowboy hat and two six-guns, and he was about to bite into one of Albion's candy bars. An ad campaign from at least forty years back.

"Can I speak freely, sir?" Adrian nodded at Bonnie.

Lester buzzed his secretary and asked Bonnie to step into the waiting room for a moment.

"Man talk," Bonnie said. "I get it."

When she was gone, Albion said, "Sorry. She doesn't have a filter."

"She's charming."

"I wish I could find a nanny who agrees with you. So what brings you by, Adrian?"

"I heard something troubling about the Ivory Coast holdings."

Albion sat back in his chair, his face tight. "Oh, please. Don't tell me there's a problem out there."

"I don't know, sir. That's why I'm here. I wanted to know if you'd heard anything, or if I should investigate the issue further."

"What exactly did you hear?"

"Nothing specific, but apparently there was an incident at the Royale Plantation."

"Christ. Not child slaves again. Tell me it's not that. Not now, for god's sake, at this delicate juncture."

"Delicate?"

Lester drew a long breath, his eyes roaming his office. At last he fixed his gaze on the glass jar of foil-wrapped chocolates before him. He reached out and tapped the lid.

"Are you familiar with these, Adrian? Marburg chocolates?"

"I don't eat many sweets, sir."

Lester removed the lid and scooped up a handful of the miniatures and rattled them in his hand like dice, then scattered them on his desktop.

"Marburg has been around for two centuries. British company, very big in India, Pakistan, throughout South Asia. Long before anyone else in the industry, they saw the possibilities of emerging markets and set up excellent supply lines and customer service. All of which makes them a perfect target for acquisition."

"You're buying Marburg?"

"In five days the deal should be complete. A few last-minute holdouts on their board that need convincing."

He thumped a finger against one of the miniature bars.

"You know, the first instant one of these melted on my tongue, I knew exactly what I wanted in life. I wanted to own the factory that made these delights. I was seven years old, didn't know a damn thing about business. But I knew what I wanted. It just appeared like a dream, a vivid dream. Did you ever have that experience as a boy? A vivid dream that pointed the way forward."

"No, sir. I'm still waiting for that dream."

He nodded in sympathy. "So on the business side, the Marburg deal offers us a chance to expand our footprint in India and emerging markets around Asia, and not just chocolate but in higher-growth sectors like gum and candy. The deal broadens our portfolio, and it should accelerate long-term growth and deliver some highly desirable returns. For Marburg, the deal gives them a chance to piggyback on our production apparatus. Faster delivery, greater scale. Just what they need in order to grow.

"But you know what, Adrian? That's just the horse manure I sling to sell stockholders on the consolidation in order to take over a company I've been dreaming of since I was a seven-year-old lad."

He stirred the miniatures with a finger.

"The one problem is that the Marburgs are Quakers."

"How's that a problem?"

"Very religious people, very moral. Any hint of scandal and they'll back away in an instant. No matter how it might benefit them financially, they'll refuse to sign. Like that, poof, it's all gone."

"A scandal like Albion using child slaves to harvest cacao beans."

"Yes, exactly," he said. "When I first learned of the issue two years ago, I addressed the problem head-on, ordered sweeping changes to our vetting procedures so local farmers who used children in the fields would no longer be associated with Albion. We made structural adjustments, tightened our oversight to eradicate any child-welfare abuses. When I was certain that chapter was closed, I invited United Nations human rights workers and independent inspectors out there to certify that there was no longer an issue with child workers.

"We started schools for local children, we've educated the adult workers, made it very clear we will not stand for such contemptible behavior again. And we've provided thorough documentation of all of these efforts to the Marburgs to once and for all put that disgraceful episode behind us. So you can imagine my dismay to hear any whisper of further scandal in the Ivory Coast."

"Yes, I can."

"Who told you about this problem? Was it Bixel?"

"I can't say, sir."

"I'm sorry?"

"It would violate confidentiality. I would lose my source. It's better if I investigate this on my own. I'll keep you informed, but I can't share anything till I'm finished."

"Is that's how it's done in your world, Adrian? Your commander gives you a direct order and you refuse?"

"Are you giving me a direct order?"

Albion's hands pressed flat against the desktop. "All right," he said. "But complete your investigation with great haste and bring your results to me and me alone, then we'll find a way to make that problem vanish. And that is a direct order."

"Yes, sir."

"Here, take some of these, see what the fuss is about."

Albion scooped up a few candies and held them out.

Adrian left Lester Albion's office with a handful of chocolates and a direct order from the boss to use any means necessary to make the Ivory Coast problem disappear.

TWENTY-THREE

Early March, en route to Zurich, Switzerland

"Who do we know in Zurich?"

Harper was calling Nick from Port Bouet International Airport in Abidjan. She'd worked her way past passport control, the two security checks, and a long, chaotic line to check her bag. Ahead of her was another tedious day of flying, ten hours, with one stop in Brussels on the way to Zurich. She was waiting in the general lounge at her gate, trying to ignore the two military guards with machine pistols who kept eyeing her.

"I'm still working on it," Nick said. "Got calls out to finance friends in Zurich who are plugged in."

"Good. We need everything they can dig up on Albion."

"You've got a plan?"

"Not yet. I need more information. I'll wait to see what your finance friends come up with."

"What do you want them to look for?"

"Anything with Albion and chocolate in the same paragraph."

"I'll do what I can."

"And the third guy on Ross's list, Adrian Naff, anything on him?"

"Nothing new. Head of security for Albion. That's all I have. His life before that is something of a blank."

"Nobody's a blank, Nick. Ross knew something about the guy. If Ross was going all the way to Zurich to interview him, the guy matters."

"I'll keep digging. Sal volunteered to dig around in some databases."

"He knows a hacker?"

"Does it himself."

"You're kidding."

"News to me too. Something he picked up in his retirement. His next-door neighbor is tutoring him."

"He any good? Sal, I mean."

"Says he is."

"Sure, go on, use him. We need anything we can get on Naff."

"Will do."

"And the apartment on Edgewater. Did Sal's CSI guys turn up anything?"

"Got a ballistics report back. The Ruger you knocked out of the guy's hand was the same weapon Jackson Sharp was killed with."

"Is that all?"

"Sal's tech guy found fingerprints. Jackson Sharp's and one other set. The second prints match the ones on the Ruger. But the Ruger guy's prints didn't ring any bells in Interpol's database. Which means Ruger Guy's never been arrested, he's not military, not a fugitive, no government job. A clean background."

"The guy I threw over the railing wasn't clean."

"There's a pattern here. Naff is a blank. Ruger Guy is clean."

"Not clean. More like scrubbed."

Nick was silent.

"And Alvarez? He been around?"

"Called twice, wanted to talk to you. I said you were out of town."

"He know about the Edgewater scene?"

"No," Nick said. "It's all cleaned up, wiped down. Sal's people disposed of the body. Like it never happened."

"You and Sal have been playing me, haven't you?"

"What do you mean?"

"That story about some outsider tampering with Alvarez's investigation, that was horseshit, wasn't it? Just to peel us away from the cops."

The line was empty for a long moment.

Then Nick said, "It was Sal's idea. I didn't like lying to you, but I went along. I'm sorry, Harper. Can you forgive me?"

"It's okay," she said, then went silent, still debating how much to reveal to Nick about her visit to Soko, the massacre, the chocolate people. Nick was already worried about her. If she told him what she'd discovered and what she'd done, he and Sal and a dozen of Sal's goons would be waiting for her in Zurich, ready to storm Albion headquarters.

"You're not going to tell me anything about Africa."

"In due time."

"Was Ross's guy helpful? Moussa Kouacou?"

"He was, yes. Very helpful."

The two soldiers were making a slow orbit around her chair. One of them was speaking on a handheld radio.

The Jetway door was open, and a Swiss Air attendant was making the preflight announcements.

She told Nick she had to go.

"Call me when you land."

"Thanks. I will."

"You sure you're all right? You sound a little, I don't know, faraway."

"I am," she said. "Five thousand miles and counting."

The two military guys were closing in.

"Got to run."

She clicked off, gathered her carry-ons, and headed toward the line forming at the door to the Jetway. Her heart had lost traction. The nasty knot on her temple where one of the guerillas had clubbed her began to throb in time with her elevated pulse.

One of the soldiers stepped in front of her and spoke her name.

"Yes?"

"You will come with us."

"My plane's leaving."

"You will come with us, answer questions."

"What kind of questions?"

The other soldier gripped her right biceps and tugged her out of the line. She wrenched her arm free, and after taking a look at her scowl, the soldier didn't try to touch her again. They led her down the concourse, one in front, one behind, a forced march past a security checkpoint, then the man in the lead directed her into a small, windowless room.

A tall white man in his late sixties sat at the head of a gleaming conference table. When Harper entered, he rose and bowed his head and waved her to a seat.

"I'm about to miss my plane."

"Sit, sit. Planes come and go. We need to talk."

His hair was thick and white and combed stiffly back. His eyes were green with an eerie shine, as if backed by silver foil.

She settled into a hard, straight-back chair at the far end of the table. The two soldiers melted away, shutting the door softly behind her.

She lightly brushed her hair over the lump. Earlier that morning at the hotel, she'd used concealer and powder to cover the spreading bruise.

"I am Roger Bellerose, deputy minister of defense and maritime affairs. Among my duties, I oversee the paramilitary forces spread throughout our country. It falls to me to monitor the advances of the guerilla forces, their comings and goings, their threats to the nation's stability. By that means I have acquired certain information concerning your visit to our nation."

Harper held his steady gaze.

"I understand that you've been quite active during your stay with us. I would like to recount the tally if I may."

"What tally?"

"You began your sojourn by brawling with a street gang and breaking a man's wrist very badly. That young man will never sign his name again or write a love letter. Then there are the events in the jungle near the border with Burkina Faso. It seems there were two casualties, both killed with automatic rifle fire.

"These men were rebels, yes, and therefore enemies of the state, but still, murder is considered a most heinous crime in our land, you see. Another man in that same location is now in critical condition, also from gunfire, and if he survives, he will walk with a limp. Still one other in the same group has suffered a severe concussion. Then there is Moussa Kouacou, a minister in our government. He is recovering from a nasty knife wound to the shoulder. That is the tally I have. There may be more I do not know of. But in such a short stay, you have created much havoc in our quiet land."

"What do you want from me?"

"You deny nothing I have said?"

"Would it do me any good?"

The man formed a narrow smile, lifted his hands, and applauded her sarcasm with a few dry pats.

"And what do you think might be an appropriate punishment for such crimes? What would the police officials in your home country do with a foreigner who committed such acts in, say, Ohio?"

"Do I need a lawyer?"

"I have been asked by certain parties to take you into custody."

"What parties?"

"I'm still debating if that is the proper course or not."

Harper was silent.

"You are fortunate the Ivory Coast has abolished the death penalty. A life sentence in the House of Detention and Correction of Dimbokro, which is two hundred kilometers north of the city . . . that is what one might reasonably expect for the crimes you have committed. The Dimbokro prison has not been updated since its construction in 1960, so you can easily imagine spending your days and nights in tin-roofed dormitories in the tropical heat. With these conditions, many convicts do not survive a single month in Dimbokro."

"Maybe I should speak to someone at the American embassy."

"Oh, no," he said. "No one at the embassy wants to speak to you."

"I have rights."

"Miss, you have only the rights I decide upon. Is that clear?"

She kept quiet.

"Do you understand that the cacao industry accounts for sixty percent of our export trade? Every year, our farmers produce well over a million tons of beans, which supplies over a third of the world's needs. It is a crucial industry both here and throughout the global marketplace."

"And all that makes child slavery acceptable?"

"Yes, yes, you Americans are very righteous. And you are also quite ill-informed. Apparently you are not aware of the great poverty that afflicts our land. A dollar a day is what our cacao farmers earn, and that is considered a very fine wage. To stay competitive against other nations with greater wealth and resources, our farmers employ every cost-saving measure they can.

"So, yes, what you say is true, some family farmers do indeed use their children to accomplish light work on the cacao plantations. Just as farmers in your own homeland, I believe, engage their children and family members for chores in the field. In our country, children who are fortunate enough to work on the cacao bean plantations have an opportunity for a better life. Sadly, it is one of the only pathways open to them. Using children for such work has been our custom for generations."

"Abducting children and enslaving them, that's your custom too?"

He smiled away the insult. "Oh, your American principles are very laudable. You can afford to be that way, I suppose. But in my country such a luxury is out of our reach. We know we must make moral sacrifices if we are to progress. You and your people have your own dark history, yet you come to our shores and preach to us as if you are free of all guilt."

"The village of Soko, have you heard of it?"

He drew an exasperated breath. "The community you mention, I believe it is across the border in Burkina Faso. Our government exerts no power over our neighbors."

"The residents of Soko were massacred because they fought back against men who repeatedly abducted and enslaved their children. And this moral sacrifice is acceptable to you, Mr. Deputy Minister?"

He continued to smile at her. Eyes cold and empty.

"All right, young woman, here is what I'm telling you. My verdict on your misconduct is the following. Henceforth, from this day forward, you will be denied access to cross our borders. You will be permitted to leave, but you can never return. Second, if it comes to our attention that you continue to make false claims against industries which are critical to our national interests, we will notify immigration authorities in your homeland that the Ivory Coast has found you to be a dangerous security threat, indeed, a terrorist wanted for murder, and our international partners should apprehend you immediately upon your arrival in their country. Your ability to travel internationally will cease, and that will be the least of your worries. Is that clear?"

Harper digested that for several moments. "You think I killed two people, but you're letting me go with a slap on the wrist."

"I don't *think* anything, my good lady. What you did is an incontestable fact. I have ironclad proof of it. And I will use the full force of that information against you if you continue to make outrageous claims against the business practices of our most valued industry."

"You know what I'm saying is true. Soko was destroyed, its residents massacred. Their killers were acting on behalf of Albion."

He fixed his gaze on her, his cold smile had vanished, and he was making no further attempt at cordiality.

"I am not a man who makes casual threats. I am warning you with all seriousness that if you continue to present spurious and damaging claims about business entities within the Ivory Coast, you will be dealt with most harshly. Now your plane is waiting, you may go."

Roger Bellerose gave her a curt nod, finished with her. He drew out his cell phone, made a call, ducked his head, and spoke quietly to someone in a language Harper had never heard.

She walked from the conference room back down the concourse. At the security checkpoint, the guards waved her through, and the gate attendant led her down the Jetway and to her seat. When the plane finally lifted off, Harper drew a long breath. It felt like the first she'd taken in days.

TWENTY-FOUR

Early March, en route to Zurich, Switzerland

Changing planes in Brussels with two hours to kill, she wandered the Pier A concourse. Jewelry shops, bars, restaurants, Victoria's Secret, Hugo Boss, Massimo Dutti, several luggage stores. She came to a halt at the window of Epicure, a fine-food emporium. An array of wines, flavored oils, hundreds of varieties of cookies, Scottish salmon, cheese, duck and goose foie gras. And chocolates.

Trays and trays, displaying a vast variety of rich Belgian treats.

She went inside, prowled the aisles till she located the glass cases where the collection of chocolates was laid out. The air was overpowering with the competing scents of chocolate and the buttery additives. On top of the counter, trays were on display, samples of every delicacy with hand-lettered cards describing every item in the poetry of indulgence.

A CRUSHED PECAN BRITTLE WITH PECAN GIANDUJA DIPPED IN MILK CHOCOLATE AND GARNISHED WITH FINELY GROUND CHILI PEPPERS.

CHOPPED, SWEETENED BRAZIL NUTS, ALMONDS, AND MACADAMIA NUTS WITH A SPRINKLING OF ORANGE PEEL, COVERED IN DARK CHOCOLATE.

A MILK CHOCOLATE FRESH CRÈME BLENDED WITH PURE, SWEET HONEY, DIPPED IN MILK CHOCOLATE, AND SPRINKLED WITH A SPICY CASSIA CINNAMON.

Ganache and truffles, pralines shaped like seashells, fish, and diamonds. Orangettes, Manon Blanc, bouchons, *pistoles*, éclairs filled with chocolate mousse and fresh buttercreams, chocolate dollops packed with pistachio paste and caramelized almonds and Grand Marnier.

At the cash register, the line was filled with smartly dressed travelers, the urbane, cultured, the business class, their faces downy white and glowing with guilty excitement. Paying their money, turning back to the concourse, some of them secretly dipping their hands into the sacks, plundering the decadent treats.

An attendant asked Harper if anything struck her fancy.

"Nothing," she said as politely as she could manage and turned away, her face flushed.

Not long ago, with no second thoughts, she would have selected a handful of sweets and relished the swoon of pleasure as they liquefied in her mouth. But after her days in Africa, after the orphanage, the trip to Soko, seeing the stone grave markers littering the village grounds, chocolate would never again be so innocent or so sweet.

Perhaps what was true for chocolate was true for every delicacy in that store. Very likely at the bottom of each food production line there was exploitation and poverty and grim, unspeakable realities. But she doubted any products shelved in Epicure were as tainted as the ones derived from cacao beans. Kidnapping, slavery, mass murder, and a conspiracy stretching across continents, one that had destroyed the two lives she cherished most.

For the next hour, she drifted through the concourse, lost in a furious stupor until her flight boarded. She took her seat, stared out her window at the tarmac slick with fresh rain, her breasts aching again, her face still prickling with heat, and the lump on her temple throbbing.

As the plane taxied to the runway, she dug a bottle of aspirin from her carry-on and dry swallowed three tablets.

She spent the flight rehashing the days since Ross and Leo were taken from her. Picking through every hour in as much detail she could recall. She'd been doing it constantly in her quiet times, retracing the steps of this torturous journey because she had a teasing sense that she'd missed something along the way. A key fact floating just out of reach in a hazy corner of her mind.

Hours later, as the flight attendants prepared the cabin for the landing in Zurich, it flashed into focus. Harper drew her iPad from her carry-on, linked to the flight's Internet, and navigated to the Epic backup service where Ross's files were stored. She entered the passwords, and once again his many pages of research material appeared. She found his JPEG files and, at the very end, saw again that single movie file.

Last week, when she'd first noticed the file, it had struck her as oddly out of place, but in the welter of calamities, she'd set that feeling aside and forgotten to watch the film.

She tapped the movie-file icon, and after a long hesitation, the video began to play. It was, she saw immediately, the attempted rescue at Royale Plantation, the film Ross had described in his notes.

The boy called Yacou and a half circle of other boys were wielding machetes that seemed outsize in their small hands. They were hacking open the cacao pods, spilling out the seeds in a clearing in the jungle. She watched as Yacou set down his blade and came to his feet, feigning nonchalance, then headed for the bushes as if to relieve himself. Just as Ross rendered it in his first-person account, Yacou next appeared a few feet from the camera. He swept aside the fronds, hesitated a moment as if marshaling his courage, then pointed at Rachel and the man named Charles and cried out, *"Ils sont ici."* Here they are.

The two African men in security uniforms burst into their hiding place, shoved Yacou aside, and behind the security guards the blond man appeared. A boxy haircut, sharp angles in his face, almost handsome except for his flattened lips and avid eyes. And yes, it was indeed the same man Harper had fought on the balcony of the Edgewater Apartments, the Ruger guy she had tipped over the railing. And on the edge of the frame was a half-second glimpse of another white man, just his ear, a quick sliver of his neck and cheek.

The next moments unfolded exactly as Ross had described. The camera ripped from Rachel Sharp's hand, tossed into the brush. Still running, its audio captured the fearsome exchange between the blond man and the two American do-gooders. And though Harper knew it was coming, she could not turn away. Ross had watched the horror. So must she.

The woman, Rachel Sharp, close to Harper's age, let loose an anguished scream, followed by a long silence, then, only a yard from the camera, slammed onto her back, blood pumping from the slit in her throat, her eyes wide and vacant.

"Madam." A flight attendant leaned over Harper. "You must turn off your device and prepare for landing."

Harper looked up into the woman's bright, clear face and opened her mouth to speak but found no words.

———

Five thirty, a half hour past quitting time on that Zurich banking street. At the Metropol's outdoor sidewalk bar, Spider was bundled up in a down parka, trying to find a comfortable position on the padded chair. Every way he moved made his left buttock throb even more. Aggravated by the endless flight across the Atlantic, wedged into a middle seat between two fat grandmothers, he had felt the blood pooling in his ass. Now, after three days on stakeout, ten hours a day sitting outside in the freezing weather, he felt the ache worsen, and it seemed to be growing claws.

Last week in Miami, the Jamaican vet who'd extracted the slug and sewed up the gouge warned him not to sit for long periods. *Sure thing, mon,* but what the hell was Spider supposed to do, pace the 737's narrow aisles for six hours, keep dodging the grumpy flight attendants, squeezing past the food carts?

This was Spider's third outing to Zurich. First time, ten years back on R & R when he was based in Düsseldorf; a second time when he'd been dispatched to take out a Russian businessman for some mortal sin Spider never learned. Spider's view: Zurich was as boring as a slice of unbuttered Wonder bread. One exception, the Niederdorf district in the lower village, part of Old Town on the east side of the Limmat River. There, along Härringstrasse, the classier hookers patrolled the sidewalks near a jazz bar he liked, the House of Spirits.

When Adrian Naff finally made an appearance, Spider could finish his business, not give his old friend a chance to explain, just take him out, then by god he'd head over to the Andorra to celebrate with a few rusty nails. Stand at the bar, let the blood drain from his swollen butt, and, when suitably lubricated, splurge on one of the street ladies. He'd choose a slender one, tall with long, black hair, close his eyes, and imagine Harper McDaniel. Then he'd spend the night spreading his all-American charm to this dreary corner of Europe.

Sooner or later, Adrian Naff had to show, and he'd have to use the front entrance. The back entry was for deliveries. No chopper pad on the roof, no side exits. Maybe when Spider was taking a piss, Adrian had passed by. Or maybe he'd blinked at the exact wrong moment, and the guy'd slipped past in a crowd. Maybe Adrian was out sick, taking a few days off. Didn't matter. Spider was patient, plenty of covert operations under his belt. You sat, you waited, you watched, you kept your trigger finger limber.

Sitting in the same seat for three consecutive days was a breach of surveillance protocol. Tactics manual said he should change his clothes, vary his appearance and location, assume his quarry was doing his own countersurveillance. But Spider didn't care anymore. Somewhere in the last few days, he'd decided he was done with this business, ready to try a new direction. Not sure exactly what, but maybe something halfway normal, four walls and a woman at the stove, kids running around in the yard wanting to throw a baseball. Retire from covert ops, finish with the endless travel, the stress, the bottomless solitude.

So screw protocol. And anyway, by god, he liked the Metropol. Liked its ambiance. Reminded him of a Paris bistro with sidewalk tables. A romantic place to take your girl, watch the flow of people, talk to her, the way ordinary people talked, the way Ross McDaniel and Harper talked. Saying nothing fancy, just regular chitchat, close, affectionate. That lucky fucker, Ross, talking with his beautiful wife. The two of them making dinner plans, sharing the events of their days, talking about their friends, about Leo, the funny shit the kid did that day.

That week of surveillance, Spider had gotten an inside look at Harper's marriage, all of it on his video feed, stored in a file on his phone. He looked at the phone sitting on the table in front of him. Maybe he'd watch a little of it again right now. That life they'd been living. An intimate view. Like nothing he'd ever seen before. Nothing like his own family, how his old man would steal into his bedroom at night with his Vietnam Purple Heart in his hand, sit on Spider's bed and tell him about the war, how ugly it was, how Spider didn't know anything about pain and terror, and the old man would pull the medal's stickpin out straight and hold it in front of Spider's eyes, hold it there for several silent seconds, then some nights he'd poke Spider with it a few times, light pokes, and while he kept talking about what a spoiled, ungrateful little shit Spider was and how he knew nothing about real pain and horror, the old man working himself up, he'd finally jab Spider with the pin, draw blood, jab him deep in his arms and his chest and his legs, jab and jab until Spider cried and writhed away. Night after night like that until, one night, Spider didn't cry and didn't writhe away. That night marking the end of his childhood.

Nothing like that ever went down with Harper and Ross and their little kid. No, this was just two calm, ordinary people. What love looked like. Sex and love and quiet dinners and talk and holding each other. All that on the video feed. All of it stored on his phone.

Spider reached out for the phone, then stopped and drew back.

No, he'd save it for later. Watch some of it when he was alone, back at the hotel when no one was around, just in case the damn thing made him cry again.

———

At the Widder Hotel, Harper settled her bags in her suite, then returned to the chrome-and-glass lobby with its zebra-striped chairs and exited onto the busy thoroughfare.

Quarter past six. She walked a block to Bahnhofstrasse, where it was a ten-minute straight shot down to the square at Paradeplatz. Dodging streetcars, finding her place in the swarm of homebound workers, she navigated the crowded sidewalk, the air crisp, the sky a soft pewter.

She glided past Cartier, Tiffany, Louis Vuitton, Hermès, Chanel, Van Cleef & Arpels, then, for no reason she could explain, stopped at the window of a swanky local shop. Another window, like the one at the Brussels airport, not chocolate this time, but belts and shoes and purses made of leather so buttery it was as if they'd been stitched from the skins of fanciful beasts that existed only in fairy tales.

On a pedestal beside the leather goods lay a silver brooch, its filigree as delicate as the wings of dragonflies, and beside the pedestal a display of watches encrusted with diamonds and pearls, and a collection of perfumes in glittering bottles shaped like ballerinas and dragons. Necklaces of gold, pendants of platinum, finely detailed bracelets and earrings.

Such abundance, such a vast accretion of bullion on display, brought to mind the gold-plated interior walls of Spanish cathedrals

sheathed in thousands of precious coins beaten flat, the alms of countless peasants, whose pooled sacrifices made such splendor possible.

She turned and pushed on through the evening crowd, her destina-
tion fifteen minutes ahead, less than a mile. All she meant to do was
cruise past the building, give it a quick look, test the air for vibrations,
glimpse the employees, look into their faces, those men and women
exiting the front doors of the headquarters of Albion.

Just a quick flyby, then she'd return to her suite at the Widder,
order a dinner on a silver tray, and haggle with her conscience for a few
hours of sleep.

Twenty yards away from the seven-story building, she halted and
watched as two armed guards in uniforms climbed down from an
armored van parked at the curb. The uniformed men lowered a stainless steel drum from the rear of the van, and when they had it settled on
the sidewalk, one of them rolled the container through the wide front
doors while the second man followed.

Harper slipped forward and watched the two uniformed men enter
the building and turn left in the lobby, then disappear down a long corridor. She stood for a moment, then rejoined the flow of the crowd, an
idea clicking into place.

TWENTY-FIVE

Early March, Zurich, Switzerland

The next morning Harper woke to the smell of coffee. It took her a hazy moment to remember she hadn't ordered any, hadn't hung out the order sheet on her door last night. She lay still, heart revving, listening to the passing street sweeper, its big brushes grinding against the pavement.

That street cleaner had stolen into her final dream of the night, morphing into a brigade of Russian-made tanks rumbling down the thoroughfare. Jamal Fakhri's tanks. In the surreal logic of her dream, Jamal was still alive and had hunted Harper down to exact revenge. He was riding atop the turret of the lead tank and somehow he'd spotted her standing in the hotel window. Fakhri waved his arms to the others behind him, directing them toward Harper. As she watched in horror, they turned in unison to point their big guns at her hotel room window.

She'd jerked awake, pulse roaring.

Still roaring now as she rose from the bed, rubbed her eyes.

She sniffed again. Definitely coffee. Maybe a passing room service cart in the hallway. Barefoot, she padded into the front room, the chilly bedroom tiles giving way to the sleek wood of the sitting room, oak inlaid with a maze of golden maple. Covering the walls was a dark-mahogany paneling, and in the center of the room, a cluster of leather chairs and matching settee arranged around a wide TV.

The heavy green drapes were open. Not how she'd left them last night. On the bar the coffee maker belched and trickled coffee into the pot. A cup and saucer sat beside the machine. On the glass-topped desk, a laptop computer she didn't recognize was open, its screensaver playing a loop of busty blondes in bikinis flashing toothy smiles at the camera.

In her flannel pajamas, Harper was now fully awake. With four quick steps, she slipped to the drapes, swept them aside. No one there. And nowhere else in the room to hide.

As she turned from the window, the toilet in the powder room flushed. She cut around the settee, pressed flat against the bathroom wall, and listened to the clumsy sounds of someone banging around in the small room.

A moment later, the door swung open and a short man stepped into the room, wiping his hands on his trousers. He wore a baggy long-sleeve T-shirt. He mumbled to himself as he continued to dry his palms on his gray pants.

From the bar she grabbed a bottle of Bordeaux by the neck and raised it. He caught the movement, halted, then turned to her. Deep-blue eyes, large ears, a nose that took up half his face.

"Did I wake you?" Sal Leonardi looked at the bottle, poised to strike. "I should've called, I guess."

She lowered the wine.

"You just walk in here, into my locked hotel room?"

He blinked at her as though he didn't comprehend the problem. "Those card keys, they're a joke."

"You're incredible."

"Sorry, sorry. I didn't mean to wake you. Tried to be quiet. You were sawing some big logs in there."

He grunted and headed to the desk. She set the bottle on the bar and followed.

"Found some interesting stuff on Naff. Like for one thing, he's twelve different guys at once."

Sal settled into the desk chair, tapped a key, and the loop of buxom babes disappeared, replaced by a page of print. Running down the left margin was a row of thumbnail photos.

"See," he said. "Same guy, different bios. Found a dozen so far."

"I'm not following you."

"These are passport photos. Took me a week to dig them out. Once I had a photo of Naff, I ran face-recognition code to find the rest.

"What you got here is four US passports, two Canadian, one French, two Swiss, three British. Different birthdays, cities of origin, date of issue. Guy's a chameleon. Beards, mustaches, glasses. I like the wig, this one here."

He tapped a finger on the screen. A man in a Paul McCartney mop with a metallic green tendril of hair drooping across his forehead.

She stared at the faces. After years of training alongside Deena, reading eyes, catching the elusive clues in faces, Harper had learned to spot slippages in the mask, the micromoments that revealed glimpses of authentic character.

With Naff, it was more than wigs and glasses and fake mustaches that made these faces different from one another. More than makeup. This man seemed to have masterful control of muscles in his mouth and cheeks, a lift of eyebrow here, a smug narrowing of eyes, warping himself into a nerdy introvert, a braying bully, a haughty snob, a playboy complete with a sleazy, come-on smile.

And there were other, subtler portraits more difficult to label. There was one man who seemed so hollowed out by heartache it made the world beyond his skin unbearable to behold. He could barely bring himself to look into the camera lens.

"This guy here." Sal tapped the last thumbnail. "Now this is the asshole you worry about. One you don't see coming."

The man in the final photo still had Naff's dark eyes, strong chin, his straight nose, but somehow he'd drained his features of content. They expressed nothing. They barely reflected light. He'd made himself so anonymous he'd be able to stand in plain sight and be all but invisible. Look at him as long as you like, memorize him, then turn away and try to picture this unremarkable man, and you'd fail. Too much like everyone else and nobody at all.

"Creative guy. Having a little fun. Got to like that in a spy."

"What makes you think he's a spy?" she asked.

"All these passports, what else? The guy's a field operative. Slippery as an electric eel with twice the voltage."

She leaned closer to the screen. Felt Sal staring at her inches away.

"You know you got your mother's looks," he said. "That smoky, pissed-off thing, like you can't decide if you're going to kiss the guy or scoop out his eyes with a melon baller."

Harper shook her head, holding back the onset of a smile.

"You got lucky with the looks," he said. "Don't see a trace of your dipshit old man. I apologize if you're close to him, which I doubt, 'cause somebody sure as hell fired a Colombian stink rocket up that guy's ass."

"I'm having trouble picturing you as a hacker."

"I'm a beginner is all, but I'm getting better. Numbers were always easy, computing in my head, logic. Like the work I did for Tessalini, keeping his books.

"See what happened, I retired, moved to South Beach, next thing I know I'm looking around for a hobby, way to fill my days, turns out my next-door neighbor, guy you saw when you came over, Chinese guy, he writes code for video games, just a kid, nineteen, twenty, name is Kong, can you believe it? I should've introduced you, you would've liked him.

"Anyway, so we hit it off, Kong and me, he shows me a few moves, simple coding, Java, JavaScript, and bang, right from the get-go it seems easy, and I'm pretty good at it, which surprised the hell out of me. Like I woke up one day, I could speak German."

With that, they ordered breakfast, and Sal laid out everything he knew about Spider between bites of Swiss breads, Zopf and Bürli, and a heaping plate of bratwurst, fried potatoes scrambled with cheese and eggs. Shoveling it in, backhanding his lips between bites. Caveman manners.

First, Nick had finagled a copy of the security video from the Aqua, captured a decent image of Spider and Harper entering the building together last week. Then Sal had used the same facial-recognition software to track down Spider's name and online presence.

Harold Anderson Combs, thirty-nine, born in Indiana, graduated high school, dropped out his first year at a local community college, joined the army, flunked out of Ranger School at Fort Benning, deployed to Iraq and Afghanistan, two tours. Exited the service, joined Aegis Defense Service, a private military contractor headquartered in London, spent five years on its payroll.

"This is where it gets interesting." Sal's eyes narrowed, and he leaned forward as if about to whisper. "These Aegis people, their encryption is so shitty a grade-school kid could crack it on his lunch break. So I go inside Aegis, prowl around, get access to travel docs, payroll, the usual stuff. Looks like Spider was pulling down one hundred forty K, plus year-end bonuses in the ten-K range. Not bad for a douche bag. He floated around Europe, took trips to Jordan and Abu Dhabi, a week or two, and other hot spots in the neighborhood, went back to Baghdad for a month, Yemen, Libya. Short stay in Syria.

"Kind of work he did, they use weasel words for everything, don't call anything what it is straight out, but it's clear enough the guy's a mercenary, a hired gun running interference for American GIs in the Iraq bullshit war, doing paramilitary actions too sketchy for straight military.

"Then, last year, our boy drops out of sight. Two months off the radar. Last seen in Yemen."

With a few keystrokes, Sal brought up a short video.

"You've probably seen one of these. On the news lately they're dime a dozen, jihadi propaganda, captured civilians held for ransom."

Sal scooted back, let her step close to the laptop screen.

Three men sat stiffly side by side on a rough bench. Their hands and feet in shackles. All three were dressed in tattered fatigues and had sleep-starved eyes. Behind them hung a black tapestry decorated with white Arabic writing.

Gaunt but defiant, Spider and Naff sat upright, shoulder to shoulder, and beside them, hunched forward and hugging himself as if to hold his guts in place, was a third man Harper recognized but couldn't place.

"Surprise, surprise," Sal said. "These two butt munchers were both hopping down the same bunny trail."

As the film played on, the third guy turned his head to the right, revealing a gaudy crucifix tattooed on his neck. Harper closed her eyes.

Jesus god. It was the man who'd lured Ross McDaniel to Denny's in downtown Miami and sold him a tale of his wife's murder in the African jungle and tricked him into launching a probe into the criminal activities of an international corporation. An act that resulted in Ross's murder and the murder of his son. The same man whose body she'd seen sprawling in a recliner at the Edgewater Apartments.

Following an off-camera command, that third man raised his head and looked directly into the lens and spoke his name: Jackson Sharp.

"The fella my guys disposed of," Sal said. "That apartment, Edgewater, it belonged to his mother. Old lady died a few years back; Sharp kept up with the rent. Probably used it as a safe house, though it didn't turn out so safe. I didn't get a chance to dig up much on him, but when I get a minute, I'll keep trying, see where it leads."

She shut her eyes, tried to fit the pieces together. These three knew each other, worked together. Soldiers of fortune. Hired guns.

Sal shut the laptop and swiveled around to face her.

"Let me ask something, sweetheart. It's just the two of us, nobody listening in. I been giving you all these goodies you wouldn't know if it weren't for me. So in fairness, it's time to reciprocate."

"How?"

"Give me something."

"Like what?"

Sal looked around the room, ran a stalling finger across his lips. "Now don't get pissed," he said, his eyes coming back to hers. "But what I want to know, how's a smart girl like you get mixed up with a half-assed outfit like the CIA?"

She stepped away from the desk, took a seat in a leather chair. Her legs failing.

Sal dragged a chair over and sat knee to knee with her. "You're mad. You're upset. I blew your cover. Hey, what can I say, I'm a snoop. I got an incurable itch to learn about the people in my life."

"I was never in the CIA."

"Okay, sure, you want to split hairs, then it's the DCS, Defense Clandestine Service, arm of the Defense Intelligence Agency, answers to the president, secretary of defense, senior policy makers. Other words, asshole buddies with the CIA. But okay, the difference is important to you, let's call it DCS.

"So how's that happen, a girl like you dabbling in espionage, a special operation, whacking that bag of pickled dicks, Jamal Fakhri? I pronounce his name right?"

She nodded.

"So how's that happen?"

She said nothing, not believing this.

"You thought it was going to stay secret? Well, yeah, far as I'm concerned it stays that way. I don't plan on telling anybody. I'm just curious. Indulge me. How's it happen?"

"How did you find out about this?"

"It's all out there if you know where to look. I searched your name, raided your e-mail, just trying to get a feel for this granddaughter I didn't know. Then one thing led to another, before I know it, I'm seeing traffic between you and some jamoke inside the government. Classified stuff I can't penetrate.

"So I go next door again, ask for help. Kong never asks why, bless his soul. Once I'm inside the servers at the DOD, I track down some back-and-forth between you and some person, sounds like he's your handler. Had to read between the lines, guess a little. The two of you calling something 'the main event.' All very cryptic, but I saw it was going down in Italy in October, then you and Deena, there you are, the two of you shooting pictures in Rome in October, turns out to be the same time this Jamal character was knocked off. So, yeah, I had my suspicions, but I didn't know for sure, not till just now, your reaction.

"I'm sorry I broke into your e-mail, but honey, your protection's for shit."

Harper sat motionless in the chair, her breath fast and shallow, staring at this man who'd dredged up her inviolable secret.

"I was recruited," she said.

"I figured. 'Cause of the photography business, the people you and Deena hung out with. You can walk into rooms normal spooks can't. Hear things, see things."

She nodded.

"Hey, don't get offended, I'm on your side. What I read, this Jamal character, guy was worse than Ted Bundy and Charlie Manson rolled up together."

"Much worse."

"But the DCS people, they had to convince you, right? Take a chance, risk your life? So how's that happen? They have something on you, something they held over your head, turned you into Mata Hari."

"No."

"So why'd you agree?"

"I wonder the same thing."

"This was before you got together with Ross?"

"A couple of years, yes."

"So you're single, your mom is the international celebrity, you're living in her shadow since forever. Maybe you were looking to strike out in a new direction, find something important, give your life some pop? These guys come along at the right time. That how it was?"

"Maybe a part of it."

"They probably showed you pictures, piles of bodies. That's how they work. Babies starving, flies on their eyes, like that. All the people Jamal wasted. They said you could make a difference."

She looked away.

"They give you training? That place, the Farm, or whatever it is."

"Six weeks."

"And what, they trained you for this one mission, or were you planning to do this kind of work full time?"

She hesitated, looking off toward the rising light in the far window. It was the dark secret she'd harbored for years. But Sal already knew most of it, and there was something in his eyes, an empathy, a gentleness that melted her resistance, so in a breathless rush, she unburdened herself.

TWENTY-SIX

Early March, Zurich, Switzerland

In his twenties, Jamal Fakhri was a darling of the tabloid press. A wealthy playboy, educated in London and fully Westernized, he dated models and film stars and royalty and frequented swanky nightclubs in Monte Carlo and Paris. That's when Deena met him and snapped the photograph that would make the cover of *Time*.

"The Next Wave of Arab Leaders."

When his father died, Jamal grudgingly returned home, assumed the throne, and tried some halfhearted democratic reforms, but after a serious drought caused food shortages, and the shortages set off street protests that became riots, Jamal lost patience and, under the sway of his generals, began a series of ruthless crackdowns. In the next three decades of his reign, he became a merciless tyrant at home and a patron of jihadist groups abroad. Tel Aviv in his sights. Shopping for nuclear materials stolen from poorly secured Russian stockpiles.

The intel community viewed Jamal's son as his nation's savior. A temperate young man with democratic ideals and a strong following in the military. If the father could be removed, there was every hope Jamal Junior would step up and lead the country out of darkness.

"So let's assassinate the dad," Sal said.

"Except nobody had access. Jamal was never seen in public."

"Until Deena lured him out."

"He was a vain man," she said. "Deena wanted him for *The Last Bloom*. She wanted to have another look at him, try to capture the essence of a despot who'd murdered thousands of his own people."

"My daughter, the artist," Sal said with a wistful smile.

"Deena got word to Jamal and he agreed to a photo shoot. An informant inside Jamal's regime sent word to the Americans. The beast was leaving its lair. That's when DCS came to me, made their proposition. After Deena and I finished the photo shoot, I was supposed to bat my eyes at him, flirt, lure him away, schedule a rendezvous. Jamal went for it, so there I was in Rome in the same room with the guy."

"Took a lot of nerve, walking in there with a knife up your sleeve."

"The knife was for protection, that's all. I was there strictly as bait. Get Jamal alone in a hotel room, lead him on, maybe get him undressed, vulnerable, then a two-man team enters a front window, takes him down."

Sal made a dubious grunt. "Doesn't sound like much of a plan."

She halted, shut her eyes.

On that sunny day the Rome hotel room had been harshly bright. That's how she remembered it whenever the scene replayed unbidden. As it replayed now. A stunning, aching glare filling the room.

Jamal knocked on the door two hours early, wrecking the timetable. In that small hotel room, there was no way for Harper to notify the ops team. Jamal's goons were stationed down in the street, others in the hall beyond the door.

As instructed, she'd tucked the knife beneath a bed pillow. Though she trusted her hand-to-hand skills, she had to admit that having the razor-sharp knife was calming.

Jamal came in, they brushed cheeks, then he wandered the room silently, checked the closets, the bathroom, even looked under the bed.

He told her he'd arrived early because his desire for her was so great he could not wait another minute, then added with a rogue's smile, "And for a man in my position punctuality can be fatal."

Sweat began to trickle down Harper's ribs. The clock on the bedside table seemed frozen. Jamal caught her glancing in its direction.

"You have other obligations?" he asked.

"Of course not. I'm all yours, as long as you'll have me."

Two hours to string him along. No way she could manage that except to take him into her bed, make it last. An intolerable thought.

So she talked, told him how well the photos had come out, how excited Deena was, how handsome he looked, far more striking than his younger self. Trying to keep the tightness from her voice.

She asked him to sit down, relax, but he refused.

Jamal was silent, listening, showing no interest in her rambling. He took off his coat, unslung his shoulder holster, hung the rig on a chair near the bed. He opened the wine he'd brought, poured two glasses as she continued her nervous chatter. She sipped her wine. He tasted his. It was three in the afternoon. The sun blazed bright. Its enormous orb seemed to be poised just beyond the hotel window.

She was dizzy, on the verge of panic. Her weeks of training seemed to have drained from her mind. This wasn't one of the contingencies they'd prepped her for.

Jamal finished his wine, set the glass aside, and came to her, drew her up from her chair, took the goblet from her hand, flung it against a wall.

He clenched her in his arms, fastened a hand over her mouth.

"No more talk," he said. "You want me. I want you. It is simple between us."

He steered her to the bed with the arrogance of ownership.

At the bedside, she broke away, said she needed a bit more wine, keeping a purr in her voice, saying she was nervous. She apologized but said she needed more warming up.

He stepped back from her, peered into her face for a few seconds, a few seconds more, boring into her mask, until an ugly recognition seeped into his eyes. His shoulders stiffened.

She should have seen it coming but didn't.

With a quick uppercut, he clipped her chin, and the room spun. He shoved her onto the bedspread, went to the chair, and drew his Glock.

Came back to the bed, pressed the pistol to her throat.

"What have you done?" he asked her. "What trap have you set?"

The pistol dug deeper against her throat, cutting her air.

She endured it as long as she could, her mind clarifying: he was making her choice unavoidable.

She gathered herself, sketched the move mentally, then, with the blade of her right hand, chopped his wrist, broke the pistol loose. Grabbed it from the bedspread, flung it away, and twisted onto her side. Then, in one fluid motion, she drew the knife from beneath the pillow and came up slashing.

Gashed his cheek, redrew his mouth, and while he staggered backward, bloody and growling, opening his mouth to roar for his guards, she sunk the blade into his chest. Jamming it to the hilt. With her left arm she held him upright, not looking at his face but feeling his body sway, then loosen in her arms, and loosen some more until he'd sunk away.

Sal was staring at Harper with growing concern, waiting mutely for her to tell the story she could not speak aloud.

She said, "So I did it myself. I took him out."

He nodded, approving. "Because you had no choice."

Harper had told herself that a hundred times, for all the good it did.

"Does Nick know any of this?"

"Not unless you told him, Sal."

"So what's the problem? You did it, you escaped, it's over."

"When I did it, I felt nothing. It was just mechanical, a movie starring someone else. That's what worries me."

Sal watched her for several moments, then sighed.

"That's how it works," he said. "The body makes some chemical, it's like moral Novocain. Makes you temporarily numb so you can do what's necessary to save your ass. What you need to do now is get over it. The world's a better place without that shit-breath."

"Not really," she said. "Jamal's son took over, he's not the savior everyone hoped for."

"Well, listen, I for one got no problem, what you did. My view, best justice is personal justice."

"It wasn't personal."

"Sure it was. You were defending your family."

"What?"

He stood up, made a slow circle around the room as if to walk off some memory. He came back to his chair and sat again across from her.

"Look, sweetheart, I'm sure you're as patriotic as the next person, ready to answer the call of your country, but I'm guessing in some roundabout way you took this on because of Nick. How his family was killed. Fakhri and his thugs raiding villages, burning, raping. Sunnis, Shi'a, Alawites, Christians, everybody killing everybody else. People say the Mafia's bad. Mafia's nothing next to those fucking religions.

"So that's what I'm saying. Killing that asshole was your way of defending your family."

Sal had mined her deepest vein. She had no secrets left.

"Do I have that right? It was about Nick. At least a little bit."

A single nod. Yes, by god, he had it right.

"You ever tell your husband about it?"

She said no. The only secret she'd never shared with Ross.

"Nobody knows?"

"Just you."

"Well, it stays here. You and me, our secret."

"It better."

"Don't know why it upsets you. You should be proud. That was one bad cocksucker." He gave her a long, appraising look. "And I'm sorry to say it, sweetheart, but from the looks of what you're into now, these guys, Naff and Spider, you're going to need to get yourself another knife. With a very sharp blade."

Outside the window, the street cleaner was making another pass. The rumble of its brushes no longer calling up the image of tanks.

"Can you hack Albion's computer network, see what they're hiding?"

Sal said he had tried. Secure beyond anything he could breach. Kong was off at a gamer conference, so the forecast wasn't good.

"You broke into the Defense Department but not Albion?"

"Kong did that, not me. And anyway, private corporations buy the best encryption. They build walls, put more walls behind those, walls and walls and walls. All it takes is money, you get all the walls you want. If I had a month, maybe Kong and I could work our way inside."

"We don't have a month."

"So what do we do?"

"Go old-school," Harper said. "Walk in the front door."

"A break-in?"

"Nick says you have connections everywhere. All over the world."

Sal shook his head, a sad smile forming on his lips. "Nick exaggerates," he said. "But sure, I know a few people who know a few people. What exactly do you need?"

She told him what she'd been thinking about, and after she was finished, he looked at her in silence for several moments. His eyes the sharp blue of the early-morning Zurich sky.

"You'd do that, all by yourself?"

"Nick will help."

"Sounds dicey," he said.

"Not if we do it right."

Sal rose from the laptop, came over to her, laid a hand on the meat of her shoulder, and took a solid grip.

"Okay," he said. "I'll get on the horn, see what I can arrange."

PART THREE

TWENTY-SEVEN

Mid-March, Zurich, Switzerland

For two days Harper and Nick rehearsed the scheme while Sal worked the phone, arranging details. She and Nick studied the floor plans Sal had managed to secure. Traced their route through the maze of offices, conference rooms, and administrative suites until both had the layout memorized. They targeted the two offices most likely to produce the results they were after. Gamed out every contingency they could imagine, picked apart the plan, found soft spots, worst-case scenarios, and came up with plausible work-arounds.

Nick unboxed the Apple computer they'd overnighted to the hotel room. Same model used throughout the Albion offices. Sal laid out the tools, a plastic spudger to jimmy loose the frame, a pair of suction cups to pull away the LCD screen, a T6 torque screwdriver. He demonstrated the method for removing the RAM access door, opening the magnetized glass to reveal the screws that held the bezel in place. He guided her, layer by layer, to the hard drive, showed her how to free it from the nest of cables and wires.

According to Sal, it should take no more than five minutes, but the first few times she tried, Harper couldn't break ten. Slowly, by repetition, she shaved away the minutes, got it down to four.

The plan was not without risk, but if they didn't draw attention, there was a chance they might unearth enough evidence of Albion's African crimes to expose the architect of the massacre at Soko. That person, Harper was convinced, would be the brains behind the murders of Ross and Leo.

Across the room, Sal said, "I don't know if this is the right time, but I found something you need to see."

Nick had just left for the neighborhood deli to pick up sandwiches.

Sal got up from the desk, his laptop frozen on an image that at first she didn't recognize. She sat in Sal's seat and stared at the screen. It came to her in slow and painful stages. The doorway leading to the kitchen. The gas range with a pot on a burner. The clock on the far wall. All of it from their cottage on Margaret Street in Coconut Grove. The house where she'd fallen in love, the house where Leo was conceived, the house that burned to the ground.

"It's a video," Sal said. "Kong sent it. As a favor to me, he's been working this thing, digging around. I don't know how he found the damn thing. Snatched it out of the cloud somehow. Those cameras spying in your house, what they recorded was sent on the wireless signal. It's there, then gone. No way to access it later unless some idiot decided to save all those hours onto a hard drive, then what they saved got backed up. Kong tracked it down, found the ISP then the IP. That's all I know. He's not big on details, explaining how he does what he does. You want me to leave you alone?"

Steam rose from the pot on the cottage's kitchen stove. The clock showed six. A bird on the bird feeder outside the window. Morning in South Florida, another day dawning at the McDaniel house.

"You can stay," she said.

She pressed the "Start" arrow, and the life she'd been living a few weeks earlier resumed, the life she'd treasured, the life she'd lost forever.

It was her family's last week together, Ross and Leo and Harper, their daily habits in the wood cottage on Margaret Street, every slow hour recorded from three angles. Bathroom, bedroom, living room. Somebody had pieced it together in one continuous stream. Crystal-clear audio, high-definition black and white.

The McDaniels woke, they dressed, ate, talked, performed their household chores. Harper breast-fed Leo. Ross used his cell, set his laptop up on the dining table, and typed. They laughed, Ross brushed her long black hair, something he enjoyed, something Harper found strange and wonderful and quietly sexy. They undressed, they touched each other, they kissed, slid into bed, pulled up the sheets, made love.

They showered, brushed their teeth. The two of them gave Leo a bath. Laughed some more. Leo giggled, Leo wailed, Leo slept at her breast. Harper sat in the wooden rocker Deena had given her as a baby-shower gift, back and forth, back and forth, a look of utter contentment.

With talons clawing her heart, Harper fast-forwarded through the long nights, the dark patches, the house empty. Then one morning, Jackson Sharp appeared in their living room.

Harper paused the video and drew a breath and looked over at Sal. His head was bowed, staring down into his lap.

She unpaused the video.

Leo was in his crib, Harper off somewhere, probably the grocery. Harper turned the volume all the way up and had to replay the three-minute segment several times to be sure of what she heard.

Jackson Sharp stood stiffly just inside the front door, as if preparing to bolt. He asked Ross if he'd made any progress.

"Some," Ross said.

"Well, I dug up a couple of names for you," Sharp said. "The man in charge of Albion's entire security staff. Adrian Naff. And his boss in

Zurich, she's a woman named Bixel, Larissa Bixel. These are the ones you should go after."

"I don't go after people," Ross said. "Apparently you've got the wrong idea about what I do."

Sharp backpedaled, apologized, said he was only trying to help, speed things up. He didn't understand the investigative-journalism game.

"Obviously not," Ross said. "By the way, let me ask you something, Jackson."

Harper leaned close to better see the look on Ross's face. One she didn't recognize. A steely clamp to his jaw, eyes flickering, bulldog tough.

"What's really going on here?"

"What do you mean?" Jackson said. "Like what?"

"Something you aren't telling me. An ulterior motive, the real reason you wanted me to go after this story."

"My wife's murder isn't enough reason?"

"Was the woman in the video actually your wife?"

"Damn right she was." Jackson drew back a step, glanced around the room. A man ready to flee.

"The reason I ask," Ross said, "I can't find any evidence you were married. None at all."

"Okay, maybe not legally, no marriage certificate, all that garbage, but we lived together for years. What's the problem, man?"

Ross said, "There's another thing. You said you quit your job teaching history at Gables High. There's no one named Jackson Sharp on the Dade County teachers' rolls. In fact, your actual work history, what I could find, is very intriguing. A stretch in the army, then a consultant with an international security outfit."

Jackson swallowed, took a breath, face going hard. "Okay, I stretched the truth a little. I was protecting myself."

"A little? Or a lot?"

"This is bullshit. You've been investigating me? For christsakes. Hey, just forget it, smart guy. Just forget the whole goddamn thing. I'm sorry I ever came to you."

Ross said, "I tried to think what possible reason you might have to sic me on this story. Why would you lie to me, why are you still lying? Only thing I can come up with is that you're using me in some kind of con. I'm your stalking horse. I dig around, make phone calls about Albion, I hit a trip wire, and somebody at the home office discovers their secrets are about to go public."

"You're fucking crazy, man. You're a fucking loon."

"I put pressure on Albion, threaten to expose their crimes, so you can wring something out of them. Hush money maybe. Am I close?"

"Fuck you, man. Just fucking drop the whole thing."

"How's it supposed to work? Once they pay you to keep me quiet, then what? You come to me, say it was all a big lie, I'm supposed to stop what I'm doing? Or were you going to find some other way to shut me up when the time came?"

"Drop it, asshole. You better hear what I'm saying. Drop it now. I'm done with you. Step away."

"No, Jackson. I'm not dropping anything. Not by a long shot. I'm just starting to dig."

Jackson stormed off. Ross made notes, made phone calls. She couldn't hear what he said. Harper came home. Ross cheerful, hiding his encounter with Sharp. The man she'd married was not the simple, transparent Ross she thought she knew. How had she missed this? She loved this man, thought she knew him thoroughly. But she'd missed it badly. He'd concealed this part of himself so well she'd had no idea about the battle he was waging, his toughness, his courage. With her photographic subjects, Harper prided herself on seeing past their veneers, but her special skill had failed her with the one person closest to her. The man she loved beyond all others. Would it have mattered? If she'd seen his worry, confronted him, managed to unearth the truth? If they'd discussed the danger, made some kind of defensive plan, would he still be alive?

She went back to the video of her family's last week. Day, night, day, night. Then the morning the three of them packed up an ice chest and towels and headed to the beach. The house empty.

Another day, another long afternoon. Leo sleeping. Harper in the kitchen making a big salad for dinner, broiled salmon on top. Ross came in, touched her cheek, she turned and stepped into an embrace. They kissed. They checked on Leo. Ross undressed her. He feathered his hands across her bare breasts. Standing beside the bed, she shivered. She unbuckled his belt. She tugged his jeans down, she stripped off his T-shirt. He was erect. She touched him there, ran her hands along its length, took a grip, tugged him like that toward the bed, a funny moment, suppressing their laughter. Naked together on top of the bed-spread, kissing, exploring with both hands.

"Know why I love you?" Ross said, hands still moving.

"My mind?" Harper said. "Or is it my long legs?"

"Both of those," he said. "And everything in between."

"That's it? That's all you've got?"

"And what a perfect mother you are to Leo. Especially that."

"Am I?" she said.

"Oh yes. Oh yes."

His hands on her, his hands on fire.

Spider had viewed all this. Saved it to his hard drive so he could view it again.

Gut twisting, Harper couldn't watch the lovemaking. She looked out at the Zurich snow beyond the hotel window, coming down harder now, bright in the sunshine, waves of snow.

When she looked back at the laptop, Ross was in the bathroom shaving, a towel around his waist, Leo strapped to his chest facing forward. Their last night. Harper dressing in her black cocktail dress. Heading out to the charity event.

She felt her pulse ticking faster.

She watched herself snapping the three photos through the crack of the bathroom door. Ross nicking himself. Their final conversation. Ross mentioning chocolate. Chocolate, and the strange look on his face when he said it. Worry mixed with resolve. Harper kissed him and kissed Leo on his nose and left.

Only a minute later, Ross went to the front door, answering a knock.

Pistol drawn, Spider Combs pushed inside, forcing Ross backward.

"Take whatever you want." Ross clutched Leo to his chest. "There's not much."

"I'm not a goddamn thief," Spider said.

Harper froze the video. She didn't need to see more. Not now. Maybe never. She didn't need to hear his final words, didn't need to see Leo's face, didn't need to see Ross trying to shield his son, their last desperate seconds. Didn't need to watch anymore. Maybe she'd watch it all someday when she was stronger, less emotionally vulnerable.

If such a day ever came.

TWENTY-EIGHT

Mid-March, Zurich, Switzerland

At 4:30 p.m. on Friday, the armored van was delivered to a side street two blocks from the hotel. Wordlessly, a man in a blue banker's suit stepped down from the cab and handed the ignition keys to Nick.

She and Nick had two hours to familiarize themselves with the equipment and for Nick to practice handling the rig in the downtown Zurich traffic. It was a Mercedes diesel, more van than truck, bullet-proof windshield, slits for side windows, and solid panels in the rear. Sleeker than a Brink's truck but just as armored.

They climbed aboard and, exactly as they'd been told, found the regular driver and his partner trussed up in the back of the van. Gagged and blindfolded, wrapped in duct tape, two husky men. According to Sal, their names were Hans and Roger. The Albion building was the first stop on their regular route for Kintana Destruction Services, a mobile document-shredding company that serviced eight banks and thirty other corporate offices in the Zurich area.

The uniforms Harper and Nick wore came from more of Sal's magic. Yesterday he'd summoned a tailor to the Widder to take their measurements. Two hours later, the yellow jumpsuits arrived, perfect fits, each with shiny snaps, buttoned pockets, and elegantly embroidered logos, identical to the ones Hans and Roger were wearing.

Their photo ID badges were also exact duplicates. Today Harper would be Sarah Ann Pearson and Nick was Herbert Osle.

Paradeplatz square on Bahnhofstrasse was the headquarters of UBS banks and Credit Suisse and Albion International. In medieval times, it had been a pig market a half mile beyond the protection of the city walls. A few centuries later, the Paradeplatz was one of the most expensive pieces of real estate in Switzerland, and one of the main crossroads for Zurich's tram network.

At six thirty, with the streetlights flickering on, Nick eased the big van across four sets of tram tracks into the loading zone just outside Albion's front doors. It was an hour past quitting time, the thoroughfare no longer thronged with workers heading home or to neighborhood bars. Only a few stragglers hurrying past. Just inside Albion's double front doors, a security guard spotted them and stepped onto the sidewalk.

Nick reached over and gripped Harper's hand. She turned to him, saw the strain in his eyes.

"You're not nervous?"

"No," she said. "I'm not."

"Well, that makes one of us." He tried to smile.

"In and out. Keep it simple."

"Now that you know Spider was the triggerman, shouldn't we be going after him? Is this even necessary?"

She watched the security guard standing stiffly outside the door. A few wispy flakes of snow had begun to swirl down from the gray sky.

"We'll deal with Spider later," she said. "I need to know who hired him, who pulled his strings, and who was responsible for the things that happened in Africa."

At the rear of the truck Nick used the van's lift gate to lower the sixty-gallon stainless steel bin. From the doorway of the Albion building, the security guard watched Nick attentively as he maneuvered the container onto the sidewalk and swiveled it around to push it before him.

Nick handled the bulky unit exactly as instructed by Angela Giger, former employee of another Zurich mobile document shredder. One more contribution from Sal, Angela had appeared at their hotel door two nights ago. A cousin twice removed of one of Sal's former partners or something similarly convoluted. The promise of two thousand euros brought her to the Widder, and after accepting the cash and a vodka martini, she mapped out the choreography of a typical document-removal session in a Zurich office building, never asking why they wanted to know such a thing.

Document shredders were scrupulously methodical. For a seven-floor building like Albion, they followed a thirty-minute timetable. Start at the top floor, work back to the lobby. Just barely time enough for Nick to empty the blue bins stationed at the end of each hallway while Harper attacked the two computers they'd targeted.

Security guards patrolled the empty corridors at ten-minute intervals. To stay ahead of the patrols, she and Nick had to time their work perfectly. In and out in thirty minutes, four minutes per floor.

As Nick approached the door, the security guard blocked their way, FREDERICK emblazoned above his jacket pocket. A fringe of silver hair rimmed his bald pate. He had the flushed and bloated face of an inveterate schnapps drinker. He wanted to know where Hans and Roger were.

"Off today," Harper told him. "Roger, on holiday. *En vacances.* Hans, *en congé de maladie.*" Out sick.

After a moment's hesitation, Frederick leaned in and examined both their IDs, gave them a challenging look, then grumbled something and slipped back to his guard post inside the front door.

Nick rolled the document drum across the lobby and onto an elevator with Harper following close. Behind the security desk were three younger guards engaged in a spirited conversation. As the elevator doors slid shut, she saw Frederick pick up a desk phone and punch in a number, his focus squarely on her face.

"Up, up, and away," Nick said.

They rode to the top floor, where the executive suites of the president and four VPs were located. Lester Albion's computer was her first goal. Before them, the carpeted hallway was silent, the after-hours lights dimmed. A two-man security team rounded the far corner and passed them, nodding as they went by.

Located at the far end of the hallway, a blue plastic bin held the confidential papers designated for shredding. As they'd drilled, Nick headed that way, and Harper waited till the guards boarded the elevators and the doors shut, then turned back to the presidential suite, her heart accelerating.

The outer door of the office was unlocked, the heavy double doors to Albion's office stood ajar. She pushed them open, entered, unzipped her fanny pack, arrayed her tools on Albion's blotter. A glint of light caught her eye, and she looked up to see Ben Westfield smiling from the far wall. An Albion advertisement from so far back in time that Westfield's face was baby smooth, yet his eyes already blazed with the manly vitality that would define his career.

Harper got to work. She tipped the iMac backward and settled it onto the desk and began to pry loose the glass. Working smoothly, her practice sessions with Sal still fresh. Minutes later she was snipping the last of the connecting wires from the hard drive when the voice called out.

"*Arrêtez!*"

Harper's hands froze. She looked up.

Frederick stood in the doorway. He'd drawn his sidearm, but it was still aimed at the floor. Behind him stood a stocky guard with red hair and yellow-tinted glasses. His handgun was still holstered.

"Who are you, what are you doing?"

This was one of the worst-case scenarios she and Nick had rehearsed, but for several seconds the words they'd scripted snagged in her throat.

"I was instructed that Mr. Albion wanted to recycle his hard drive. It's part of our regular service."

"No, this is untrue. I telephoned Kintana and spoke with Julia, the dispatcher. Roger and Hans indeed reported for work this afternoon. You are a fraud. You will raise your hands and come with me. Police will be called."

A sheen of sweat had appeared on Frederick's forehead. Dread quivered in his eyes as if he'd never drawn his weapon or confronted an intruder. A safe, uneventful career thrown into turmoil.

"Come around from behind the desk. Keep your hands aloft."

Harper set down the pliers and stripped off the surgical gloves and let them drop on the desk.

"There's been a mistake," she said. "Julia misinformed you. Herbert and I are the official replacements. You must call the Kintana offices again and this time ask to speak to my supervisor, Margaret Bauer." Buying time with a lie.

He stiffened and a flash of worry crossed his eyes. The possibility that Frederick might have mistakenly accosted two honorable workers and would now suffer a public humiliation deepened the flush in his face.

Behind the two guards, Nick edged through the office door. In his right hand he held a black leather sap—a last minute gift from Sal. *Take it, take it, I've seen how these things go wrong, crazy shit flying in from nowhere.*

Nick raised the blackjack above his shoulder, eased forward.

She managed to keep her face empty as Nick took another step, cocked his arm, drew a breath, and nailed the chunky guard on the edge of his skull. The man gasped, plowed into Frederick's backside.

Frederick lost his balance, heaved toward her, and his shooting hand came up and his pistol discharged, an earsplitting blast, the slug tearing a ragged groove across the desktop, spraying splinters and debris into Harper's face, missing her arm by inches.

Nick stepped in and clubbed Frederick, hit him again and again until the big man's legs buckled and he wilted to the floor. Nick stooped over the man and continued to pound with the blackjack, sickening thuds.

She shouted for him to stop, but he struck the man twice more before she rounded the desk and seized his arm and shook loose the sap.

Nick was panting, his face pale. He looked at her with bewildered eyes.

She kneeled, rolled Frederick onto his back, and felt his throat for a pulse. Faint and slow but still ticking.

Nick hobbled across the room and dropped into a leather chair.

"Is he . . . is he okay?"

"Barely."

The other guard stirred.

She dug through the fanny pack, found the flex-cuffs Sal had insisted they take along. She zipped them tight around the guard's wrists and ankles. Nick was slumped in the chair.

"I thought he shot you," Nick said. "I thought you were hurt. Isn't that what you wanted, to put him away? Isn't that how we do things now?"

She stared into his eyes, trying to see beyond the blur of rage.

"Need to move," she said. "That shot, somebody had to hear it."

She cuffed Frederick. Felt again for his pulse. Still faint and slow.

Rolling the collection bin, Nick followed her to the elevator. Inside the car, he settled against the opposite wall, keeping his distance.

"I fucked up," he said, eyes down. "I'm sorry."

"We're okay. We skip the other floors, I grab Naff's hard drive and go."

"We could leave now," he said. "Just walk out. Why risk it?"

Fourth floor, third.

"You go to the van. Roll the bin back, don't talk to the guards, don't even look their way, just put the bin inside like everything's normal, then warm up the engine. Five minutes. If I'm even a second longer, you leave."

"We can't separate. I won't do that."

She held out Albion's hard drive. Nick shook his head.

"Take it, Nick. Go back to the truck and wait. Five minutes, no more than that. Promise me."

The elevator door opened in the lobby, and Nick took the hard drive from her, slipped it into a jacket pocket, and rolled the stainless steel bin across the lobby.

One of the guards rose and called out for him to halt.

"Go on, Nick," Harper said. "I'll take care of this."

Nick continued to the door and pushed through it onto the sidewalk. It was dark outside, snow coming thicker. A layer of it building on the street.

The guard, a stocky man with a bushy mustache, was hurrying after Nick, but she intercepted him at the door.

"We straightened everything out with Frederick. He spoke to the wrong party at Kintana and received bad information."

"Where is he? He doesn't answer his radio."

"He and his partner found a tray of leftover tarts and are having a snack."

"What floor?"

"Five," Harper said.

The young guard gave her a long, suspicious once-over.

"You wait here," he said. "Don't go anywhere."

"I have a schedule, other businesses to attend to."

"You will do as I say and wait exactly here."

He pointed at a spot on the floor and marched to the elevator, and Harper stood in place until the doors closed, then she trotted down the corridor to Adrian Naff's office in the security suite.

Naff's name was etched on the double glass doors. Lights off, door unlocked. Oddly trusting, though she supposed there was little of value to pilfer in a food conglomerate's headquarters. Computer hardware, office supplies, but not much else to entice a thief.

As she'd done in Albion's office, she arrayed the tools, tipped the computer onto its back, and set to work. Moving fast but with a measured focus. When she lifted off the monitor glass and was looking for a place to rest it, she saw the book.

It lay facedown on the left side of Naff's desk. Deena's piercing eyes were staring up at her, and Harper's own face in a smaller frame below Deena's. It was the back jacket of *The Last Bloom*.

She swung around, half expecting to see Naff standing in the doorway. An icy wave of prickles passed across her shoulders. No one was there. The corridor quiet, only the hush of the big building swelling around her.

So Albion's chief of security had Harper in his sights, already making a study of her. Just as she was making a study of him.

She drew a long breath and got back to work, digging through the strata of Naff's computer until she'd reached the hard drive. Checked her watch. It had taken only four minutes. Hustle out the front doors and still make her deadline with Nick. She snipped the last of the wires, disconnected the two remaining cables, and drew out the unit, the size of a deck of cards.

She stripped off the gloves, tucked away her tools, slipped the hard drive in her jumpsuit pocket, and headed back to the lobby. As she rounded the last corner, she halted and drew back.

The guard who'd questioned her earlier was talking to a man in jeans and a black turtleneck. Topcoat over his arm. His profile was all she could see, but it was all she needed.

She'd studied a dozen different versions of him in the passport photos Sal had uncovered. Dark eyes, strong chin, wearing his jet-black hair swept back. Resembling the version of Adrian Naff she'd seen in the hostage video. A bit frayed at the edges, but tough, a cool-headed pro.

The guard's gaze strayed from his boss's face, and before Harper could draw back, he'd caught sight of her and was motioning in her direction, pointing, then beckoning her to join them.

She came forward, Naff's hard drive suddenly heavy in her pocket. The men watched her silently.

When Naff spoke to her, it was in English.

"Austin tells me you and your partner are subbing for Hans and Roger today."

"Correct."

Adrian Naff regarded her with frank, unguarded curiosity. In that instant, she caught a whiff of melancholy in his eyes, a dreamy faraway look that revealed more about his character than he probably intended. A man whose work did not have his full attention.

He leaned toward her and read the ID pinned to her uniform. She cut a look to her watch. Six minutes had passed. If Nick had followed her directions, he was well away.

"As you see, my name is Sarah Ann Pearson," Harper said.

Naff didn't seem to recognize her. Maybe the uniform was throwing him off or her long hair tucked under her cap. That book-jacket photograph on his office desk was a couple of years out-of-date, a soft-focus flattering shot in full makeup, not at all how she looked tonight, her face grown gaunt and pale.

"You're American?"

"My father, yes, but I am Swiss."

"I believe I've seen you before."

"It's possible, I suppose, but I would have remembered you."

"Oh, really? And why is that? Am I so memorable?"

The guard was looking back and forth between them with uncertainty. Was this flirtatious or something else entirely? Harper wasn't sure herself.

"Your smile," Harper said. "It's rather unique."

"How so?"

"As if you practice before a mirror to fine-tune its authenticity."

By slow degrees, the grin vanished, and as his eyes cooled, she thought she saw in them a first spark of recognition.

"And you found everything in good order tonight?" Naff asked as if buying another moment while he rummaged his memory.

"Everything was fine, sir. Now I must be going. Many more documents to dispose of this evening."

His eyes roamed her face with a sharpening focus, on the threshold of calling her out.

"Good evening, gentlemen."

She made it to the door. Reflected in the glass, she saw Naff marching in her direction. She pushed through and stepped onto the snowy sidewalk.

The van was gone. Nick had obeyed. She glanced up Bahnhofstrasse, then back the other direction. No sign of him. At a fast clip she headed south, back toward the Widder.

Behind her, Naff called out for her to stop.

She kept walking, the hard drive tapping against her thigh.

Two more steps, he was beside her, his shoulder brushing hers.

"That took a lot of nerve, McDaniel."

"I have nerve to spare." She kept her stride steady.

"What were you looking for, if I might ask?"

"Just getting the lay of the land."

"I'd like to hear how you pulled it off, those uniforms, the rest of it. Let's go back to my office and we'll chat."

He took a light grip on her upper arm, but she shrugged it off.

"I have a previous engagement. Sorry."

"You're a cool customer, aren't you?"

"Touch me again and find out."

A half block ahead, the Kintana van rounded the corner and came coasting down the snowy street toward her.

"You know, I have orders to remove you from the playing field. Permanently."

"Whose orders?"

"You have any idea why someone would want you killed? Because I don't follow orders I don't understand."

"Can't help you," she said.

"Does questioning orders make me a bad soldier?"

"In this case, I believe you're making the right call."

"Well, you would think that, wouldn't you?"

"My ride's here. I'll be in touch."

"I'm counting on it."

The van pulled up, door slid open, and she climbed aboard.

She slammed it behind her, and as the van pulled away, she watched Adrian Naff lope alongside, calling out to Harper to stop, get out, she was in danger.

The van accelerated down Bahnhofstrasse, leaving Naff behind.

She looked over at Nick. But he wasn't at the wheel. Nick was lying on his back on the rear floor, duct tape wrapping his wrists and ankles, more duct tape over his mouth. A gash on his forehead, his eyes wild. He was thrashing against his restraints. Hans and Roger were gone.

At the wheel, Spider smiled at her.

"I always had a special fondness," he said, "for a woman in uniform."

TWENTY-NINE

Mid-March, Zurich, Switzerland

Larissa Bixel marched into Lester Albion's office red-faced and winded as though she might have sprinted from the elevator. Helmut Mullen followed in her wake, his hair unruffled, his tight smile in place.

"Well, we're all here," Adrian said and turned to Albion.

It was one in the morning. Half an hour earlier, when Adrian phoned Bixel to tell her she was wanted in Lester Albion's office immediately, all she'd said was "This better be good."

"Oh, it is," he said. "And bring your boy Helmut."

Albion didn't look up at the new arrivals. He was studying the screen on the laptop Adrian had set up. Scrolling through dozens of his recent e-mails and files, everything Adrian rescued from the backup system, checking to see if any corporate secrets might've been stolen.

"I believe we're okay," Albion said to Naff. "I don't think we've been severely compromised. A few financial specifics about the Marburg transaction I'd rather not be made public, but they'd only be minor embarrassments. Other than that, I see no problem with what was taken. Certainly no top secrets, not that we have any of those."

"What's going on?" Bixel said.

"Shall I fill them in?" Adrian asked.

Albion waggled his hand, get on with it. He had on a rumpled white shirt and beltless trousers, and his eyes were still puffy from sleep. With a finger, he traced the scar that ran the length of his desktop. On his face was a wistful, distracted look, as if he were bidding farewell to a dear friend.

Behind Bixel, Albion's young daughter peeked through the open door and asked if it was time to go yet.

"Not yet, sugar, just a few minutes." When she'd gone back to the waiting room, Albion apologized for the interruption. His wife was away, and he couldn't leave the child unattended.

Adrian swiveled the laptop around and brought up the videos. He'd spliced the three security clips together to show Albion the extent of the incursion. He tilted back the screen, and Bixel and Helmut stepped close to the edge of the desk to watch.

A woman and a man about her age, both dressed in the uniforms of Kintana Destruction Services, entered the building, passing a few feet in front of the security desk, then stepped into the lobby elevator.

Cut to Albion's office, where the same woman entered and set about methodically excavating Albion's computer, eventually extracting his hard drive. A few moments later, Frederick Perse, a veteran Albion guard, appeared in the doorway, his gun drawn, and confronted the woman. Frederick was backed up by a younger guard Adrian didn't know well. Enter the woman's male accomplice, sneaking in behind them, raising a sap and striking the younger guard. Bumped from behind, Frederick fired his weapon, the slug grazing the desktop inches from the woman's arm.

"Stop the video," Bixel said.

Adrian pressed "Pause."

"Who is this person and what is she after?"

"Her name is Harper McDaniel. I think you know why she's here."

Bixel stiffened and shot Helmut a withering glare.

"You're telling me you know this woman, Adrian?" Albion said. "This intruder."

"Yes, sir, she came to my attention earlier in the week."

"And you know what she was searching for?"

Naff said, "Ms. McDaniel wants to know the same thing I'd like to know, the same thing you might want to know as well."

"And what is that?"

"Maybe Ms. Bixel can tell us, or Helmut."

"No, Adrian. Whatever it is, I want to hear it from you."

"All right," he said. "I believe Ms. McDaniel is searching for details about a series of events in Africa that Bixel and Helmut are trying very hard to conceal."

Bonnie opened the office door again and said, "Okay, time to go, Daddy. My teachers at school won't like that my father wakes me up in the middle of the night, drags me to his office, has me sit in the waiting room with nothing but magazines that are all words and no pictures."

"One second, honey. I promise. A couple of things to finish."

Bonnie stabbed a finger at the floor in front of her.

"There's blood on your rug, you know that, Daddy? Somebody was bleeding in your office. Was it you?"

"No, it wasn't me, sweetie. Now please, go sit down."

"Was Mommy here? Did she scratch you again?"

"Bonnie, please."

"Mommy's getting a divorce," Bonnie announced. "She can't take Daddy anymore. She moved out."

"Bonnie, stop it. Please."

"I'm tired," she said. "I'm supposed to be in bed."

"Helmut," Bixel said. "Entertain Bonnie for a minute, will you?"

Helmut shot the child a cold look, and Bonnie said, "You're that scary man. You hurt people and enjoy it. Daddy's afraid of you. He doesn't know what your job is, but you're always around. Isn't that what you said, Daddy? This is the man, right? The one you call Helmet Head."

Albion rose from his chair. "All right," he said with a deep sigh. "Enough of this. The three of you stay and look at the rest of the video if you like. Sort this out, get your story straight. But I don't want to hear any more about Africa. At this late date I don't care what happened over there. All I want is for the three of you to fix whatever is wrong, smooth over anything you have to so we can complete the Marburg transaction. If any one of you screws this up and that deal is jeopardized, you're finished at Albion. Now do what you have to do. Whatever it takes. But I'll hear no more about any of this. Is that clear?"

———

"Why the long face?" Spider said. "Aren't you glad to see me? Old friends in a foreign land?"

Spider steered with his knee while he tugged open his parka so she could see the pistol he was holding in his lap. Aimed her way.

She looked back at Nick lying perfectly still, his eyes on hers, questioning. What now?

"All day I've been lusting for a big, greasy cheeseburger. You hungry? I bet you are, the big night you're having."

Spider turned off Bahnhofstrasse and crossed the Limmat River on the Quaibrücke bridge, then looped left, heading into Altstadt. The Old Town.

"Where are you taking us?" Keeping her voice quiet, almost a whisper, the way she might have spoken to Ross while Leo was sleeping nearby.

"My hotel," he said. "It's not the Widder, but it works for me."

"How did you find me?"

"Karma," he said. "Wasn't even looking, but there you were."

"Karma."

"I was watching for somebody else, a guy who did me wrong, and day after day I'm waiting for him to show, who walks by but my favorite lady. So I pay my check, follow till you get back to your hotel.

"I find a café nearby, wait to see what you're up to, your comings and goings. For a few days it was nothing unusual, then, boom, I'm there this afternoon across the plaza, drinking espresso, I see this tall woman come out of the Widder, looks a little like you only she's wearing a uniform, and I'm about to go back to my espresso, but no, it wasn't just any woman in any uniform. It was you. So I grab a taxi, follow along, see what kind of trickery you're up to, then you and the brother go into the Albion building, leave the van outside. I wait till Nicky boy comes back out and take him down. I need some duct tape to keep him quiet, so I let the guys you abducted loose, and that's it. The whole story. Like I said, karma."

"Who were you waiting for when I walked by?"

"Look, here's my hotel now. You'll like it, it's kitschy, a bit of Americana in the heart of Zurich. Good burgers too. We can order room service when we get hungry. And if I know us, we will get hungry."

He looked over with a sleepy smile. Ran a hand through his thick, red hair, combing it back.

"You think you're going to rape me?"

He pulled the van into a narrow side street two blocks off Limmatquai and killed the engine. He sat staring out the windshield for several moments chewing his gum.

"Rape? Oh, hell, no, I'm hoping we can get to know each other better. We got started off on a bad foot." Still looking straight ahead he said, "Come up to my room, we talk, get some room service, have a bite to eat. Just talk, see what we got in common. I bet it's more than you think."

Harper's mouth was dry, lungs tight.

"Look, I know it's weird, me showing up like this," he said. "But I'm not nuts. I was just hoping we could give it a try. A real conversation, share our backgrounds, get to know each other better. I mean, yeah, I know you a little already, and I like what I see, but I think you've got a negative first impression of me. I'd like a do-over."

"I'm not going anywhere with you. Not to your room, not anywhere."

"Okay, yeah, I know, maybe I'm rushing things a little. I get it. So here's a thought. Maybe what we could do, we take a stroll down these cobblestone streets. It's romantic, medieval architecture, all that, we could stop in a club. You're young, you like to dance, right? We get sweaty and loose, a couple of drinks, then back to the hotel, see how you feel. Bet you're in a better mood for talking."

"Who do you work for? Who paid you to kill my husband and child?"

"Huh?"

He took his hand off the wheel and looked at her. Face half-hidden in shadows, but she could see a twist in his mouth. All his sleazy charm gone.

She said, "Don't bother denying it. I saw the video you made."

"What video?"

"The one from the spy cams you hid inside my house. What was that about? What did you need to know? How far the infection had spread? Was that it? Find out if Ross talked to anyone else about what he'd discovered, then you'd have to kill them too. Is that it?"

"I wish I knew what you were referring to. You're scaring me with this crazy talk." But his eyes and voice said otherwise. He had the slippery look of a cornered animal.

"Who shot you in the parking lot of the Aqua? Was it Adrian Naff?"

"Whoa. Where you getting this stuff?"

"You and Naff and Jackson Sharp were buddies, comrades in arms. I saw that video too, the three of you held hostage by some jihadi group, you were pleading for ransom."

"I don't remember pleading. But, boy oh boy, you've been a busy girl."

"The massacre in Soko, you were part of that, weren't you?"

He looked at her blankly. "Now you totally lost me. Never heard of any Soko."

"Listen to me, Spider. You're done, you're finished. Your only hope is to let us go and try to make a run for it."

He chuckled and waved away her bravado like a bad smell.

"Look, you think I killed your husband and little boy," he said. "But you're wrong. I hated what happened to them. I liked your family. The way you and your husband acted when you were together, that's how it's supposed to be between people. What you had with him, maybe it could happen again with someone else, out in the future somewhere, I mean, like it might take a while, you'd need to get over your grief and loss, but it could happen, right? You think that's possible?"

"With you? Is that what you mean?"

"You think I'm stupid. But I'm not stupid. I've had a successful career. I even went to college."

"Yeah, you dropped out your first year."

"Wow." He smiled at her. "You really been checking up on me."

"That's right."

"I'm flattered. What else you find out?"

Harper didn't respond.

"Maybe you read about my old man, how he died. That made the papers."

Harper looked straight ahead out the windshield.

"No? You didn't find out about my dad? Well, somebody killed the cocksucker. Blew his face off with his own shotgun. Stuffed his corpse in a drainage pipe. I was just a kid at the time, thirteen, fourteen."

Spider looked at her, eyes in shadow, just a gleam in the dark, nothing she could read.

"Cops went through the motions, but the old man was such a mean-ass drunk, always in trouble with the law, beating the shit out of my mother, picking fights in bars, drunk and disorderly half his life, so as far as the cops were concerned, him getting murdered, it was good riddance."

Harper cut a quick look at Nick. Lying still, listening to Spider.

"You want to know a secret? I never told anybody this before. It was me who did it, killed the son of a bitch, my start in life, how I went off in the wrong direction."

"Oh, that's how it is," she said. "Your shitty childhood gives you a license to murder anybody you feel like? That what you're saying?"

He smiled at her. "See what we're doing now? This kind of back-and-forth is what I was talking about. Sharing our pasts, opening up, revealing who we are. That's a good thing, a healthy thing. But it would be a lot easier if we went inside, more comfortable, sit in chairs, have a glass of wine. How about it? I don't want to bully you, but we should go in."

She took another glance at Nick. He gave her a gloomy look, then closed his eyes and turned his head away.

Harper settled back in the seat and watched the snowflakes swirling in the dark. A frigid hand gripping her heart.

"So what do you say, Harper? Give it a try, go up to my room, talk some more? How bad could that be?"

THIRTY

Mid-March, Altstadt, Old Town, Zurich, Switzerland

The lobby for the Hotel California was on the second floor, up a narrow flight of stairs. Harper in front, Spider following close. Framed posters on the wall featured American bands from the sixties. Led Zeppelin, Grateful Dead, The Doors. Garish yellows and reds, harsh overhead lights.

The young man behind the reception desk wore a brown-and-red uniform. He looked up as they entered the small lobby, checked out Harper, gave Spider a knowing nod, and got back to the newspaper spread out before him on the counter.

They waited in silence for one of the elevators to arrive. On the walls were posters of the American West. A large desert scene covered each elevator door, boulders and saguaros, wide expanses of sand, the paintings labeled Red Rock Canyon and Death Valley.

"I know you're jumpy," Spider said. "But there's no need. It's going to be just fine. You'll see."

She was silent, coiled, watching for the opening that was bound to come.

"I'm not like this normally, so forward with women," he said, keeping his voice low, intimate. "It's your fault, really. The way you are. That animal energy you project."

Yes, animal energy. She felt it rising inside her like black steam.

The elevator arrived and she stepped aboard. Spider followed, leaned across her to press number five. She looked down at the brief flash of his exposed neck.

When the doors closed, Harper stepped away and planted her back against the opposite wall.

At the second floor, the doors drew open, and a squat woman in her sixties in a maid's uniform rolled her cart into the car, separating them. Harper on the right side, Spider left. He gave her a warning look: don't try any shit.

As the doors closed, the woman punched the button for three. She stared at Spider then and at Harper. Gave Harper a commiserating shrug. In a side tray of the cart there were cleaning supplies and sheets of hotel stationery and envelopes. In a second tray, a collection of ballpoint pens emblazoned with the hotel's logo.

Her move hidden by the cart, Harper pocketed a single pen. Spider smiled at her as the doors opened at three. The maid bid them *bonne soirée*, and rolled her cart into the corridor.

"Five-eleven," Spider said when they'd stepped onto the fifth-floor hallway. "Left around the corner, third door on your right."

Across the hall from 511, a BBC newscast was filtering through the door, another devastating terrorist attack in Germany. Harper stepped aside and Spider used the key, swung open the door, and gestured for her to enter. His room smelled of a citrusy cologne. His bed tightly made with crisp hospital corners, suitcase open on a luggage stand, contents folded, portioned off in neat sections.

"I'm a neat freak," he said. "Too many years in the military. I don't like messes. But you're neat too, right? Organize your drawers, your closet. Something we have in common."

Harper went to the window and drew aside the curtains and looked out at the snowy street below. She could see the rear doors of the Kintana van a half block away. Nick would be shivering, frightened, battling against the wraps of tape, the numbing cold.

"Red or white?" Spider held up two bottles. "I seem to remember you're a red girl."

"Can we dispense with the foreplay?"

"You're making this harder than it needs to be. Why don't you sit down, get comfortable? Maybe take a look at the room service menu." He picked up a leather folder from the desk and held it out to her.

Work with what you have, her sensei said. *Use what's at hand.*

She stepped forward and took the binder from him and opened it. He didn't back away, letting her into his space. His guard down.

Hand the menu back, and while he's close, plant the pen in his throat and rip. Same as she'd handled Jamal Fakhri. Steeling herself. The icy hand in her chest tightening. A flutter of stage fright.

Spider watched her, holding his ground a few feet away.

The desk was behind him. Harper's calves and the back of her knees brushing the double bed. Not the best fighting space. So many obstacles, so many variables. A floor lamp on one side of the bed, a bedside table on the other. Phone, table lamp. A mirror on the wall beside the closet. More glass-framed posters of California scenes. Big Sur, Mendocino, the Sierra Nevada, another Red Rock Canyon in a heavy frame. Objects that could be clubs, things to be smashed, glass shattered, variables.

"Oh, and by the way," he said, drawing open his jacket, showing his holstered pistol. "Why don't you give me the pen you palmed."

Harper drew a hard breath.

"Put it down," he said. "Over here."

He patted the desktop and took two steps to the side.

She drew out the ballpoint, laid it on the desk. Set the menu beside it.

"You really hate me that much? You'd stab me with that?"

A door slammed in the hallway, voices walked past, giddy female laughter.

Spider picked up the pen, snapped it in two. Dropped the pieces in a metal waste can.

"You're delusional if you think I'm going to have some kind of relationship with the man who destroyed my family."

"You keep saying that, but I didn't do it."

"I saw you, Spider. I watched the video."

"I don't know what you saw, but it's not true. I never killed them. I wouldn't do that. I regret it happened. Deeply regret it. Now just let that go and let's have a drink? Settle us both down."

When she didn't answer, he studied her for a long moment. "Have a drink . . . then maybe, if you like, I could brush your hair, how Ross used to do it. I've got a very nice brush right here. Would you like that? I know I would."

The jolt in her chest sent a wild, skittering light through the room. The floor rocked. Spider's grotesque violation, his invasion of her marriage, befouling the most intimate moments between Harper and Ross.

"I bought it yesterday. It's a very nice brush."

He turned to reach for it, and she was on him.

Right elbow cracking against his skull sent him sprawling into the desk chair. She kept coming, chopped him in the throat, two more blows to the side of his head, then she grabbed the chardonnay. Spider rolled into her, shoulder into her gut, knocked her back against the bed.

He drew his pistol, brought it to her face, and Harper swept the wine bottle up, cracked his wrist, sent the pistol flying.

Then swung the bottle downward at his skull, but he'd moved too close, and it only clipped the side of his head, slowed him for a second, but he recovered, knocked the bottle away, sent it crashing against the side table, and he rose and closed in, face inches from hers, both fists pummeling her midsection, body blows again and again, a street fighter, nothing fancy. Still, he doubled her over.

She gasped, spun away, and as he closed again, she kneed him, missed his crotch, struck his thigh. No room to work. He kept coming, making a mournful, apocalyptic moan, as if he were abandoning all hope, throwing himself off some excruciating cliff.

She let him drive her backward into the bedside wall, flatten her there, his breath heavy, and she stayed pinned, let him crush his body into hers, grinding his hips into her loins, falling into a rhythm, and good Christ, the guy was dry humping her, grinding and grinding, the fantasy in his head taking charge, savagery and sex intertwined for him, and as he slowed his rhythm, she felt him harden against her, and she went with it, sexual judo, fed his make-believe, became the slut unable to resist, and tilted her face forward, fit her lips to his wild mouth, his hot breath filling her, but he resisted, mouth hard, lips shut, disbelieving, then seconds later his vanity undid him, and he softened, thought she was yielding.

The kiss went deeper, his tongue testing her lips, then plunging into her mouth, a French kiss from this man who'd murdered sweet Leo, strong, loving Ross.

She lifted her arms high above her head as if to surrender further and found the edges of the desert scene above her, the metal frame, slipping her thumbs behind it, lifting it up and off its hanger, then sucked his tongue deeper, held it there, squirming briefly, and she bit down hard, whipping her head to the left, then right, ripping his tongue, then thrust him away with her hips and brought the Red Rock Canyon down on his skull, the glass shattering, a lost cry from Spider, slamming him again and again until the frame broke apart, then used her fists and feet, snapping the chopping blows, the heel thrusts, knocking him back into the desk, shattering one of its legs.

Spider was down. Face torn, a wedge of glass snagged deep in his cheek, a splinter in his right eye. He blew a blood bubble, and she side kicked his face. Heard the flattening cartilage.

She knelt beside him, checked his throat, felt a thready pulse. He was hanging on. She looked out at the snow swirling down. With Nick freezing, there was no time to measure the moral costs. She gripped his throat in both hands, crushed. Held on a minute. More than a minute.

His mouth sagged, his eyes came open. Staring into hers with surprise that shaded into a weary sadness and, just before he closed his eyes for good, seemed to fill with forgiveness. The patient look of a man loosening his hold on earthly concerns as his body eased into the silky warm bath of forever.

When she found no heartbeat, she pushed herself to her feet and rushed from the room, located the fire-exit stairs, slipped past the lobby floor to the basement, out a side door, momentarily lost, her heart flailing, wiping the blood from her face as she hustled through the thickening snow to the van. Threw open the door, found Nick trembling, sitting up, his hands free, working on the tape at his ankles.

She spoke his name, and he swung around, eyes desolate.

"Oh god. Are you—are you okay?"

"He's gone. Spider's finished."

"Jesus," he said, shivering. "Thank god it's over."

"But it isn't, Nick."

She knelt beside him, wrapped him in her arms, holding him tight, warming him with her own crazed heat.

"It's just beginning."

THIRTY-ONE

Mid-March, the Widder, Zurich, Switzerland

The final look in Spider's eyes, what she'd taken as an instant of forgiveness, haunted her. For the next few days she said little, stayed in the bedroom, hardly ate. Looked out the window at the March sky. Clouds and rain, more snow, then a sudden warming, the heavens turning a perfect blue. Saturday, Sunday, Monday.

She wasn't sure if Spider truly had a final epiphany. Was that even possible for a man whose trade was murder? Or was the look she saw some other thing entirely? Simply the rapid dissolution of his nervous system, the quick biological undoing of all that made him human. She'd not looked into the dying eyes of Jamal Fakhri so had no point of comparison. In any case, it was a useless deliberation, perhaps a trick she was playing on herself to occupy her mind, distract from the twist of guilt that tortured her.

Killing the killer of Leo and Ross had done nothing to assuage her grief. If anything, it made her anguish more complex, added a tinge of shame so potent it inflamed her sorrow all over again.

On Tuesday afternoon, Nick knocked at her door and called out that he needed to speak to her right away.

She'd just showered for the first time since Friday and was starting the slow ordeal of recuperation. She followed him into the study, where Sal was tipped back in the recliner, reading the *International Herald Tribune.*

"Our boy Nick has been working hard," Sal said. "This might be something we could use."

She sat at the desk and watched Nick pace the room. Since the night at the Albion building and the Hotel California, he'd apologized a half dozen times. Guilty that he hadn't fended off Spider at the van, guilty he hadn't escaped from his bonds to help her in Spider's hotel room. Guilty he'd so far contributed almost nothing to their quest.

"There's not much on the hard drives," Nick said. "Sal and I looked them over. Nothing incriminating, nothing about Ross or Spider."

"That's too bad."

"But it wasn't a waste."

She waited.

"There's one thing we can use. Albion's e-mail logs show he's done a lot of recent communication with his legal team about an upcoming deal, a takeover of Marburg chocolates."

"Okay," she said. It didn't sound like much.

"Most of that is about the structure of the deal, negotiations, the point-by-point strategy they're using to convince the Marburg board of the benefits of the deal. But there's some personal information too: Lester Albion's motivation comes across in several of the e-mails."

"What motivation?"

Sal said, "Guy's obsessed with Marburg chocolates. It's a lifelong fantasy. A very big deal to Albion. More personal than business. He's like some little kid, never grew up."

"And how does that help us?"

"I'm not through," Nick said. "The transaction is supposed to close Friday, in three days. So that's all the time we have."

"Time for what?"

"Just wait," he said. "Let me put it all out there, then we can figure out how to use it."

Nick launched into a description of the Marburg acquisition deal, revealing a side of him she'd never seen. The businessman fluent in financial jargon, the mechanics of corporate economics. In his detailed explanation, he lost her several times, and she had to stop him and make him simplify, but eventually she thought she had the gist of it.

Albion's acquisition of Marburg was a tricky deal for several financial reasons but mainly because the Marburg family were practicing Quakers, and their religious conservatism guided all their business decisions. Any hint of impropriety was anathema to them, and even if it meant making decisions that were unprofitable to their corporate interests, they were nevertheless guided by their strict ethical codes. Ethics trumping profit, a quaint idea.

"That's where the Ivory Coast comes in," Nick said.

Harper leaned forward in her chair. A prickle on her shoulders.

"There were twenty e-mails, maybe more, back and forth between Lester Albion and Edwin Marburg. Edwin is the patriarch. Chairman of the board, clearly the head honcho, even though his two sons are the CEO and CFO. It's Edwin who'll make the go/no-go merger decision.

"Of those twenty e-mails, most are about an incident in the Ivory Coast four years ago. It started after accusations from an international relief agency came out about the use of child slaves on Albion-controlled cacao plantations. They sent a couple of video people out into the jungle and got film of the slave kids. The press investigated, the claims turned out to be true. Kids as young as five using machetes to open cacao pods, deaths, lost fingers, hands, all of these kids working sixteen hours a day, frequent beatings, no school, no holidays. Cruel shit.

"Lester Albion claimed he had no knowledge of the practice and that once made aware, he worked overtime to correct the problem. Ordered reeducation of all his plantation bosses, sensitivity training, and he built schools to service the kids, increased oversight, invited a

UN humanitarian investigative team to make sure the problem was corrected permanently. He had one of his people, a woman named Larissa Bixel, send Marburg executives dozens of documents, press releases, certification notices, a huge pile of supporting material to convince him the problem with child slaves was permanently cleared up."

"And who exactly is Bixel?" Harper said.

"Larissa Bixel is the VP of global affairs, second in the corporate ladder behind Albion. Working-class background, father was a baker, so she's up by the bootstraps."

Harper nodded. "Bixel was one of the people Jackson Sharp mentioned to Ross. He was trying to get Ross to investigate the woman."

"Investigators from AVISCO, a child protection NGO, were the ones who first exposed Albion for using child slaves," Nick said. "I think it was those same two AVISCO investigators doing a follow-up who were killed on the video Jackson Sharp showed Ross. Late last year, a husband-and-wife team, Bert and Kathy Fordham, working for AVISCO, were reported missing while out on a research trip to the Ivory Coast, never heard from again."

"So that whole story Sharp sold Ross was bogus. Rachel Sharp being Jackson's wife, all that."

Nick nodded. "There's another detail I learned from a World Bank associate of mine. A couple of weeks back, I put the word out to a few friends I thought might have had some knowledge of Lester Albion. Asked them very discreetly. And I heard back from almost all of them. Mostly it was about how Albion was an obsessive guy. A micromanager. Watching every penny and nickel, everything comes across his desk. Everything."

"And the intriguing detail?" Harper said.

"It involves Ben Westfield, our actor friend," he said. "Albion's infatuated with Westfield. Well, more than infatuated. He collects Westfield memorabilia. Pricey stuff. Has his people going to auctions, buying vintage posters, old movie scripts, wardrobe items, props from the sets of his movies, souvenirs from other private collectors. Westfield's cowboy hat from *Lost Trail*, he paid eighteen thousand euros for that. And he's managed to put together a collection of every pistol Westfield ever used in a movie since *High Peak at Sunset*."

"There was a poster of Westfield in his office," she said. "An ad Ben did for Albion, it must've been forty years ago."

"I told Nick this Albion guy's like some little kid." Sal picked something off his sweater and flicked it across the room. "Those Westfield movies suck, by the way, most of them. Those three Mafia flicks, you see them? Well, don't bother. I seen *Three Stooges* episodes more realistic."

"I don't understand where this goes," Harper said. "What's the relevance?"

"I'm not finished," Nick said.

Harper raised both hands. Sorry, sorry, go on.

"Here's the point," Nick said. "Edwin Marburg and Albion are both members of the Westfield fan club. Marburg's not as far gone as Albion, but he's a fan. He prefers Westfield's recent war movies, while Albion is more into the early stuff, the spaghetti westerns, the Chicago cop movies. And the five Westfield directed. *Ocean of Blood*, all those."

"Those cop movies are a joke," Sal said. "Ten minutes in, I walked out of that first one, *Johnny Danger*, or whatever the hell it was. There was no cop ever born as pure as that guy. What a load of shit."

"And your idea?" Harper said.

Nick picked up a chair, carried it across the room, and sat across from her. He was flushed with eagerness. Eyes lit.

"You call Ben Westfield, get him to fly to Zurich right away, we'll set up a meeting with Albion and Marburg. They'd be thrilled at the chance, flattered as hell. The story is Ben's decided to make a movie about the chocolate industry, he's doing research, needs their input. Gets us in the door."

"And do what?"

He sighed and shook his head.

"I don't know. That's as far as I've gotten, just the structure of it. The creative part, that's your department, Harper."

"How do you figure that?"

"You came up with that Kintana plan."

"That almost got us killed."

"You'll think of something."

"You will," Sal said. "I can hear the wheels cranking from over here."

"Westfield's a busy man. He's probably making a movie."

"He'll come if you ask him, Harper."

"Why do you say that?"

Nick hesitated for a moment, then said, "Because you're Deena's daughter."

"So?"

"He had a thing for Deena. Well, a thing with Deena."

"What?"

"A thing."

"What kind of thing?"

Nick took a long moment, eyes lowered.

"Okay." He swallowed a breath, bringing his eyes to hers. "I discovered it when we were kids. Deena and you and me, we were all in Istanbul. I think I was eight, you were nine. I remember we were staying at the Four Seasons at the Bosporus. One morning, I was up early wandering the halls, I saw Westfield come out of Deena's room, must've been six or seven o'clock. I said hello, and he ducked his face and kept walking. Apparently their affair went on for years."

"You're sure of that?"

Nick nodded. "I knocked on Deena's door that morning and asked her about it. She dragged me into her room and slapped me. Only time she ever hit me. She apologized, hugged me. And while she was holding me, I asked her again if Ben Westfield was her boyfriend, and she said yes, it was true, she had a lover. And I could never tell anyone, not you, not Dad, no one. And I promised her I wouldn't. It was our secret. For years."

"Deena and Ben Westfield. I can't picture it."

"Your mother was a tiger," Sal said. "She was a force of nature. She probably ran that show, even a macho man like Westfield."

"Look," Nick said. "The Marburg takeover deal is on track to close Friday. Albion's desperate for it to happen. It's his childhood fantasy. So if we're going to try to leverage Marburg's moral righteousness to pressure Albion, then after Friday, we lose that leverage."

"Pressure him to do what?" Harper said.

Even as she spoke the words, an idea came to her, forming quickly with the sharp-edged clarity of a photographic image.

Sal said, "I think Nick wants to get everyone together in a room, throw a bomb on the table, make the bad guys turn on each other as they're fighting for the exits."

"I think I have something," she said.

"Great," Nick said. "So share."

"Not yet. I need more time. I need to refine it a little."

"Well, if we're going to do this," Sal said, "you've got to call Westfield, get him moving."

"Just tell him you need his help," Nick said. "You're Deena's little girl. He'll come."

She nodded, the image hardening into place. It was a decent plan. It might even work.

Nick said, "We need to move. We only have two days to get ready."

THIRTY-TWO

Mid-March, Zurich, Switzerland

An hour later she made the call. Westfield's cell number was stored in her phone from last year's photo shoot—the thirty-year reunion of *The Last Bloom* group. She got him as he was leaving the makeup trailer, heading for the set. He wasn't surprised to be hearing from her. Actually, he seemed pleased, chatting away as he walked across the lot.

Told her he was starring in an action thriller about a heroin kingpin who'd escaped from a Mexican supermax prison. His character was leading the commando assault on the bad guy's mountain hideout. Tarzan with shoulder-fired missiles is how he described it. He thought the movie was even sillier than usual.

He told her he'd heard about Ross and Leo. Said he'd called Nick to check on Harper the day after it happened. His condolences must've gotten lost in the agonizing shuffle.

Hearing Westfield's voice, his deep bass, Harper was disarmed by his unadorned authenticity and dropped the lie she was going to tell him.

"I've been tracking Ross and Leo's killer."

He was silent for several moments. She asked if he was still there.

"You got Deena's moxie, all right. Tracking a killer."

"I found the triggerman and took him out," she said. "But I need to know who pulled his strings."

"You did what?" he said. "You sure you should be telling me this?"

"I'm sure."

"Okay, okay. How can I help?"

"I'd like to put you in a room with the suspects, see what happens."

"Is there a script?"

"I'm working on it."

"Sounds like serious business."

"I wouldn't call you if it wasn't."

"And you think I can help?"

"A couple of the principals are your fanboys."

"Run into those idiots everywhere."

Harper was silent while Westfield continued to talk.

"Sure, I'll take a few days off. They can shoot around me. My plane's in a hangar half an hour away. I could be in Zurich by breakfast. That good enough?"

Without warning, the tears came. His warmth, his reassuring strength had given her a sense of security she hadn't felt since losing Ross. His screen persona was no act. Solid to the marrow. Deena's equal.

Her next call was to the number she'd promised never to use again.

"I need your help," she said to the familiar voice.

"Change your mind, coming back in?"

"No," she said.

"Then I don't know what I can do."

"The Rome job. I want to collect on some long overdue payback."

Silence.

"You're thinking about it."

"Need some details."

"This line secure?"

"As secure as a line can be."

She described what she knew. Didn't dress it up. A matter-of-fact accounting of Royale Plantation, the killings in the Ivory Coast, and those in Miami. Even described killing Spider. She saved Soko for last, a village massacre, fifty, sixty killed, women, children.

"You've been on a rampage."

"Isn't that how you trained me?"

"Pains me to inform you, but massacres in Africa are a dime a dozen. I'm sorry to say, these days when another one happens, our needle doesn't even twitch. No constituency for that sort of thing."

"What if the massacre was the work of one of the world's largest corporations?"

The line went quiet for a few breaths, then: "Name of that village?"

She spelled Soko.

Another pause, then, in a sober voice, "I'll need to check this out."

The connection broke, and she sat beside the window and watched the pure blue Zurich sky, birds wheeling past. Watched the trams coming and going, the streets teeming with people, her mind free, the heaviness lifting.

In twenty minutes, her phone rang.

"What exactly you have in mind?"

"Sit in on a meeting."

"Sounds boring."

"You might be able to capture a heinous criminal."

"Do that every day."

"Ever heard of Ben Westfield, the actor?"

"Sure. Badass dude, maybe a little long in the tooth these days, but somehow he still manages to kick the young punks' asses."

"Westfield's running the meeting."

"Friend of yours?"

"That's right."

"What's his stance on autographs?"

"I could arrange it."

"My friend's a big fan. Myself, I'm more into Bruce Willis. Wiseass suits me better."

"I'd rather not have to explain who you are to the people I'm working with. Including my brother. How about if we say you're Ben Westfield's personal assistant?"

"Now you're talking."

"And one more thing—well, actually make that two."

"Don't push it."

"I'll e-mail you a short video. Stars a man with blond hair and horn-rim glasses. If you could identify him, dig up any background, it could be helpful. He might have been the point man on the massacre."

"And?"

"Another gentleman named Adrian Naff. Current head of security for Albion International. Before that he worked as a contractor for an outfit called Aegis Defense Service. Anything you can dig up."

"Ben Westfield in the flesh, you're not playing me?"

"In the flesh."

"Okay then. Look for me late tomorrow."

"I don't know how to thank you."

"No one ever does."

———

She needed to refresh her memory, get the details straight before Westfield arrived, so Harper spent the afternoon on her laptop reviewing the three videos, taking notes on hotel stationery, working up a timeline, a cast of characters. Trying to visualize the connective tissue between events.

First she watched the group of child slaves on Royale Plantation. Scrawny nine-year-old Yacou chopped cacao pods for a while, then rose from the circle of boys and headed into the bush. He drew the fronds aside and pointed at "Rachel" and the other man, and called out to the security team. The two beefy black men in uniforms flanked by a white man in a blue button-down shirt, striped tie, and black-framed glasses burst into their hiding spot. Ross had described the white man as an accounting professor, but when Harper went hand to hand with the same man at the Edgewater Apartments, knocking his Ruger away, accounting hadn't come to mind. There was a second white man behind Ruger Guy, but his face was never on camera. Just a quick flash.

Then she watched again the short hostage film with Spider, Naff, and Jackson Sharp crammed together on a bench. It was grainy, probably shot with a cheap mobile phone. She reran the hostage video several times, concentrating on each of the three prisoners in turn. Only one of these men was still alive. Only one still mattered. Adrian Naff.

But she noticed things about each of the men that escaped her before. The pissed-off squint in Spider's eyes, a man enraged by his predicament and on the verge of a violent eruption. And Jackson Sharp, his shoulders hunched, cowering. More defeated than she'd previously noticed. Of the three, he was plainly the weakest, with sneaky eyes, a coward searching for an easy out, ready to confess whatever confidential information he could use to bargain for his release. Willing to betray his employer, his country, even his comrades in an instant.

Adrian Naff was strikingly different from the others. His eyes were oddly calm, locked on the unblinking camera. In the passport photos of Naff, and during her brief encounter with him, she hadn't seen this detached, unflinching expression. Undaunted by his captivity, his gaze sent a direct challenge to his captors. But it was more than simple bravery. She saw a man who'd long ago made peace with his own mortality. A man perfectly at ease with this ugly situation, which made him, in Harper's view, far more lethal than his two companions.

Sal cleared his throat. Standing just behind her shoulder.

"I took another look at the video in the jungle, the woman with her throat slit."

"Yeah?"

"I froze it on one frame to get a better look at the second white man who was with Ruger Guy and the African guards."

"What is it, Sal?"

"He had a tattoo on his neck, a crucifix."

She was silent for a moment, letting her pulse recover.

"You're sure?"

"I can show you the frame, you don't believe me."

"Jackson Sharp. The guy that conned Ross. He was there when it all happened. He was part of it."

Sal nodded.

Harper looked off at the street window again. "Which explains how Sharp got hold of the video he was peddling to Ross. He picked it up that day. Used it later for his blackmail scheme."

"Seems that way."

"Good work, Sal. Very good work."

"You watch the other video?" he said, his eyes shying away. "One shot inside your house?"

She closed the laptop and swiveled around. Sal was wearing jeans and a black V-necked sweater, his white chest hair curling out of the V.

"I watched enough."

"How much?"

"All I could manage."

"Not the whole way through?"

"No."

"I wondered."

"Why do you ask?"

"You see the part where Spider comes into the house, gun drawn?"

"That's where I stopped, yes. What're you getting at?"

"I thought maybe it was like that."

"Damn it, Sal, say what's on your mind."

"Nick told me what went down in the hotel in Old Town. What you did to Spider, god only knows what he had in mind. So taking him out, you can chalk that up to self-defense. 'Cause see, it wasn't Spider shot Ross and Leo. I mean, yeah, he was there, but he didn't pull the trigger."

Inside her chest she felt the flimsy structure of rationalizations she'd assembled begin to fall apart.

"Are you serious?"

"Sorry," he said. "But I had to tell you."

"Who was it then? Who killed them?"

"I know it's rough," he said. "But you need to look, see for yourself."

"I don't believe this."

"Watch it. When you're done, if you need to talk, I'll be out in the front room."

It took her several minutes to build up the nerve. Then she ran the video again, fast-forwarded through the days she'd already seen, came to Spider's entrance. Stopped. She felt her heart struggling, breath hard and shallow.

She steeled herself and tapped the arrow and the video came alive.

With his pistol pointed at Ross, Spider said, "Like you to meet an associate of mine."

He stepped aside and swept his arm upward as if shooing a balloon into the air.

Entering the room was a man in black trousers, black turtleneck, dark Windbreaker, and a white ghost mask. Leo gurgled with glee. A masked man had come calling. What fun.

The camera, fixed high on the wall in the far corner, recorded a panoramic view of the room. The masked man took a leisurely look at his surroundings, then drew a silver pistol from inside his jacket. A long suppressor was fastened to its barrel.

Ross said, "Hey, wait a second, will you? Tell me what you want. We can work this out."

Spider raised his hands and shrugged. Sorry, pal, too late to negotiate.

Without warning, the masked man raised the pistol, aime. fired. Ross stumbled backward. His arms were wrapped tight around Leo, trying in vain to shield him.

Ross kept his footing, wobbling, clutching Leo. The shooter stepped forward, closing in on Ross until his pistol was no more than a foot from his face. The second shot struck Ross squarely in the forehead and sent him sprawling onto the green couch.

The masked man kept the pistol raised as if debating a third shot. Spider stepped to his side, whispered into his ear, and raised a cautious hand to coax the shooter's hand down.

Spider said, "Okay, you happy now? You tied up the loose ends. You earned your merit badge. Now get the fuck out of here while I finish up."

The masked man took another slow look around the living room, as though basking in the moment, turned, and left.

Harper stopped the video, swallowed an impossible breath. Her eyes fogged over.

It wasn't Spider. She'd strangled the wrong man. The killer was someone else, a man who appeared unpracticed in the art of murder, a novice.

The spy cam distorted the perspective slightly, but Harper was pretty sure the shooter was several inches shorter than Spider. He had narrow shoulders, a sunken chest, a puny physique.

But his eyes behind the mask, oh, those eyes were bright.

That much was absolutely clear. His bright, burning eyes.

THIRTY-THREE

Mid-March, Seestrasse, Zurich, Switzerland

At the Berlang Indoor Gun Range, six miles south of Paradeplatz and the Albion building, Adrian Naff was shooting his .357 Smith & Wesson. A reliable, uncomplicated weapon that suited his temperament. With the paper target hanging forty feet away, he'd grouped six rounds in a tight cluster, mostly inside the bull's-eye. Not bad for an old-timer whose eyes weren't as sharp as they'd once been.

In the next booth, Lester Albion was trying out his new Glock 43 9mm. His target was positioned only half the distance of Adrian's, but his six perforations were scattered around the periphery of the outer circle. Not a target to take home and frame.

While Adrian was reloading, Albion peeked around the edge of the booth and stripped off his tactical ear protectors. Adrian did the same. No other shooters on the range today. All quiet.

"How's it feel?"

Albion grinned. "I love it. For one thing, the size is perfect, it's very concealable, and I like the oversize magazine catch. Easy to pop out. And the built-in beavertail design lets me grip it high and tight."

"Not too tight," Naff said. "Like I said, keep your hand a little loose, find that sweet spot between firm and soft."

"Right, right."

Lester Albion pressed the button on the automatic pulley, and his target came fluttering back. He unclipped it and held it out for Naff to admire. In the dozen times they'd come to this range on Seestrasse, Naff had managed to navigate the tricky pathways of Albion's ego. But it wasn't always easy to come up with praise to balance out his critiques.

"Well, I admit, the grouping could be tighter," Albion said.

"True," Naff said. "It should be half that diameter. And see how most of the cluster is high and to the right. Means you're still pulling up when you squeeze. Flinching just a hair."

"But overall it's good, no? Better than with the Ruger."

"Miles ahead of that," Adrian said.

This was hard duty for Adrian. He wasn't a natural bullshitter. With the young men he'd schooled in the marines, there had been no pep talks at the firing range. With those guys, marksmanship wasn't a hobby. It was life and death.

"Have another go?" Albion said.

Adrian was still reloading when Albion ran his target out to fifty feet and began to fire. Just as Adrian raised the .357, someone tapped on his back.

Wearing a set of white ear protectors, Larissa Bixel gestured curtly for him to follow.

Out in the lobby coffee bar, she led him to a corner booth and waved off an approaching waitress. She set the earmuffs on the table and leaned forward. The veins in her temple crisscrossing her pale skin were at full bulge. She gritted her teeth and sighed in resignation, as if preparing to berate a perpetual fuckup.

Adrian said, "You're looking lovely today."

She registered the remark for several seconds, then the air went out of her, and she sat back in the booth and looked past him at a far wall. Eyes flitting to the left, then the right. In such close quarters, she had to work overtime to avoid eye contact.

"This morning I spoke to one of our security guards about the incident on Friday night, and I was informed that you had a brief encounter with the McDaniel woman."

"Your information is correct."

"Afterward, you followed the woman outside."

"Also correct."

"And allowed her to depart."

"Your point is?"

She planted both hands flat on the table and studied her manicure. "I ordered you to remove this woman."

"What? Shoot her dead on the sidewalk outside the building? Is that how you would have handled it?"

"You made no attempt to follow her."

"Following her wasn't necessary. I know where Ms. McDaniel is staying. A very posh local hotel."

"What hotel?"

Adrian smiled. "So you can send Helmut over with a bouquet of flowers?"

Her glance grazed his face, then flicked away.

"Do you think this is a laughing matter, Mr. Naff? Because I assure you it is quite the opposite. Ms. McDaniel is a threat to you and to me and the entire Albion family. Her incursion into the building and her thievery should make perfectly clear that the woman intends to do harm to our business."

Naff glanced around the small café. A young couple was having coffee three booths away. Otherwise empty.

"Where's Helmut? You give him the day off?"

Bixel ran a finger inside the rim of her red turtleneck sweater as if it had tightened against her throat.

"Your boy's not very good at what he does, you know. I suppose he must have some skills, or you wouldn't keep him around, but tailing a person isn't one of them. Why was he shadowing me anyway? You worried I'm going to uncover your secrets and let Lester know what you've been up to?"

"If you know the woman's whereabouts, why are you waiting?"

"You have the wrong impression about me, Ms. Bixel. I'm not a hired gun. If you want that kind of service, use Helmut."

"I asked you a question. What're you waiting for?"

"Okay, actually there's someone in line ahead of you."

"And who would that be?"

"Lester asked me to investigate the African matter, so I've been making phone calls, talking to some people out there. Learning fascinating details about recent events on the Royale Plantation and the surrounding region."

"It would be a grave error to involve yourself in this situation, which is far beyond your abilities."

"Story of my life."

"You obviously misunderstood Mr. Albion's wishes. Have you forgotten his instructions Friday night? He made it very clear to all of us that his foremost priority was to complete the Marburg transaction. He asked to hear no more about the African situation. How can it be more plain than that?"

Naff straightened his place mat, dusted it off. Enjoying this, fencing with her, watching Bixel's growing irritation. "While I was poking around, I came across an incident in a village named Soko, a tiny place in Burkina Faso about a hundred miles from Albion's cacao plantation. My source in the Ivory Coast tells me that some months ago this village was destroyed, villagers murdered. Upward of seventy-five people, that's what my source said.

"And the kicker is there's talk that what happened in Soko is related to cacao beans. Seems very strange, doesn't it? I'm trying to figure out just what the connection is, how it relates to my old chum Spider and to Harper McDaniel.

"Oh, and by the way, did you know that Ms. McDaniel recently lost her husband and child? Victims of homicide. All indications are that it was a professional job. You happen to know anything about this? Like maybe it was the task you gave Spider?"

Her face had stiffened into a mask of speechless rage. Just as she was opening her mouth to unleash a withering response, Lester Albion arrived breathless at their booth.

"Look at this. My god, you won't believe it."

He held out his phone.

"The caller at the top, see the name. How amazing is that? Ben Westfield tracked me down and called me directly! He wants to meet, discuss his new movie. It's about the chocolate industry, an action thriller, the kind of movie he does. He thinks I can help with his research."

"Westfield?" Bixel asked.

"Hollywood tough guy," Adrian said. "Been around forever."

"He's an actor, yes, but Westfield does it all: actor, writer, director. Plays the most marvelous villains. You'll meet him day after tomorrow, Thursday at four. He wants to sit down with my inner circle. Cecil Marburg too. He asked for Marburg by name. Isn't this amazing?"

"An actor," Bixel said. "He wants a meeting? And you're doing it?"

"Yes, yes, of course I am. I'm a huge fan. Have been all my life. And out of the blue he calls me up. He's coming to Zurich just to meet us. The inner circle, as he said."

Adrian was quiet, picturing that coffee-table book still lying on his office desk, *The Last Bloom*, photos by Deena Roberts and Harper McDaniel. Ben Westfield's portraits on page one and two. Young version on the left, and on the facing page the older Westfield, handsome, rawboned, rugged, looking twice as tough as his younger self. There he was, a supernova among ordinary stars, prominently displayed at the opening of Harper's book. And now he was coming all the way to Zurich to meet Lester Albion and his inner circle.

"Out of the blue," Adrian said.

"Yes, yes," Albion said. "Out of the blue. Can you believe it?"

THIRTY-FOUR

Mid-March, Zurich Airport, Switzerland

Harper was being stalked. She felt the whispery brush of eyes following close behind as she navigated the main concourse of Zurich Airport, a slow stroll toward the VIP arrival lounge where she was to meet Ben Westfield at noon.

She'd arrived an hour early. Eager to see him again, to lay out the plan, nerves jittery from the extra cup of Jamaican coffee this morning. And now, the clear certainty that someone was shadowing her through the waves of airline passengers raised the pressure in her ears a few more degrees.

Harper stopped abruptly, swung around, almost collided with a blue-suited man with a rolling suitcase. She apologized, and he replied gruffly and marched on. She stepped to the front window of a newspaper kiosk and pressed her back to the glass and scanned the flow of travelers. Not the multicultural mix you'd expect elsewhere in Europe. These were mostly white, mostly young to middle-aged, suits and tailored outfits, briefcases and Rolexes. Men on phones, women on phones.

No one caught her eye. No one ducked away. Whoever was following her was more skilled than that. The flow continued to flow. And she rejoined it, resumed her leisurely pace, trying to hatch a plan, trying to recall some gambit from a long-ago spy film, a clever way to circle back and track the tracker, and once she had him in her sights, slide up beside him, embarrass him with some droll remark, and disarm him if necessary.

Maybe it was only the flush of hubris, but Harper was convinced she could manhandle whomever they'd sent to tail her. Her long-dormant fighting skills were fully reactivated, and she was certainly angry enough, weary of the games, ready for a final confrontation, long past ready to blow this thing wide open.

She used the window glass to keep a watch behind her. Still nothing caught her eye. Ahead she saw a women's WC, sped up to a near trot, then, at the last second, cut into the entrance.

She halted just inside the open doorway, watching the crowd stream past. Two women went by. A young couple pushing a baby stroller. A man passed. Black baseball cap, gray sweater, a briefcase. He seemed to slant his head in her direction, then kept going. A gang of Japanese businessmen came next, a red-haired family, two kids, two adults.

No sign of a watcher. Except . . .

She returned to the man in the gray sweater. His eyes angling ever so slightly toward her. It was nobody's face she recognized. But those eyes. Dark and disinterested. A bland face with a slight frown, as if he were preoccupied with snaking through the crowd, avoiding the bumps and jostles of oncoming traffic. Much like anyone else.

Except she recognized those eyes. She'd seen them before, first from the passport photos Sal had uncovered, and later she'd looked into their dark depths while jousting with him in the Albion building.

That night, in a fleeting unguarded moment, Adrian Naff had revealed himself, appraising her with eyes that seemed toughened by too many wars in distant lands, harsh places he'd never completely left.

It was Naff dogging her, hiding behind a facade of anonymity. Transformed into an unremarkable man, disappearing in plain sight.

And if she hadn't spent years apprenticing to Deena, studying the eyes of her photographic subjects, Harper would have fallen for his ruse.

She swung back into the flow. There were still a dozen gates before the VIP lounge, maybe a ten-minute walk.

She stretched taller, tried to catch sight of him above the mob of bobbing heads but saw no sign of the black baseball cap. Maybe she'd lost him. Maybe he'd aborted his mission or ducked into a concourse shop to give her time to catch up.

Two more gates, still nothing. She was angling off into a random waiting area when she spotted the black baseball hat. It was twenty feet ahead, perched atop an aluminum waste can, an offering to any passerby. She approached it. She picked it up, briefly inspected it, then put it back.

She found a slot in the river of people and kept pace. He must've known she'd spotted him, and though he might have simply discarded the hat in response, Harper had the feeling that leaving it behind was a cocky message to her. *You're in over your head, an amateur in the big leagues.*

Alert to any unusual movement around her, she continued without incident until she arrived at the VIP arrival lounge and halted at the entrance door. She was still a half hour early. If on schedule, Westfield would have landed already and started working his way through whatever passport control the rock stars of the world were subjected to.

She looked back down the concourse, vaguely disappointed Naff had vanished.

She stepped aside to let an elderly couple enter the smoked-glass doors and looked around for a café where she could sit and gather herself.

Ever since strangling Spider, she'd been battling a deep disquiet. In slack, unexpected moments, she'd felt her moral certainty unraveling. Even her desire for vengeance seemed to be losing thrust. She'd spent hours second-guessing herself, recycling the same nagging complaint: killing Spider was wrong and needless.

He might have been made to confess all he knew and simplify her quest. At the very least, she'd left a grossly untidy murder scene. A desk clerk had seen her face. Her fingerprints were everywhere. Security cameras almost certainly had recorded her coming and going. She would be caught. She would never be able to mount a respectable defense. She could barely defend her actions to herself.

From Jamal Fakhri and the street thugs and guerillas she'd cut down in the Ivory Coast and now to Spider Combs, she'd left a trail of broken men, and the guilt was beginning to cloud her clarity of purpose.

She spotted a café two gates down and headed that way, settling in behind a cluster of tall, young men in matching athletic gear. As she cut left across the oncoming flow of travelers, she glimpsed a figure breaking loose from the approaching crowd.

He was a thick-bodied man wearing dark trousers, a cream leather coat, his hair hidden beneath a blue knit cap tugged low across his forehead nearly to the brim of his black framed glasses. He was striding directly toward her, shoulders wide, hands buried in the pockets of his coat.

It was, she realized as he closed in, Ross's blond accounting professor.

She slipped left through a knot of teenagers blocking the entrance to the café and, once inside, scanned the space and took a sharp right to position herself behind a wide steel column. Hidden from the doorway.

A moment later the hostess saw her and headed in her direction with an armload of menus. Behind the hostess, the back wall of the café was a floor-to-ceiling mirror, which gave her an unobstructed view of the entrance while shielding her from the entrance.

Another customer entered the restaurant and halted. Ruger Guy pushed in behind him and, over the shorter man's shoulder, swept the café with a glance.

"May I seat you, madam?"

The hostess stood nearby and smiled uneasily at this strange woman tucked behind a steel column.

In the mirror, Harper watched as Ruger Guy's gaze caught the hostess and read the situation. He shoved the smaller man out of his way and headed her way.

In a quiet voice, Harper told the hostess, *"Appelez la police dès maintenant."* Though she doubted the police could possibly arrive in time to intercede.

Ruger Guy pressed against the hostess's shoulder and hissed in German, telling her to get the hell back to work. Then he took hold of Harper's arm and yanked her toward the door. She was about to break his grip with a windmill sweep when he prodded her in the ribs with a blade so sharp it took her breath away. With ghastly ease, the point of the blade pierced the layers of her jacket and the wool of her sweater and pricked her flesh, releasing a warm track of blood down her hip.

"No ninja bullshit this time, understand, or I will *couper votre foie en deux.*"

If there was a blade that could cut her liver in half in a single swipe, she felt certain this was it. Far sharper than the one she'd used on Jamal Fakhri.

He walked her across the concourse, the blade's point digging into the flesh just below her rib cage. Blocking the pain, Harper mapped out a countermove. But this time she wasn't going to execute it too early. With her takedown of Spider still fresh in her mind, she was determined not to make that mistake again but instead to mine this moment for everything she could, even though it meant enduring the hard sting of the knife and risking serious injury.

"Who sent you?"

"What?"

"Your boss, who is it?"

"No one. I work only for myself."

"Is it Lester Albion?"

He jerked her to a stop, kept the tip needling into the meat of her waist.

"Lester Albion is a worthless *mauviette*."

"A wimp? Unlike you, *monsieur macho*."

The crowd flowed around them, no curious looks, an orderly, impassive mob.

"You believe you are a humorist, but there is nothing funny here."

"Adrian Naff?"

He mimicked a spit.

"Larissa Bixel, then. You work for her. Boss lady."

His silence lasted a second too long. Then a loose smile came to his lips, and his eyes disconnected from her and swept the far end of the concourse as if he were readying himself for the plunge of the knife.

She slipped to the left, a simple glissade, and chopped her hand at his wrist. His grip held firm, but he was a half second late in recovery, and his knife swiped through empty air, the force of his swing bringing him forward. She landed her right fist in his throat, and he coughed hard and stumbled backward against a passing electric cart and was thrown to the ground.

"Nice work."

Adrian Naff, in a yellow sweater and his reclaimed black baseball cap, stood beside her. A few feet away, the commotion with Ruger Guy was escalating as he pushed aside an elderly woman in a flowered dress, who'd stopped to offer assistance.

"I wondered how long you'd give him before you put him down," said Naff. "Are you hurt?"

"Not your concern."

"That was a nasty-looking blade."

"What's his name?"

Naff gestured for her to follow, and he turned away and cut through the crowd, halting at the doorway of a bar. He took a longing look into the cheery atmosphere of the lounge done up in a soft golden decor.

"An ice-cold pilsner would be good about now. You up for a drink?"

"I want to know his name."

"You always this pushy?"

"You don't know the half of it."

"You made me, didn't you?"

"You're good, but you can't mask your eyes."

"I came back to see if I could help. It's my fault this happened, the guy with the knife. I mentioned to someone that I knew where you were staying, said it was a posh hotel, but I didn't tell them it was the Widder. They must've called around, figured it out, got on your trail today. That was pretty reckless, you know, not using an alias to sign in."

"What's that man's name?"

"Okay, okay. The man with the knife was Helmut Mullen. I don't know if that's a pseudonym or what. I do know he's a blackhearted bastard with dubious credentials."

"He works for Bixel."

Holding her gaze, Naff smiled at her shrewdness. "Well, yes, it's true Ms. Bixel uses Helmut's services from time to time. But I wouldn't dignify the arrangement as work."

"Where do you fit in?"

"Excellent question. I've been trying to get a fix on that myself."

"You said you're supposed to kill me. Why?"

"I was hoping you could tell me that."

"You still planning to try it?"

"Sure you don't want a drink? Have a nice, civilized discussion."

"I'm meeting someone." She glanced at her watch. "I'm late already."

"Rain check, then."

"Not likely," she said and headed into the crowd.

THIRTY-FIVE

Mid-March, Widder Hotel, Zurich, Switzerland

Ben Westfield's penthouse at the Widder Hotel had a white marble fireplace, white leather couches, a Rauschenberg silk screen on the living room wall, a sumptuous white bedroom with intricate woodworking on the cabinets and around the transom windows, and a balcony that occupied the entire roof of the hotel and provided a 360-degree view of Zurich and the distant mountains.

Sal said, "At six thousand a night, I was expecting dancing girls."

"They arrive after midnight," Ben said. "You're welcome to stay."

"Past my bedtime. Anyway, my dancing-girl days are long gone."

It was seven thirty, and the four of them had finished their in-room dining. Her appetite dulled by the knife-wound throb in her side, Harper dabbled with the cauliflower soup, then pushed it away.

Westfield wore a skintight white turtleneck and faded jeans and scuffed-up hiking boots. He was a few inches over six feet, unbowed by age, lean with ropy muscles and the powerful hands and wiry body of a climber who masters sheer rock faces without ropes or pitons. There was a vigorous glow shining through his tan, and his noble face showed the honest weathering of a lifelong devotee of outdoor sports. His gray eyes were younger than the rest of him, with the clarity and penetrating focus of the world-class marksman he was reputed to be.

From his earliest days, he'd no doubt been the kid picked first for every sandlot team. And today, Westfield was still the man you wanted on your side. After a round of brandy, the men settled back in the plush furniture and turned to her expectantly.

"As I said on the phone, Ben, you're describing a movie to them. You're pretending you need their help with your research on cacao farming and the chocolate industry. To fill in the holes in your story."

"And the real purpose is?"

"I want to look each of them in the face, see whose eyes I recognize."

"That's it? That's your plan?"

Harper rose, walked to the fireplace, brushed her hand along the mantel.

"I'll explain the rest of it," she said. "But first you need to see some of the evidence."

While Nick and Sal moved away to a respectful distance, Harper showed Ben Westfield the three videos, narrating as little as possible. First Yacou's betrayal of the two aid workers, the man named Helmut Mullen bulling through the jungle foliage, the brown-haired woman slamming to the ground, throat slit. Then she played the short hostage tape with Naff, Sharp, and Spider crowded onto a bench backed by an Arabic tapestry. And last she ran the video of the final hours of the McDaniel family. She didn't skip the scene of Ross and Harper's lovemaking, but played it without comment straight through to the end. She watched over Ben's shoulder as Spider entered and the masked man followed him inside and fired the fatal shots.

When the scene was done and the laptop screen went black, Ben tipped his head back, stared up at the ceiling, then shut his eyes hard, as if trying to erase the barbarity he'd just witnessed.

With his eyes still closed, he said, "I'll do whatever you want."

He shut the laptop, rose, and walked to the fireplace. Harper glanced back at the sitting room. Either Nick or Sal had shut the door, giving the movie star and Harper a little privacy. She watched Ben Westfield as he paced in front of the fabricated fire, shadows flitting in his eyes like the tattered remains of gloomy memories.

"Listen, there's something I need to tell you."

He stopped pacing, turned to face her.

"I know already," she said.

"Do you?"

"Nick told me. You and Deena were lovers. I'm not surprised. The two of you are a lot alike."

"We were, yes. But there's more."

He cleared his throat, and his eyes looked inward, as if searching for another way to proceed. Finally, he sighed to himself and came to sit beside her on the couch. He reached out and took her right hand and turned it over as a fortune-teller might, or a suitor about to propose.

"Deena was always terrified of what was swimming in her veins. She meant Sal, of course, his shadowy background, the violence he committed as a boy. It frightened her that some of that might be lurking in her own bloodstream and might surface any moment. And she was scared to death she would pass on Sal's tendencies to her offspring. It's why she planned on never having a child. Warren wanted a family, but he couldn't convince Deena. Maybe some small part of her hesitation was because of her career. She didn't see how children fit in the life she was living. But more than that, she was frightened of what her children might become. She simply couldn't bring herself to do it."

Harper looked at her upturned hand cradled in Ben Westfield's. The unreality of the moment sent her mind hurtling off into some airless, woozy void. Deena was so indomitably secure in her beliefs it never occurred to Harper that she might have floundered over anything.

"But when you came along," Ben said, "she was ecstatic."

"Was she?"

Westfield bent forward, lowering his eyes to the level of hers. "Nothing but the truth for you," he said.

"It's easier than navigating a trail of lies."

He considered that for several moments, looking toward a darkened window.

"Truth is Deena had a rough postpartum. From the very start, she loved you passionately, but it was a bewildering time for her. Ecstatic one minute, terrified the next. Poor Warren was no help."

His straightened, and his eyes swept the room, ticking over each piece of furniture and item of decor as if all of it had just then solidified around him.

"When I met your mother, she'd come to Hollywood to shoot a portrait of my first wife. Margie Seybold. You've heard of her."

"Of course." Mansfield, Monroe, Seybold.

"Margie was the star with the big studio contract. I was a two-bit nobody in cowboy shoot-'em-ups. Margie was resolved to have a Deena Roberts photo of herself hanging alongside Mick Jagger and John Lennon and the others in some art gallery back East. For two solid weeks, Deena spent every waking hour with her, and in all that time Deena couldn't get the shot she wanted. She said she couldn't get Margie to reveal her true nature. I think the reason was Margie didn't have a true nature.

"She'd been a knockout since she was a kid, and from ten, eleven years old, she was put on display, day in, day out, and never learned to do anything but smile and pout and strike a pose. So there was nothing below the surface to reveal. During those two weeks, Deena took a couple of random shots of me, and one of them came out okay, and lo and behold, she wound up using that one in an exhibition at some trendy LA gallery.

"Don't ask me why, but that photo gave my career a boost, probably opened some doors that wouldn't have opened otherwise. But Margie was livid, and that two weeks with Deena was the beginning of the end for Margie and me. And the beginning of my connection with Deena."

Harper felt a sudden calm. Nothing to do but watch and listen and absorb what she sensed was coming. A spreading warmth in her chest like the first flush of whiskey hitting the blood.

He blinked hard and shook his head as if waking from a trance.

"Sorry, sorry, I got sidetracked. So the thing I was trying to say was that after you were born, I failed Deena. I didn't realize how hard motherhood would be for her, and I simply let my work and the drumbeat of my career seduce me away from her at the most important moment of Deena's life. It was a betrayal of loyalty. A desertion of the worst kind. Later on, as much as I tried to make it up to her, the damage was done. What trust she had in me was shattered."

He took another distracted look around the room.

"Look, Harper. Maybe this is the wrong time. Maybe this is the exact worst time I could've chosen, but Deena's gone now, and you and I are here together in the middle of this shitty situation. I don't know, but I feel like it's important to lay it all out for you."

"So do it."

He drew a breath and said, "Warren Roberts isn't your father."

The silence that followed sent an ache deep into her chest.

When she spoke, her voice was thin and faraway.

"You are," she said. "Ben Westfield is my father."

He nodded. Yes, yes, yes.

Her first reaction was ridiculous. Well, hey, this solved a lifetime of puzzles. Her height, for one. Towering above Warren, a full foot taller than Deena. A different body type than either, rangy, long limbed in a family of petites and bantamweights. And it explained Warren's cool disinterest in her welfare and Deena's own businesslike mothering approach. It opened up endless reconsiderations. And yet somehow the disclosure also felt like a reprieve. A burden lifted, a fresh start.

A moment later, when the full impact hit her, the sheer absurdity of it made her giddy. An impulsive burst of laughter broke from her throat. The idea that she was Ben Westfield's daughter was so preposterous she couldn't stop herself. She laughed harder and harder still. Shaking, gasping for breath, bending forward, holding her stomach, a series of uncontrollable hiccups of laughter. Ben Westfield, screen legend, man's man, Deena's lover, her goddamn father.

He lay a hand on her back, warm, comforting, trying to draw her back.

For a moment amid the laughter, Harper broke free of her body and floated somewhere overhead, looking down on this opulent room, this strange spectacle, and she knew her laughter was grossly inappropriate. An insult to Westfield's sincerity. She tried to bring it to a halt, but the laughter wouldn't slow. One after another the guffaws rolled and rolled and rolled up from her belly in irrepressible bursts until she thought she might faint. Her vision fogged, an iron fist clamped deep in her gut.

Then with a sputtering gasp and a deep gulp of air, she stopped. She wiped her eyes, looked up at Ben. He'd stepped away from the couch and was watching her warily from a few feet away.

"It's true," he said. "I'm sorry to drop it on you this way."

She nodded.

"Warren has always known you weren't his," he said, "but as far as Deena knew, he didn't suspect me."

She eased back against the cushions, glanced at the closed door.

"And Nick?"

He nodded.

"Deena told him. I don't know why. She never explained it."

"And Sal?"

"Nobody but Nick, and now you."

"Yes," she said. "Now me."

And those were the last words she managed until morning.

———

At ten, as Ben and Harper were leaving for the Albion meeting, Sal met them in the lobby, asked to speak to Harper alone.

Sal guided her to a quiet corner in the Widder lobby.

"What's up?"

"Wanted to wish you luck."

"In private?"

"Well," he said. "There was something else."

He motioned to the zebra-striped chairs nearby, and they sat.

He looked off at the sunlight streaming through the plate-glass windows, people on the sidewalk outside shuffling through the new snow, and he blinked hard as if to clear his eyes.

"One thing you learn you get my age, the work I did, living around tough guys with guns, you can never be sure, somebody walks out the door, maybe this is the last time you see them. This right here."

Harper waited.

"I don't mean to be morbid, but you know, my age, these ideas take shape, they're hard to ignore."

"Are you sick, Sal?"

He waved away the thought, then shrugged.

"No, no, it's not that. I mean, yeah, I had a brush with cancer, some polyps a year back, but they dug around in there, got it all, they think. No, this is something else, just a feeling I had. You love somebody, you start looking at them, and I can't help it, but I think, like, what if they got hurt or had a heart attack, a stroke, or god forbid they got shot and killed and this was the last time I ever saw them. It's just that time of life for me, is all. It's not a premonition about what you're doing today or nothing like that. It's just how I been feeling lately."

"About me."

"About you, yeah."

"What you're saying is you love me."

Sal straightened up, looked around the lobby, flustered. "Sure I love you. Sure, sure. You're my granddaughter, for christsakes. Of course I do."

"But it's more than me being your granddaughter, isn't it?"

"Okay, okay," he said. "I'm being a sentimental old schmuck. Just ignore me, okay. Good luck today. That's all I meant to say."

"I love you too, Sal. Sure you're my granddad, but it's more than that. I love who you are."

"Jesus, listen to us. A couple of sappy douche bags."

She rose and bent forward and gave Sal a kiss on his cheek. First time she'd kissed the old man. And not, if she could help it, the last.

THIRTY-SIX

Mid-March, Albion building, Zurich, Switzerland

"Isn't it beautiful?"

Lester Albion swept his hand toward the far wall of the conference room. In the center of the space stood an eight-foot-tall fountain with dark melted chocolate cascading from tier to tier, seven tiers in all, the rich, earthy odor of the concoction flooding the room. Around its base were dishes heaped with fresh strawberries.

"This particular chocolate is Marburg's finest *grand cru* champagne truffle. Arnold, my chef, hasn't slept in days, perfecting the recipe so it flows smoothly. Go on, dip a berry. Taste a bit of paradise."

Harper hung back behind Ben Westfield's shoulder. Everyone's attention was focused on the movie star. Everyone except Albion's young daughter.

"This lady doesn't like chocolate, Daddy. She looks allergic." Bonnie Albion was smiling up at Harper. A menacing grin. The girl seemed to have taken an immediate dislike to Harper, as if somehow she knew Harper was here to take down her father. The girl's bright-blonde hair was cut in a harsh pageboy. She was dolled up in a blue velvet frock and black patent-leather shoes. A slash of garish red lipstick ineptly applied.

As though the two were old chums, Albion gripped Ben Westfield's elbow and steered him with possessive delight across the room to meet Edwin Marburg.

Marburg was a tall, skeletal man with a sour mouth and watery eyes and an ill-fitting gray suit. Then came Larissa Bixel, who shook Westfield's hand while her eyes dodged left and right, never settling on anything for more than a half second. Bixel was a blocky woman, who'd tried without success to hide her massive arms and shoulders beneath an oversize tunic sweater. Flanking her was Mr. Helmut Mullen, who gave Ben's hand a perfunctory pump while eyeing Harper with a bitter we're-not-done-yet smile.

No one seemed surprised to find Harper McDaniel accompanying the movie legend. She suspected that Adrian Naff had made the connection between Westfield and Harper and cautioned his colleagues that there was some kind of trickery afoot. Perhaps they'd even devised their own counterstrategy, setting a trap for Harper that they'd spring once Albion had finished hobnobbing with the star.

But as long as Edwin Marburg was in attendance, Harper was fairly sure she and Ben were safe. None of these people would dare jeopardize Albion's merger plans by committing a crude act of violence in front of the priggish Marburg.

When Albion drew away from Ben to consult with Adrian Naff, who'd just arrived, Westfield bent in Harper's direction.

"We're outnumbered. Where's your friend with the badge?"

"Late as usual."

Lester Albion clapped his hands and turned to face the assembly. It was then that Harper noticed his eyes were lit from within as if by a fierce blue flame. As he spoke, welcoming them to this gathering in honor of Ben Westfield, Harper studied their smoldering intensity. She'd seen those eyes only briefly before, but that was all the evidence she needed.

She leaned close to Ben and whispered the revelation in his ear.

He absorbed her message and straightened, staring across the room at their host.

"You're sure?"

"I am."

"Now it is my great honor and personal thrill to introduce my life-long hero, a man who has brought to life some of my favorite characters, strong men, determined men, larger-than-life heroes, as well as some of the most twisted and inspired villains ever seen. I give you, ladies and gentlemen, the master of his dramatic craft and the driving force behind many of the finest films of our time, Mr. Ben Westfield."

After a patter of awkward applause, Albion herded the group to the conference table, where yellow nameplates marked their spots. Westfield was positioned at the head of the table, Marburg at the opposite end. Albion, Bixel, Mullen, and Naff sat side by side across from Harper, and beside her was a single, empty seat with a blank yellow card. Bonnie fluttered around the table like a high-strung sparrow searching for a safe roost.

Harper drew her iPad from her purse and laid it on the table before her, the video of Ross's murder cued up.

In a blind flurry this morning in the hours before dawn, Harper had scribbled ten pages detailing the events in Miami, Africa, and Zurich. She'd pared those ten down to four and presented them to Ben at breakfast.

"Before you read them, let me sketch out the plan."

When she had finished, Ben nodded.

"And after we're done, how the hell do we get out of there alive?"

"Not to worry. A highly skilled friend of mine from law enforcement will be there and have our backs."

He'd read through her notes and handed them back. That's all he needed, he'd assured her. He was a one-read-through veteran.

"As you know," Albion was saying, "Mr. Westfield has come all this way to pick our brains so that we might provide him what assistance we can concerning his latest film project, which will center on the industry we all know and cherish, the business of chocolate. Ben, if I may call you that, you have the floor."

The conference room door swung open and Lavonne Jones entered. Her hair was stacked in a five-inch pile of Rasta braids, and her costume for the day was a royal-blue knee-length dress embroidered lavishly across the breast with thread as gold as the late autumn sun over the plains of Kenya. Even on an average day, Lavonne was statuesque, but today, for drama's sake, in heels and with her shoulders drawn back and her chin tipped up, she seemed positively regal.

Harper motioned Lavonne to her chair.

"Mr. Westfield's personal assistant," Harper announced, "always makes an entrance."

When Lavonne was seated, Ben came to his feet, ticked his gaze across each face in the room, then drew a long, fortifying breath. Albion smiled around the table as if basking in the glow of Westfield's eminence.

"The film story I'm about to describe to you will begin shooting this spring. I believe the narrative is solid. It's the details that need work, the nitty-gritty factual stuff. Which, as Lester said, is why I'm here. So you, a group of highly knowledgeable folks, can prevent me from making a damn fool of myself."

Albion laughed and said, "I seriously doubt that's possible. But we're happy to help."

Ben nodded at Albion with a pinched smile as if to caution him against further interruptions.

"Okay then. Our movie opens in a small village in the jungle. Primitive folks going about their daily lives. Huts, open fires, kids playing in the dirt, everyone terribly poor, but they're happy enough, making do. There's love here, deep family bonds. Camera moves back and we see a handful of African lads standing shirtless at the edge of the village looking warily out into the jungle.

"Music rises, tension in the air. The men are holding machetes and wooden staffs, apparently on guard. Then we get more peacefulness of the village, normal routines, old women stirring pots of stew. We're only half a minute in, credits slow rolling.

"With a blast of gunfire, a group of men with automatic weapons storm the village. They're white, they're in uniform, a paramilitary look. With their AK-47s, they take out the men guarding the perimeter, then wade into the helpless village itself. Firing, firing, firing, kids screaming, kids splattered, mothers running with their babies into the jungle, cut down. I know, I know, it's raw, ugly stuff. Somewhat gory. But we'll do it tastefully—there are ways. The right director, the right cinematographer.

"So that's a minute in, just the opening. Now we cut to a coffee shop in modern day Miami, two men speaking in a booth. The contrast is jarring and delicious. Bright, affluent first world with palm trees, a warped echo of the third-world scene we just saw. One man is showing the other a video on his iPad. We just get a glimpse of it, but it's clearly in a jungle, a quick image of that village where we just were.

"Man number one is describing a massacre to man number two. Dozens murdered. What he wants to know is, Will man number two investigate, write about it for the newspaper? The journalist stares at the video, winces like he's about to be sick. Finally he says yes, I'll look into it.

"Then we get a quick montage as the final credits are scrolling. Journalist on the phone, typing on his laptop, he's at his computer reading through old newspaper clippings. He's researching, researching.

"In that montage, we see the journalist's wife and young son living a happy, modern, busy life. Until one night, the wife is away, and two strangers barge into the house and shoot the journalist dead. His son, not even a year old, is gunned down too.

"This is the setup. Five minutes in. Everything is on the table now, all the elements that will pay off later in the movie. It sounds like a lot to cram into five minutes, but believe me, we do it all the time."

Bonnie crowded in between her father and Bixel and said, "This is boring. Isn't it boring, Daddy? I thought his movies were fun."

Albion wiped his mouth to smooth away a grimace.

"Helmut," he said. "Escort Bonnie to the waiting room, and stay with her if you please."

"I believe I'm needed here, sir."

Albion looked at Bixel, prompting her with a jerk of his head.

Bixel said, "Do it, Helmut. We'll be fine."

Scowling, Helmut rose. Bonnie ducked away from his encircling arm, fleeing to the fountain, where she seized a handful of strawberries and dunked them in the molten chocolate and plopped them in her mouth as Helmut guided her roughly out the door.

Lavonne leaned close and murmured, "Nice folks."

Across the table, the fire in Albion's eyes burned the stark blue-white of an acetylene torch. Embarrassed by his daughter, or alarmed by Ben Westfield's unfolding story, hard to tell. But those eyes, Harper was certain, were the ones behind the white ghost mask. Lester Albion was the scrawny man who'd followed Spider into their house on Margaret Street and destroyed her family.

Harper swallowed back the acid burn of rage and tried to ease the clench in her throat that made breathing all but impossible. She tried to imagine the world as seen through those burning eyes, his twisted reasoning, his failure of conscience, tried to fathom what grotesque need he'd satisfied in gunning down Ross and Leo. A merit badge. That's how Spider had seen it.

When Ben resumed, he sailed through the rest of the story. The murders, the heroine's derring-do, her trip to Africa, the discoveries that led her to Zurich and to the doorstep of a giant multinational corporation.

While Ben spoke, Albion's forehead began to glisten, and a pink glow colored his cheeks. Unblinking, Marburg looked on with pursed lips and the straight-backed sanctimony of a Victorian preacher about to lay waste to his sinful flock.

"Okay, our heroine discovers a small, highly regarded chocolate maker is the target for acquisition of the corrupt corporation, and since the owner of that small prestigious company is a deeply pious man, the deal would surely explode if he learned his business suitor is using child slaves and committing mass murder to cover up the fact."

"Now wait just a minute," Albion said.

"Not quite done," said Westfield. "Juicy parts still to come."

Ben cleared his throat, shot Harper a get-ready look, and continued, describing a video the heroine discovers that shows the murder of her husband and son by two men.

"And in one final revelation, our heroine learns that the CEO of the corporation responsible for the African massacre was the very man who murdered her husband and child."

Across the room, Albion scooted his chair a few inches away from the table. Bixel's gaze had finally come to rest and was fixed on Harper with such poisonous loathing that the air between them seemed to ripple. Only Adrian Naff appeared blithely unaffected. A half smile played on his lips, eyes downcast.

"Is all this true?" Lavonne said quietly.

Harper nodded that it was. All too true.

At the far end of the conference table, Edwin Marburg pressed his hands flat on the table and heaved himself up from his seat.

"I believe I've heard quite enough," he said.

"Oh, I'm almost finished. Just one final reveal."

"Mr. Westfield," Marburg said, "in addition to being a very competent actor, you seem to be a man of prodigious cunning."

Ben nodded his thanks.

"At this moment it would interest me greatly to know if this yarn you've been spinning is indeed founded on actual events."

"I'm afraid it is."

"You can prove this?"

"We have the video of the murder of Harper's husband and son. Would you care to see it?"

With a growl, Albion pushed away from the table, knocked his chair over. His right hand unbuttoned his suit coat.

Marburg said, "I would indeed."

Albion, his face bloated with rage, turned on Westfield. "There's no such video. It does not exist."

Harper opened the cover of the iPad, brought the screen to life. "Well, why don't we all have a look," she said. "You apparently don't remember, Mr. Albion, but you took off the ghost mask you were wearing. Your face was visible for several seconds."

"That's preposterous. These are lies, disgusting fabrications."

"Then let's look at the video."

"You're all lying." Albion's flush was as purple as a new bruise.

At the far end of the table, Marburg watched with stern fascination. Albion seemed adrift. Publicly humiliated by his childhood hero, his good name vilified before a crucial business rival. His darkest secret laid bare.

"After you shot Ross twice," she said. "You were about to fire a third time, but Spider stopped you. Do you remember that?"

Albion's mouth opened, then shut. He swiped a hand through his stringy hair. His eyes were loose and uncertain.

"When Spider stopped you from shooting, that's when you removed the mask. If you don't recall doing that, it's because you weren't thinking straight. You must have been so exhilarated by what you'd done."

"None of this happened," Albion said. "The mask, all that. It's a damnable lie."

"Let's watch the video, then. See for ourselves."

Albion cast a helpless look at the faces around the table. No one would meet his gaze. He turned his head away from them and looked longingly back at the chocolate fountain. "This is ridiculous," he said. "An outrage."

There was a quaver of uncertainty in Albion's voice. He hadn't removed the mask at all, but would he remember that? He seemed unsure, so Harper pressed her bluff.

"Killed two people, then you took off the mask like it was too hot, too cramped. A bit small for your face."

She caught the fleeting moment in his eyes. That instant of authenticity Deena had trained her to see. Albion's blue-white rage was the tantrum of a child forever trapped in a stunted man's physique, a boy with dreams too grand and silly for the world he occupied. Nothing he could do, not even murder, could satisfy his hunger, attain the impossible grandeur he'd witnessed on the movie screen and cultivated in his outlandish imagination.

"Never, never, never. I wouldn't do such a thing. That would be idiotic. Am I crazy? Am I a fool? I built all this. Everything you see around you, I built it. Would I endanger all this?"

"You murdered my husband because he discovered the massacre you masterminded. Those villagers were preyed upon for years, their children kidnapped and taken away to work on your plantation to cut your labor costs, and those villagers had endured all they could handle and were fighting back and trying to expose you. So you ordered them slaughtered. Dozens and dozens of innocents.

"You came for my husband because his investigative work threatened to reveal all that. And after you shot him and my son, you took off the ghost mask and showed your face."

"I didn't. I'm not insane. None of this is true. None of it."

The room was silent for several moments, then the door swung open, and Bonnie came bouncing into the room.

"Helmut ran off," said Bonnie. "He was listening at the door. That's called eavesdropping. I was eavesdropping too."

"Go back to the waiting room, child."

"You were talking about that ghost mask. I heard you."

Albion gave her a stricken look. "Hush, Bonnie. Go back outside. Bixel, take her away. Do it now."

Bixel rose and went for the girl, but Bonnie ducked away from her grasp.

"That was my favorite mask, Daddy. Casper the Friendly Ghost. You borrowed it to take on that trip and you promised to bring it back but you never did."

The room was painfully silent. Albion's mouth quivered.

"Mr. Albion," Lavonne said, coming to her feet. "Put your hands above your head and keep them there."

Albion recoiled, eyes drained of light. He looked around the room, as if searching for an exit, and when he saw none, he took a long swallow of air, and his right hand flashed inside his coat and came out with a sleek automatic.

"Don't be an idiot, Lester," Naff said, rising.

"You underestimate me," Albion said. "Everyone does. They take one look at me, see a small man, and think I'm weak. But I'm not weak. I'm a powerful man. Powerful."

Harper said, "Look at the video. Tell me how powerful you look while you're murdering a baby in diapers."

She held out the iPad.

Albion aimed his pistol and fired a single shot, blowing the iPad out of Harper's hands. As the reverberations of the blast died away, the room was silent. Immobilized, Albion seemed stunned by his own rash act.

Then gradually he came to, his eyes hardened, and, as if taking a count, he ticked the pistol over each person around the table.

When he reached Bixel, standing beside him, Harper made her move. She rounded the end of the table, pushing past Westfield, and in the moments that followed, took in only disjointed fragments. A frenzy of shouts and the excruciating thunderclaps of Albion's pistol firing, and firing again, and then again and again.

Naff hit, Westfield hit and hit again, Ben staggering to the side, falling away. Lavonne shot and, with a small gasp, falling hard. As Harper rounded the table, Albion pointed her way and put one slug in her leg as she flung herself on him, hammered his wrist, a solid blow, but somehow he held to the pistol, got off another shot that tugged hard at the same leg and instantly deadened her hip and thigh, and another round that fired a spike of stunning cold through her right arm, and, with half of her numb, she shouldered into him, fortified by her sweet Leo, her fine, noble husband, powered by the pressure that had been building for these last terrible weeks, feeling no pain, no weakness as she rammed him backward, pressed flat against him, her chin locked over his shoulder, levered his shooting hand up into the air with her one good arm, and drove him back and back into the chocolate fountain, crashing into it, the metal tiers screeching, breaking apart, then clattering to the floor, and Albion collapsed on top of the wreckage and struggled in her grip, sprawled on his back in the warm brown chocolate, the fountain's auger continuing to turn, stirring the remains of the chocolate, stirring and stirring.

He clawed at her face as she jammed his head back into the warm pudding, held him there, faceup, drowning him in the brown African sauce, his body going limp, his disembodied eyes swimming just below the surface. From the corner of the room little Bonnie screamed in terror and delight as though rooting her father on, screaming with the wild abandon of a child on the steep swoop of a carnival ride.

Down and down and down, plunging . . . Harper watched bubbles flood from Albion's mouth. She drew a long breath and caught herself. She jerked his head up from the pool of chocolate, released him. Albion limp and gasping. Someone drew Harper away and laid her on the cold wood floor, where she writhed in sorrow and release.

Chocolate in her mouth. Chocolate in her eyes. Dark, rich chocolate.

THIRTY-SEVEN

Mid-May, Puerto Viejo, Algorta, Spain

One of Nick's pals, Salvador Aregoa, a young, flamboyant Basque financier, owned a half dozen homes around the globe. One of them, a private rock-walled villa in the small fishing village of Algorta, was perched on a cliffside overlooking the busy harbor of Bilbao, Spain. It was there, after being released from the UniversitätsSpital, one of the better hospitals in Zurich, that Harper recuperated from her wounds.

For the moment, she had no desire to return to the United States. Too many ghosts were wandering the city of her birth. In fact, as the days passed, she'd been growing increasingly uncertain if she'd ever return.

The family life she'd so long imagined and hungered for had been a fleeting daydream, a glorious two years. All of it demolished in one brutal night, and Harper forced into exile, sent back to wandering the globe as Deena had done, rootless, on some endless indefinable quest with her new family assembled on the fly. Her oddball band, a father she was still struggling to accept, a grandfather who had proved himself more useful and more kind than she could ever have expected, and a Russian orphan boy, who was closer to her than any blood kin could ever be. Not the family she'd wanted. Not the one she'd dreamed of and briefly enjoyed. But a family still, one whose bonds had been tested in the flames of risk and violence.

In the hectic jumble of these last weeks, Harper had let go of one family and embraced another. If neither act were as yet complete, it was clear enough the process was moving forward with an inevitable momentum. Her grief was resolving, her heart freshened by the challenges of these new loyalties, these new trials of love.

Nick came and went from Bilbao. His official leave of absence had ended, and he was back at work for the World Bank. Flying off to New Zealand one week, Shanghai the next, and recently spending a two-week stint in Turkmenistan. Sal returned to Miami Beach but sent her daily texts that invariably included real estate listings within a few blocks of his condo with versions of the same refrain: "You can't live in rented rooms forever."

By the third week in May, Harper put aside her crutches for good, her left leg healing nicely. But her right arm still throbbed when she lifted it shoulder-high. Tony, the British ex-pat who was handling her physical therapy, visited the villa three times a week and put Harper through a grueling three-hour regimen of stretching and weight lifting. Back in Zurich, in four separate operations, her shattered humerus had been pinned back together, but the surgeons warned her the arm would never be quite the same. After weeks of PT, Tony predicted that she might regain as much as 80 percent of her original range of motion, though he doubted her fastball would ever have quite the pop it once had.

"How about her punching strength?" Nick had asked.

"Your sister is a boxer?"

Harper said, "As long as I can hold a camera to my eye, I'm fine."

On the villa's patio on a rare sunny afternoon, in that perpetually rainy region, Harper and Nick went over their game plan. What they would and would not tell Detective Joe Alvarez when he arrived later in the day.

Alvarez had already interviewed her once in Zurich shortly after the shooting in Albion's conference room. But she'd pretended to be muddled from the pain meds and managed to dodge most of his questions. Since then, he'd been sending her regular e-mails to update her on the progress of his investigation. Having viewed the spy-cam video of the shooting of Ross and Leo, Detective Alvarez was trying without success to locate a Casper the Ghost mask that might have been discarded in the immediate area of the murder scene. He and his men had gone door-to-door in her old neighborhood, and he'd enlisted Geneva Carlson's help at the *Miami News* to run stories prominently featuring the mask. So far nothing. It didn't seem a promising approach to Harper.

Immediately after the shootings, Lester Albion was taken into custody and held briefly in Lenzburg Prison, thirty kilometers west of Zurich. But after only seventy-two hours behind bars, Albion was released, his lawyers arguing that Albion was simply defending himself against a malicious attack on his character that had turned physical. The statements of those present at the shooting were so contradictory that the authorities found it difficult to know exactly what had taken place before the shooting began.

Larissa Bixel claimed that Harper McDaniel and Ben Westfield had set up the meeting to make spurious public accusations against Mr. Albion, perhaps in a nefarious attempt to derail his business dealings, and when Albion refuted each of their claims, Harper became enraged and charged at Mr. Albion, as did her cohorts, Mr. Ben Westfield and an African American woman who drew her own weapon. Lavonne was hit twice in the hip. After several hours of surgery, she was rolled into a recovery room, the last place she was seen. Subsequently, the Swiss Federal Police were unable to establish Lavonne's true identity or the method of her entry into their country. Neither Harper nor Ben Westfield could help them with the mystery.

Young Bonnie Albion agreed with Bixel's claims that her father was only defending his life against the bad men, and though Adrian Naff sided with Ben and Harper, the criminal judge in the case was inclined to give Mr. Albion, a Swiss citizen and esteemed member of the community, the benefit of the doubt. The Swiss judicial system, Harper learned, was out of step with the rest of Europe, rarely sending violent offenders to jail. The prevailing view was that prison sentences were of limited value in lowering the risk of reoffending. So at that moment, Lester Albion was living in and working from his townhouse in Zurich's Seefeld district along the lakeside under a lax form of house arrest.

After Albion's release, Larissa Bixel provided to the Swiss Federal Police and Interpol a trove of e-mails and text messages sent to her by Helmut Mullen, incriminating him in the slaughter of dozens of African villagers as well as the shooting of an American, Jackson Sharp, in Miami, Florida. And though it wasn't referred to in the e-mails, Bixel said that Mullen was also responsible for the strangulation death of Harry Combs, aka Spider. She claimed she'd been suppressing this information until after the Marburg deal was complete for fear of causing a scandal that might result in Mr. Marburg withdrawing from the transaction.

Guilty of withholding criminal information, yes, but Ms. Bixel had an understandable fiduciary defense for her actions, according to the same judge who released Albion. No criminal indictment for Bixel. But a full-scale, international manhunt for Helmut Mullen.

It was late afternoon, siesta time ending in the village below, and Harper was standing at the stone balustrade, looking down on the maze of steep cobblestone streets of Algorta and the small plaza where Café Usategui, the local bar, had moved all the tables from its musty interior into the sunny courtyard. The streets swarmed with locals in their black shawls and berets, everyone in a festive mood, as always seemed the case when the sun made a brief appearance in the Basque country.

"Westfield's coming for a visit," Nick said.

"Is he?"

"Arrives tomorrow. I said he could stay here if he wanted. I hope that's okay."

"It'll have to be okay now that he's invited."

"Why so hostile? You don't want to see him? He said you've not answered any of his e-mails, so he's worried."

"He needn't be."

"And he's feeling very guilty about dropping the news on you back at the Widder. It must've been a shock."

"One of many shocks," she said.

"Harper, talk to me. What's going on with you? You're so withdrawn, you're off somewhere like I've never seen you."

She watched a black dog running along the small beach below. A full-out gallop, long ears flopping. No human calling it and not chasing seagulls. Just a dog reveling in the sunshine and the empty beach. The mutt reached one end of the sandy strip, turned, and galloped back to the other. Harper felt a pang of jealousy for the dog, its freedom to play, to simply let loose.

"You wouldn't understand."

"Try me."

She'd been storing up the words for weeks. Unable to utter them aloud until she was absolutely certain they were true.

"I'm not letting go of this. I can't. I won't."

The black dog stopped at the far end of the beach, panting. He looked out at the harbor, then flopped on his side and rolled onto his back, paws to the sky, rolling right and left.

"What're you saying? You're going after Albion again?"

"Him, yes, and Mullen, Bixel, Naff, all of them."

"Why?"

"How can you ask that?"

"You're still seething. Of course. So am I. Sal and Ben too. It's terrible. It's unfair. But Harper, it's done. It's over. We're talking about the

Swiss courts, here. Without new evidence, there's nothing you can do. Nothing anybody can do."

"Isn't there?"

"Oh yes, sure. Become an assassin? Knock them off one by one? That's not you, Harper. You know that's not you."

"Isn't it? Are you so sure of that? Because I'm not."

"So that's why you're pushing Ben away. You're afraid he'll bring you to your senses."

"It's not that."

"Then what is it?"

"This is my issue. It's nobody else's problem. I can't put you or Ben or Sal in danger again. I won't do that, let you risk your lives for this craziness."

"So you push us away? That's your solution?"

"Leave it alone, Nick. Let me handle it."

He shook his head, either in refusal or frustration, she couldn't say.

Alvarez arrived at four, sweating heavily from the walk up the grueling stairways that led from the Algorta train station. He carried an overnight bag and his brown sport coat, rumpled from his flight and the journey from the airport. His shirt and pants were disheveled too, and his face looked twice as worn as when she'd last seen him.

Nick greeted him at the front door and led him out to the patio. They sat together beneath a striped umbrella that shaded the wrought iron table where Nick had laid out small plates of *pintxos*, chorizo, and *angulas* from the Usategui, a pitcher of *tinto*, and another of iced tea. Alvarez chose tea, guzzled an entire glass, and poured himself another.

"First time in Spain?" Nick asked him.

"Way back when, my first wife and I took a bus tour for an anniversary, our fifth I think it was. Didn't visit anywhere around here. Madrid, Seville, Barcelona, those were the places. It's a pretty country."

Nick tried to make more small talk, burn up some time, but Alvarez simply grunted when it was his turn to reply. Ready to get to business.

"I'm short on time," he said. "Got to fly out tomorrow. This is strictly a courtesy call. More courtesy than you probably deserve."

Nick nodded. "So I guess we should start."

"Tell me about Jackson Sharp."

Nick glanced at Harper. If Sharp came up, they'd planned to deny knowing anything about him. Alvarez caught the look, read it correctly.

"You tell me everything you know about Sharp, I give you some good news. An even trade. Otherwise, I head back to the train station."

Harper shrugged a question at Nick. He shrugged back, go ahead if you like.

So Harper told Alvarez about finding Ross's research notes, her trip to Sharp's Edgewater Apartments, seeing him dead in the recliner, her fight with Mullen. And stopped there.

Alvarez shook his head, not satisfied.

"After Sharp's name came up in Ms. Bixel's report, we tracked down his address, had a look inside the apartment, Edgewater, that place. Very curious scene."

"How so?" Nick said, his tone a trifle too breezy. Not a good liar.

"The place was disinfected, totally sterilized. We got one of the best forensics squads in the country. Plenty of practice. But in this case, they found no blood, no hairs, no bodily fluids, spit, sperm, zero.

"That never happens, an apartment where someone was living, it's not possible. Even a crime-scene cleanup crew, a good one, after they're done, there's going to be some microscopic this or that left behind. But not in Sharp's place. Rent paid in advance for six months. But no clothes in the closet, no food, no personal items of any kind, not even hangers, mirrors clean, not a spatter of toothpaste, a flake of snot. Even the drains were sterile, the traps, the toilet. Furniture was scrubbed, cabinets, refrigerator. That just doesn't happen."

"Maybe Sharp was OCD," Nick said. "A clean freak."

Alvarez gave no sign he'd heard, looking past Nick into Harper's eyes.

"Share what you have," she said. "We'll give you the whole story on Jackson Sharp."

"Including where you disposed of the body?"

"*That* we don't know," Nick said.

"We'll play fair," said Harper. "You have my word."

Alvarez considered that for several moments, looking down at the harbor where a container ship was idling through the channel a half mile north of the small bay of Algorta, heading into the bustling Bilbao port.

The detective dug through his overnight bag and drew out a file folder. He slid it across the tabletop to Harper. She opened the folder, looked at the photograph, closed the folder, and slid it to Nick.

"The mask," Nick said. "You found it."

"A kid, eight years old, pulled it out of the trash the day after Ross and Leo were murdered. A dumpster behind a Coconut Grove restaurant. He took it home, put it in a drawer, forgot about it. His mother came across it two weeks ago, remembered hearing about a mask in the news, called one of the TV stations, WSVN, the blood-and-gore guys. They sent a camera crew out. Called Miami PD on their way to the kid's house so they'd get a big scene, full of cops.

"When we got the results back from the crime lab, there were fingerprints, the kid, his mother, others we couldn't identify, and a lot of smears of this and that. Mixed in with all that there's Albion's DNA, saliva around the mouth hole, more DNA around the eyeholes. So there you go.

"Federal prosecutor filed extradition papers immediately. I'm on my way to Zurich to give a statement in the first hearing. Prosecutor warned the case could take six months, a year, to work through the appeals process. But he's confident the Swiss will comply. There's a solid treaty with the United States, and this case satisfies the dual-criminality statute, which means the Swiss treat murder similar to how the United States does. So it might take a while, but Albion's going down."

Nick laid a hand on Harper's arm. "That's good news, very good news," he said. "Isn't it, Harper?"

"We've seen Swiss justice in action already. Why should this time be different?"

"Judge that freed Albion has nothing to do with this case. It's going to happen, trust me, Albion will serve serious time."

"Okay," she said. "One down."

Alvarez gave her a careful look. "What's that supposed to mean?"

When Harper didn't answer, Nick jumped in.

"She's not satisfied the whole truth's being told. She thinks Mullen is their scapegoat. They're using him to cover their own tracks."

"Oh, sure, I get it. You're still on a vigilante kick. Going to be like old Grandpa Sal when he was a kid. What was it? Killed like six, seven guys, mutilated their corpses. That's your agenda now, pull a Leonardi, take out all these guys?"

"You want to hear what I have to say about Jackson Sharp or give me a lecture about genetics?"

She told him about the hostage video of Sharp and Naff and Spider. Three guys who knew each other. Naff going off to a legit job, Spider freelancing his paramilitary skills, Sharp partnering up with Helmut Mullen. She told him about the video that showed Sharp in Africa alongside Helmut Mullen, the two of them murdering the Fordhams, the husband-and-wife aid workers who were filming the child slaves. Sharp was along for the massacre at Soko too, used the video the aid woman was shooting in an extortion scam against Albion. He decided he needed someone who could put the screws to Albion. Somebody to get their attention and make them hand over a pile of cash to Sharp to keep it all quiet. His home base was Miami. He looked around him, thought Ross fit the bill, a bulldog with a megaphone.

Alvarez said, "A lot of bad guys in this story. But for my money, Sharp's the sleaziest. Knew he was putting Ross in Albion's crosshairs but didn't give a shit what happened to him."

Harper watched Alvarez look off at the harbor. Saw in his eyes a flicker of anguish she hadn't noticed before. This was the world he'd chosen, where every day the crimes of the past worked on him like a dark, relentless undertow as new crimes came crashing ashore, one after the next after the next, piling atop him. Alvarez out there in the deep water, struggling to free himself from the awful tidal pull that threatened to drag him under while more waves kept pounding the beachhead.

"Where's his body?" Alvarez said at last. "Can you give me that much?"

"It's gone," she said. "Disposed of. A cleanup crew sanitized Sharp's apartment. A friend of a friend suggested their services."

"A friend of a friend?" Alvarez said. "That would be Sal."

"Friend of a friend."

"That's it, all you're going to say?"

"All there is to say."

"Well, they did a damn good job. You get a chance, send me their business card."

Maybe it was too little, too late, but Harper drew a deep breath and went with it.

"I've given you a hard time," she said. "From the first night on, I made you an adversary. I'm sorry. And I want to thank you, Alvarez. For your work, for not giving up, and for not throwing the bunch of us in jail. I was wrong about you. You're a decent man."

He brought his eyes back from the distance and looked at her with a half smile. His eyes had closed off. The cool dispassion she'd seen in them that first night had returned. The detective was back on the job.

"A little friendly advice," he said. "From here on, watch yourself, Ms. McDaniel. Because I will be."

She gave a quiet sigh.

"Is there anything else, Detective?"

There wasn't.

THIRTY-EIGHT

Mid-May, Guggenheim Museum, Bilbao, Spain

Ben Westfield arrived late morning on Friday. He was walking with a cane, a gift from the ingenue costarring in his latest movie. Though he claimed he didn't need it anymore, that his left leg was fully recovered, he'd said he'd become fond of the sleek wooden stick during his six-week recovery. Good for fending off overzealous fans and yappy dogs.

After a shower and a light lunch, Ben asked if they wanted to go with him to see the Guggenheim Museum. Because the weather was still clear, they decided to make the half-hour trip into town.

Shaped like a surreal schooner, the wildly eccentric structure was built along the Nervión River near downtown Bilbao in what had once been a seedy part of the port area but had become gentrified in the years since the museum's construction.

Harper reluctantly tagged along, telling herself to relax, embrace the experience, get to know her father better, this kind, honest, talented man who was trying his best to make peace. But for reasons she didn't fully grasp, she was sulky and unforgiving, although she could not name exactly what it was Ben Westfield might be guilty of.

To make matters more distressing, since exiting the train, she'd had several brief flutters of panic, an uneasy sense that once again she was being spied on. She kept glancing around to locate the stalker until Nick asked her what was wrong.

She told him it was nothing. After so many weeks of living in near isolation at the cliffside villa, she'd become oversensitive to crowds. And maybe that was truly the reason for her jitters.

When they arrived at the Guggenheim, the three of them cruised the spacious plaza that wrapped around the museum, stopping to admire the enormous sculpture of a long-legged spider made of iron. Once inside the museum, Ben led them directly to the Richard Serra permanent exhibit in a cavernous exhibition hall with rounded corners and a towering ceiling.

This exhibit had been on Ben's wish list since meeting Serra at a Malibu party years earlier. The two men had hit it off and stayed in touch ever since. Fast friends now, Westfield visited Serra in New York and in his San Francisco home, and on several occasions Serra had stayed in Ben's La Jolla estate. In the last few years, Ben had traveled to several of Serra's US exhibits and was awed by his new friend's talent. But so far he'd not found a free moment to see Serra's premier work, *The Matter of Time*, which was a centerpiece of Bilbao's Guggenheim collection. It was, Ben informed them, seven interlocking sculptures, large-scale abstract sheet metal assemblies that were constructed of weathered steel.

"That's an alloy," he said as they stood at a distance taking in the dramatic sculpture. "That reddish patina is a kind of organic secretion that the steel creates to form a protective layer. It looks like rust but in fact it retards damaging corrosion. And as that top layer wears away, it regenerates continuously. Living steel."

"Like a callus," Nick said.

"More like a kind of molting," said Ben. "Even metal can change, grow, develop." He winked at Harper.

To her the towering sculpture with parallel wavy walls that snaked halfway across the hall was less beautiful than it was menacing. Groups of people were entering its narrow, sinuous lanes, walking warily between the warped and tilting high walls of the sculpted sheet metal, navigating its serpentine paths as if the sculpture were a carnival spook house. She watched a young couple disappear into the maze of elastic curves, then reappear in an unexpected location further on.

"I'm going back," she announced.

Ben peered into her eyes.

"Back to the villa?" Nick said. "You're not feeling well?"

"No, I'm okay. I'll just wait outside."

"We'll all go," said Ben. "Come back when you're feeling better."

"No, no, go ahead. Explore all you want. It's a pretty day. I'll just sit out in the sun."

"You're sure?"

She said she was.

"Okay, if that's what you want. We'll be out as quick as we can."

"Don't hurry, please. You came all this way. Take your time. I'm just feeling . . . I don't know. Claustrophobic or something."

Nick gave her a buck-up pat on her good shoulder and headed off, following Ben into the interior of the sculpture.

She found a spot outside the front doors with a view across the river toward the Universidad de Deusto, a Jesuit college that was reputed to be the Harvard of Spain. She watched the flow of tourists and locals strolling along the waterfront. After a few minutes, the smell of *tortilla española* from a nearby café enticed her to rise from her bench and wander in that direction. Maybe she was only hungry.

She was on the steps down to the riverfront walkway when she heard the first screams.

A throng of people, women wailing, men barking at their children to keep up, were flooding out of the front doors of the museum. Harper trotted back against the flow of the panicked crowd. She stepped in front of a college boy, blocked his way, and asked what was going on.

"Terroristas," he said and tore away from her.

She waded through the crowd and pushed into the museum. Guards stood atop the ticket counters and were calling out for everyone to remain calm, but no one was listening. A herd of Japanese tourists passed her in a tight formation, and behind them another tour group of elderly ladies were being shepherded toward the exit by an impatient Spaniard, who hurled a steady stream of curses at his clients.

Harper jogged down an empty corridor, cut through a roped-off exhibit of ancient pots and vases, and located the corridor where they'd traveled earlier, retracing their steps to the vast exhibition hall where she'd left Ben and Nick.

Screams and deep grunts of exertion led her the last few yards until she reached the spot where she'd last seen them. Deep in the interior of the labyrinthine structure, she could see the sheet metal shiver and shake, and she heard the thuds and hollow chimes of the metal ringing as if someone was hammering it with their fists.

She forged ahead, entering the closest entrance that seemed to lead toward the clamor, but after only a few steps, she was already disoriented. The high, curving walls and the narrowing and widening path before her created the sense that the ground was no longer supporting her.

She thought she heard Nick's shout. The *kiai* he'd mastered as a boy on the workout mats. A deep-throated battle cry meant to release a fighter's stored energy. Another *kiai* and then another.

As she hustled toward Nick's voice, the slanted walls, the false openings, the changing light and the deceptive slants of the open spaces confused her, sent her in directions farther from Nick's cries and the grunts and hoarse curses that answered him.

She broke into a run, but it seemed like she was getting nowhere. The walls closing in and widening, shifting right, then veering left, she made wrong turns, came to dead ends, had to run back the other direction, lost and with a rising dread that she would be too late.

She scraped her forehead on a wall, bounced off another, rounded a corner, and saw figures in the distance. She was bruised, scuffed, bleeding, and out of breath. Her injured right arm ached anew with every pump of her heart.

The light was frail and gray back there, making the shadowy figures little more than blurs of movement. They seemed to be wrestling, punching, gouging, grabbing for handholds, trapped in a tight box of steel. A body lay facedown on the floor nearby, one arm outstretched, reaching for his cane. Her father, Ben.

As she closed to twenty yards, she saw a second man lying on the floor behind the two fighters. Then a muzzle flash, and the chimes of a slug hitting the weathered steel and ricocheting twice more inside the tight passage.

The shooter saw her and released the person he'd been pistol-whipping, let him crumple to the floor and settle in beside the other two sprawling men.

He aimed at her as she came forward, the pistol glinting in a sudden shaft of sunlight.

"Run, Harper, run!"

Nick's voice. She saw her brother struggle to his knees to the left of the shooter.

"She won't run," Helmut Mullen said.

Harper came closer.

Mullen said, "We meet for the final time."

"One thing I don't get," she said. "Bixel's the one who turned you in. Why come for us, not her?"

"Bixel's next. You started this. You die first, you and these others."

To Mullen's right, the man lying on his side turned his head, a ragged gash across his forehead. Adrian Naff.

She'd closed to ten feet. Nick was wobbling upright behind Mullen. He came to his full height, drew back his right fist, and launched a feeble punch. Mullen bobbed his head, slipped the blow, and hacked Nick on the skull with his pistol. Brought his aim quickly back to Harper. She halted five feet away. Nowhere to go but forward. Dodge, feint—maybe there was a chance. But no time to chart her moves. This was about instinct and timing and maybe a lucky distraction.

Harper said, "And another thing I don't understand."

"We're not doing that tired-out confession thing," Mullen said. "I have nothing to say to you."

He lifted the pistol a few inches to better sight along its barrel. She was watching his eyes, looking for a telltale signal that he was about to fire. Timing her dodge to that. Betting her goddamn life on Deena's training.

When his sighting eye tensed, she ducked her head, dived, and rolled across an empty span of floor. Coming to her feet, she saw Mullen stagger to one side, the crooked handle of Ben Westfield's cane hooked around his ankle, and Ben tugging hard.

Harper crashed into him, a roundhouse knee into his ribs, then three quick strikes to his head and throat. His pistol fired three or four times, deafening her, but the rounds sailed into the faraway spaces of the exhibition hall. Another knuckle blow to his throat, and as Mullen coughed and sputtered, she axed his wrist with the blade of her right hand, the pistol breaking loose and skittering down the passageway she'd just crossed. She cocked her right hand, thrust its heel into Mullen's long, straight nose, and heard the harsh crunch. His back was plastered against one side of the narrow passage, blood streamed into his mouth.

She kneed him in the groin. He growled and slashed a fist at her face, clipped her chin, jarred her backward, struck her again in the jaw, and the daylight flickered and faded, but she caught herself, didn't go down, but bulled back into him, flattening her body against his, coming well inside his roundhouse blows. She grabbed both his ears, slammed his head into the steel wall, slammed it a second time. Another knee into his crotch, then another.

His eyelids fluttered up and down like the slow wings of a dying butterfly. Adrian Naff was beside her, his eyes woozy, but he took Mullen from her hands and manhandled him against the wall, gut-punched him three times, then spun him around and locked his wrists in handcuffs.

THIRTY-NINE

Mid-May, Clínica IMQ Zorrotzaurre, Bilbao, Spain

Ben had a mild concussion, which he claimed was his seventh, apparently averaging one per decade. Starting with a bicycle crash when he was ten, little Ben versus a drunk's pickup truck. Since then, most had been on movie sets doing his own stunt work.

"I know the cure," he said. "Three shots of Gray Goose. I'll be fine."

His thirtysomething female doctor was trying with little success to suppress her delight at having the celebrated actor as a patient. "I think is best you drink only wine the first days."

"Okay, Doc. That's a reasonable compromise."

"I will have an excellent bottle of *Garnacha* sent up, Señor Westfield."

She smiled at him and decided she needed to feel his pulse again. Her long, delicate fingers encircling his wrist, her eyes going dreamy as she felt the thump of the movie star's heart.

Adrian Naff appeared in the doorway and asked to speak to Harper.

She joined him in the corridor. He'd abandoned his hospital gown and was back in street clothes, his forehead heavily bandaged.

"Should you be walking around?"

"I wanted to see you, explain why I'm here." A smile flitted across his lips, coming and going so quickly she couldn't read its meaning.

"Okay, I'm listening."

"I was tracking Mullen while apparently he was tracking you. I didn't figure out what he was up to today until Westfield and your brother appeared. If I'd intervened sooner, no one would have been hurt."

"Everyone's okay. Nick'll be out of action for a few days, but he's all stitched up. Nothing too serious."

"And Ben?"

"If he can pull himself away from a lovesick doctor, he should be out tomorrow."

"Good."

"Why track Mullen? Why not just take him into custody?"

"I was hoping he'd lead me to you. I wasn't sure, but I was hoping." The heat in his eyes made her swallow. "Well, here I am."

"I want to help you."

"And how could you possibly help me?"

"You're planning to finish what you started, aren't you?"

"What would that be?"

"Bring down Albion, Bixel, the whole gang. Me included."

"I don't follow."

"Yes, you do. It's an admirable goal. But you'll need help. Someone on the inside. Someone who knows a little of what's going on."

Naff looked down the corridor, watched a passing orderly. When the orderly was out of earshot, Naff said, "What's going on is more than Africa, more than that one massacre. That's bad, sure, but it's nothing compared to what else they're into."

She drew a breath. She didn't have to try to read his brown eyes. His drawbridge was open, the castle vulnerable. This wasn't one of his roles. This was the man she'd glimpsed before, a man who'd fought in foreign lands he'd never truly left. A man with more layers than he'd shown to Harper or, she suspected, to anyone.

"What I'm saying is Albion's into some major shit all over the world. And I don't mean Lester Albion, I mean the whole company."

"What do I care about any of that?"

"You want to take Bixel down. You're probably thinking get her alone somewhere, dark alley, put a round in her skull, and sure, that would be satisfying. But if you truly want to destroy the woman, there's a better way."

"I'm listening."

"Dismember her."

"And how would someone do that?"

"She's a dangerous woman, devious and powerful and a hell of a lot smarter than Lester. But if you rip apart her empire from beneath her, you've accomplished something more worthwhile than just removing the woman."

"And let's say I buy any of this, what do you get out of the arrangement?"

The smile was there again, his eyes homing in on hers, getting inside her, reading her, turning the tables.

"What do I get? I get to see more of you."

"Very funny."

"Not meant to be."

"How do I know you're not trying to send me on a fool's errand? Keep the idiot chasing her tail?"

"Only way you'll know for sure is to take me out for a test run."

She considered that for several moments. "I'll let you know."

"While you're thinking it over, let me give you something else to chew on, a place you might start."

"What place is that?"

"You ever heard of Puglia?"

"Italy. The heel of the boot."

His smile darkened as a troubling thought seemed to cloud his eyes. "No, forget it," he said. "Bad idea."

"Don't toy with me."

"I'm sorry. Just too chancy. You could put yourself at serious risk, still not make a difference."

"You're one slippery bastard."

He looked down the gleaming hallway. Hospital gongs and messages in Spanish repeating from the overhead speakers.

He sighed. Harper wasn't sure, but he looked honestly torn.

"Okay, here's what I can do," he said. "You got an in-depth look at the chocolate business. If you're sure you're up to it, I can point you in a new direction, something even more corrupt."

"Is that possible?"

"Oh yes."

Down the hall the same orderly was marching toward them again, this time talking on a cell phone. Eyeing his approach, Naff reset his feet, his hands rising.

When the man passed, Naff drew a breath, relaxed his shoulders, his gaze returning to Harper.

"You were telling me about something more corrupt than chocolate."

Naff found a fresh smile and leaned forward as if to whisper in her ear. Or perhaps inhale her scent.

"Olive oil," he said and turned and walked away.

ACKNOWLEDGMENTS

The dashing Dan Gibson was very helpful in teaching me about the goals and operations of the World Bank. And much thanks to Martin Feather, who spent a good deal of effort and time educating me about material that, alas, didn't wind up in this novel but will certainly show up in future Harper McDaniel episodes. Laura Crovo-Lane suggested a colorful and crucial detail that gave the ending far more pizzazz than it would have had otherwise. Les Standiford, my dear friend and an excellent writer and editor, did his usual thorough job of pointing out scenes and situations that could be improved. For thirty years I've depended on Les's insights, and he never lets me down. His comments are always spot-on, pointing out things I should have seen myself but didn't. Ann Rittenberg, my literary agent, listened thoughtfully to my earliest clumsy descriptions of this book and encouraged me, giving me confidence to strike out in this new direction. Later on she continued to counsel me wisely, then read multiple drafts and helped in countless ways to improve the finished product. The final polish would not have the same luster without the help of Liz Pearsons and Ed Stackler, two real pros. And without the insights, patience, and close reading of the manuscript at every stage along way—not to mention the loyal emotional support—of my wife, Evelyn, this book would never have seen the light of day.

ABOUT THE AUTHOR

Photo © 2007 Maggie Evans Silverstein

A winner of the Edgar and Shamus Awards, James W. Hall is the author of twenty novels, including *The Big Finish*, the latest in the Thorn Mysteries, as well as four books of poetry, two short story collections, and two works of nonfiction. Born in Hopkinsville, Kentucky, Hall holds a BA from Florida Presbyterian College, an MA from Johns Hopkins University, and a PhD in literature from the University of Utah. He divides his time between North Carolina and Florida.